WHEN JUSTICE CALLS

JAMIE MCFARLANE

FICKLE DRAGON PUBLISHING LLC

FREE DOWNLOAD

Sign up for my newsletter and receive a free Jamie McFarlane starter library.

To get started, please visit:

http://www.fickledragon.com

"Rosita, wake up. Sister Marta is coming." Amalia Rouca shook her older sister gently. The two lay together on a single mattress within the pantry of the parish food kitchen.

"Go back to sleep, Ama," Rosita whispered in Spanish, pushing her sister back with a shoulder. "It's too early."

Ama pulled her knee up to her chest, placed a foot into Rosita's back, and pushed her from the bed. "No. Sister Marta said we had to get up before everyone else if we wanted to sleep here."

Rosita groaned. Light streamed into the room as the pantry door opened. The staunch figure of an aged nun stood silhouetted by kitchen lights.

"Rise and shine, my quiet little urchins." Sister Marta's voice cracked as she spoke.

"Yes, ma'am," Amalia answered quickly. "We were just getting up."

"You're both filthy," the sister observed as the girls scrambled to their feet. Brushing past them, she grabbed for the small bag that held the girls' only worldly possessions. "We'll run wash and get you cleaned up after we prepare the breakfast."

Amalia knit her brows in confusion as Rosita lunged for the bag the nun had grabbed. "That's mine," Rosita exclaimed as Sister Marta yanked it from her grasp.

"Father Timothy reported that a few items had gone missing in the narthex," Sister Marta said. "You wouldn't know anything about this, would you, Rosita?"

"No!" Rosita said defiantly, even as the sister pulled at the drawstrings holding the bag closed.

In a single, last-ditch attempt to intervene, Rosita moved to wedge her body between the woman's arms and the bag. The sister was not so easily defeated and brought a heavy hip around, blocking the girl.

"Now, what would a couple of street children be doing with this?" Sister Marta withdrew a brass candlestick. "You do know that stealing from the church is a sin? Father Timothy will be quite upset when he hears of your transgression."

Amalia looked at the aging woman, wondering what she would do. The night before they'd met the father and found him to be a gentle man. She hated that he would think less of them. What had Rosita been thinking?

"No," she whispered without even knowing she had.

This caught Sister Marta's attention and she turned to Amalia, her face softening. "Dear child, perhaps Father Timothy does not need to hear of this. After punishment, restitution ..."

Sister Marta collapsed to the floor. Looking up, Amalia saw her sister standing over the large woman, brandishing a can of tomatoes.

"Rosita. What have you done?" Amalia whispered in shock. "She is a sister."

"We did not leave our home to be beaten by an angry old nun," Rosita said.

Sounds in the adjacent kitchen caught the girls' attention and they froze, staring at each other.

"Marta?" a woman's voice called and then trailed off as she moved out of the kitchen.

"Grab food," Rosita demanded, wrenching the bag from Sister Marta's hand and stuffing the candlestick back in.

Amalia reached for the well-stocked shelves and had just grabbed two cans of peaches when the door was pulled open.

"Marta?" a woman Amalia did not recognize asked, her voice rising in horror. "What have you done?"

"Run!" Rosita demanded. As she bolted from the room she threw her shoulder into the woman's soft mid-section.

Amalia needed no further prompting and followed her sister as they made a mad dash out of the building.

It was dark as they exited into the church's courtyard. Even so, they saw a few lights on in the residences. A shout from behind only served to spur the girls as they continued their sprint from the property, and they didn't slow until they could no longer run.

"Why did you hit her?" Amalia asked, leaning over with hands on her knees. "She would have allowed us to stay. We shouldn't have stolen the candlesticks."

"You are my responsibility, Ama," Rosita said, also gasping for breath. "When I was out last night, I heard Sister Marta talking to the father. They were going to call child services. We would have been sent home to Guatemala. We have no one left, Ama. We cannot go back. You must trust me."

"Then what are we going to do, Rosita?"

"I will think of something. What did you get?"

Amalia shrugged, looking at the cans in her hands. "It was the first thing I grabbed."

"You did well, Ama," Rosita said, showing off a long loaf of bread. "Are you hungry?"

Amalia's stomach growled as the two emerged from the alley where they'd slept. It had been a couple of days, the food they'd stolen was almost gone, and they were becoming desperate.

"Hey, look at this," Rosita said, picking up a tire iron and a cheap scissor jack that had been discarded in the alley. Both tools were heavily rusted.

"No one will pay for that," Amalia said. "We only got two dollars for the candlesticks. What do you think they'll give for that rusty old crap? We should sell our phones. Mine only has twenty minutes left on it. Who are we going to call anyway?"

"No one will pay for phones with only a few minutes left either," Rosita said. "And you're missing the value." She shrugged the drawstring of her bag onto a shoulder and held the jack and tire iron out.

"I don't get it," Amalia said.

Rosita pointed at an older, but immaculately maintained truck that had just pulled to a stop on the street in front of an apartment building two blocks away.

"With these, we can get something the shop will pay for," Rosita said.

"You want to steal a truck?" Amalia asked, confused.

"Tires."

"And they'll pay for those?"

"Of course," Rosita said confidently. "Everyone needs tires. See how shiny the wheels are?"

"He looks big and he has a dog." Amalia worried aloud about the truck's occupants as they walked down the street toward the truck.

"Be brave. The dog cannot escape through the windows," Rosita said. "And big men cannot catch us. We run too fast."

The two paused as the man disappeared into the apartment building. He reappeared on the second floor and it was then that Rosita grabbed Amalia's arm and pulled her to the opposite side of the truck, hiding them from view.

Amalia flinched when the dog inside the truck barked, lunging at the window. She stared at it as Rosita placed the jack on the ground and attempted to work it. Each inch they moved closer to the truck seemed to rile the dog even more, but in the end, her sister had been right. It couldn't escape from its prison.

"Make sure he's not coming back," Rosita demanded, placing the tire iron on the first lug nut.

Amalia peered around the truck. The truck's owner was talking to another man at the door to one of the apartments. She continued to watch until they both disappeared inside.

"We need to be fast. I think it's a drug deal," Amalia whispered. "Why else would he have a dog? I bet it's guarding his stash."

"Maybe. I need your help. This is stuck," Rosita said pushing unsuccessfully on the tire iron. Amalia dared another glance back and not seeing either man, helped push on the tire iron. Their combined weight was sufficient, and the nut started to turn.

Together, the two girls worked feverishly to remove the lug nuts, finally jacking the vehicle up far enough to pull the wheel off.

"Someone's yelling," Amalia said as Rosita unexpectedly moved to the other side of the truck. "What are you doing?"

"There are two of us. We take two tires," she said.

"They're fighting," Amalia answered. "We need to run while we can still get away."

Rosita pushed against another stubborn nut. "Help me."

Unlike the first wheel, the second wheel seemed to know it shouldn't be removed and resisted the sisters at every turn. Amalia constantly checked over her shoulder, looking for the man who she knew would come back at any moment.

"I've got it," Rosita finally exclaimed at the same moment two men came around the corner of the apartment building, heading their way.

"He's here. Run!" Amalia said.

Rosita pushed her tire from the vehicle and rolled it down the street. "Get the other one."

Amalia ran to the other side of the truck, grabbed the second tire and quickly followed.

At first, the tire felt impossible to move, but as it picked up speed, it became more stable. A shout from behind spurred Amalia on and she looked over only to see her sister release the tire she'd been pushing and dart into the alley.

"Run, Ama. Get away," Rosita called over her shoulder.

For a moment, Amalia was stuck in indecision. She was running hard and the tire was tracking with her. She gave it a final push, angling for the alley. It was then she felt a shove from the side. She stumbled and became entwined with the wheel, which rolled over the top of her, slamming her and the tire into a pile of garbage, the tire coming to rest on her leg.

"Get off, pervert," Amalia screamed defiantly in Spanish as the man attempted to pull the wheel from her leg.

"Don't give me that," he replied in English.

Amalia watched the man's thick muscles tighten as he pulled the wheel off her. They'd had no business stealing from him. If he decided to hurt her, there was no one to stop him.

"Take it," she said, defiantly, using fear to fuel her anger.

"Who's going to pay for the damage?" he asked, his face flushed as he cut off her tirade and pulled her up from the pile where she lay.

"Not my problem, shit-stain."

"Watch it, or I'll hold you for the cops," he said. The two stared at each other for a moment and the man's face softened. "Dammit. How about ten bucks if you help me get my wheels back to the truck."

He pulled a ten-dollar bill from his pocket and showed it to her. She tried to grab it, but he was too quick.

"Fine," she agreed, and started rolling the wheel back to the truck.

Ten minutes later, she rejoined her sister at the end of the alley.

"What happened?" Rosita asked. "Why'd you help him?"

Amalia smiled and flashed the ten-dollar bill at her sister. "Today we eat."

———

Rosita lay against the cardboard walls of their temporary new home. The two had followed a homeless woman into an abandoned warehouse and discovered the unused shelter. They would move on in the morning, but it would do for the night. She reflected on how things had gone from bad to worse since they'd arrived in Sutherland with their uncle, moving in with him and his girlfriend. Things soon turned bad and the girlfriend kicked them all out. For a few days, the three had lived in an old car until one day, their uncle simply walked off.

A shout sounded somewhere within the shanty town of card-board box homes. Since arriving, they'd witnessed a multitude of fights between the drunken residents. The only safety they'd found had been in hunkering down and hiding from view. Rosita pulled Amalia even closer and ran a hand over the younger girl's short-cut hair, trying to provide comfort.

A new shout, closer this time, alerted her to a potential problem and she shook her exhausted sister, worried they might have to make a run for it.

"What?" Ama whispered, instantly awake.

Rosita didn't answer but held a finger to her mouth.

"Little bunny foo-foo, hopping through the forest, scooping up the field mice ..." A man's voice grew louder as he approached and roughly shook the box they were in.

Ama mouthed *"Run,"* and Rosita nodded in agreement, crouching in front of the closed flap. When the box was shaken again, Rosita bolted with Ama close behind. Strong arms wrapped around Rosita as she exited.

"Run, Ama!" Rosita shouted, struggling helplessly against the man's grip.

Amalia, spurred on by Rosita's panic, wriggled around her sister and squirted out into the aisle between the rows of makeshift homes. A large hand swiped at her back, but she twisted and scrabbled away.

Fear fueled her run as she fought to gain her feet. A second hand grabbed her shoulder, but she slid from beneath it and ran with every-thing she had. Behind her, Rosita's screams echoed, both cursing her captors and encouraging Amalia to flee. Tears streamed down her face as she jumped over her drunken neighbors and dodged junk-filled shopping carts.

An angry voice threatened but she was too terrified to even process the words. She focused only on the freedom promised by a wide warehouse exit. She didn't dare a glance backward but knew she was outdistancing her pursuers. Her breath came in ragged sobs as she wondered how she might possibly survive without Rosita.

Cool night air filled Amalia's lungs as she grabbed the rusty metal door frame and launched herself into the alley. She skidded to a halt, almost running into the front of a vehicle blocking her way. The headlights were blinding and she spun around, her shoes slipping on sandy gravel.

She dodged a shadowy arm that grabbed for her and turned to flee, only to run into a blonde-haired man, who easily wrapped her up.

"Oh no you don't, field mouse," he said. His voice was calm and he smelled of black licorice.

A sharp prick drew her attention and she looked over to see another man, thumbing the contents of a syringe into her arm. The world grew fuzzy and then dark.

⊏══⊐

"Ama. Ama." Rosita's voice was insistent, but Amalia did not want to wake. Rosita was always waking her up.

The scents of gasoline and body odor accomplished what her sister's voice had not. Ama's eyes flew open and she became aware of the rattling and shaking of the heavy vehicle in which they were riding. Rough, unfinished wood cut into her palms as she pushed herself to a sitting position.

More people than just Rosita sat next to her in the dim interior. There had to be at least six pairs of legs touching her own and she drew her knees up to her chest in an attempt to gain some personal space.

"Rosita, I'm scared," she whispered. "Where are we?"

"Bad men have taken us," Rosita said. "You must be brave."

"Where are they taking us, Rosita?"

"It does not matter. We will fight them. Do you understand? It would be better to die fighting than to let them hurt us," Rosita said resolutely.

Amalia laid her head on Rosita's shoulder and became aware of the soft sobbing of some of the other girls within their wooden prison.

"Do you know where they are taking us?" she asked aloud.

"To hell," a girl answered back.

"You're frightening her," Rosita said. "Stop."

"She is right to be scared. We have been captured by the devil himself."

The conversation was cut short as the truck bumped to a stop and changed directions.

"What's happening?" Amalia asked timidly.

"They're storing us like we are melons being brought to market," the girl said. "They will put us in the building and then sell us."

Rosita grabbed Amalia's hand and squeezed. "We will fight, Amalia."

"They will kill you," the anonymous girl said.

A small breeze and dim light wafted into the small holes at the top of the crate as doors to the truck were opened. Amalia stood and peered out through one of the openings. A forklift approached, rolling from the warehouse into the back of the truck. Their prison lurched as the forklift made contact and lifted the box into the air. Beneath her feet, Amalia felt off balanced, the forklift's tines not wide enough to fully support the size of the box it was lifting.

"Help me, Rosita," Amalia said, jumping against the side of the box, inadvertently stepping on one of the girls who still sat on the floor.

Instead of complaining or helping, the girl moved aside.

"What are you doing, Ama?" Rosita didn't need an answer. With her sister's weight on the unsupported side, the box tipped slightly and then bumped back down onto the tines as the lift operator shifted into reverse.

Together, they threw themselves against the wall of the box. Amalia heard creaking and felt the end of the box dip even further. The operator, recognizing the package's peril, slowed and started to lower the tines. The girl who'd been brave enough to speak to them earlier joined the effort, throwing her weight over to the lower end. The box toppled from the forklift, breaking open like an egg and spilling its contents onto an opening between the truck and a poorly lit warehouse.

"Run, Amalia, run!" Rosita called as the sisters picked themselves from the crate's rubble.

Amalia stumbled when she fell between the truck and the warehouse dock, scraping her chest as she slid to the ground. There would be no better chance at freedom. She ignored the pain in her palms and knees as she scrabbled from beneath the truck and once again ran for her life.

A light at the front of an adjacent building hinted at freedom and she darted through the shadows and across pavement. Daring a glance over her shoulder, she saw Rosita running only a few yards behind her. Her chest heaved with exhilaration; they would live. The sound of popping surprised her and she watched Rosita fall to the ground.

"Rosita!" Amalia stopped and turned, running back to her fallen sister.

"No, Amalia," Rosita said, coughing blood. "You must run for your freedom. I love you, sister."

The pavement next to Amalia erupted. Chips of asphalt were thrown into her face, about the same time she heard popping sounds again.

"I can't leave you," Amalia cried.

"Live for us both, sister," Rosita said. "Do not let them take you."

Another round of gunfire stitched the ground beside them and

Rosita jumped. Tears erupted from Amalia's eyes as her sister drooped in her arms.

"We got one," a man yelled, still fifteen yards away. "There's one more. We'll grab her. She's not moving."

Amalia kissed her sister on the forehead and laid her gently onto the ground. Jumping up, she ran, spurred on by more gunfire. Each time a bullet slammed into the pavement around her she flinched, but she refused to stop. Crossing into the light at the front of the next building, she pounded on the doors.

A man appeared in the hallway and waved at her, walking forward. He would let her in. He would save her.

She continued banging on the door frantically as he approached. There were two sets of doors between them, but the first set wasn't locked. As the man approached the outer doors and fumbled with a ring of keys, Amalia's heart leapt with hope.

"Little bunny Foo Foo needs to learn her place." Amalia's hopes were crushed. She didn't need to turn to recognize the blond man's voice behind her.

The man trying to unlock the door looked surprised as the glass in front of Amalia spiderwebbed. A small circle of blood appeared on his chest and he stumbled back, falling to the ground.

Amalia screamed and jumped aside. Her sister's voice softly whispered in her mind, "Run!" So Amalia did what she was best at. She ran.

I STARED at the grimy beige door sporting the number '1C.' It was a cool spring day but I was sweating bullets, the scene all too familiar. I'd done my fair share of raids in the service, but today I was unarmed and without a team. Steeling myself, I knocked. I must have hit it too hard because the 'C' loosened and swiveled downward, its waving motion slowing as time passed.

"What do you want?" a raspy voice asked from behind the door.

Finkle, owner of Sure Bond, had assured me this job would be easy. Sitting in his office, he'd been convincing. Buster Dowdy, a lightweight – Finkle's words, not mine – had missed his court date. He was a known drunk and in lousy physical shape. All I had to do was take him to the police station and Finkle would pay me three hundred dollars. Not bad for an hour's work. At least that was the theory I was operating under.

"Dowdy? It's Henry Biggston from Sure Bond," I said. Even to me, my voice sounded weak and I cleared my throat, already knowing I'd need a second shot at it.

"Go away! I don't want any!"

"We need to talk to you about your court date. I'm from Sure Bond. Chester Finkle asked me to come down here."

Finkle was my uncle and had given me a job after I'd come back from my last tour in Afghanistan.

"Gimme a second." The sound of someone wading through beer cans preceded that of a door chain being released. A wave of putrid air assaulted me as the door opened and exposed a pear-shaped man dressed in a heavily stained, wife-beater t-shirt that missed covering his stomach by several inches.

Dowdy had bloodshot eyes, a red-veined bulbous nose and a face covered by several days of beard growth. He leaned against the door jamb and said, "So talk."

I nearly gagged as his breath assaulted my senses.

"Buster Dowdy?" I asked.

"Yeah, so what if I am? Shit, kid, you said you needed to talk, so talk."

I sighed. If there was one thing I'd learned in the service, it was that the more a man postured, the less they had to back it up.

"You missed your court date. Let's take a ride to the station and get it worked out."

"Oh, did they have that already?" Buster asked, feigning an innocence he didn't wear well.

"It was two weeks ago," I said. "We'll go down to County and they'll get you a new date." I was stretching the truth. Buster would have to spend at least a night in lockup as Finkle wasn't about to re-bond him.

"Wait here, I'll get some clothes."

I relaxed. I'd been anticipating a confrontation. While I'd seen my fair share of action, I wasn't the sort who looked forward to it.

The apartment complex was in a rough part of town and I wasn't thrilled to be standing in the open. "How about I wait inside?"

"Suit yourself. Just need to use the john." Buster moved his bulk through the room, grabbed a shirt and disappeared through a door at the back of the apartment.

I scanned the room. It was trashed. My best guess was that my arrival had awakened Buster. Empty beer cans were strewn about near the single chair that occupied the room. It sat in front of an old CRT-style television. I felt sorry for the big man, I couldn't imagine living like that.

The sound of heavy grunting came from behind the door where Dowdy had disappeared.

"Dowdy? You okay in there?" I called. "You hurt?"

Buster's voice sounded far away, "Everything's fine, no problems in here."

"Are you sure?" I could feel things heading south, but Finkle had warned me about 'going too hard.'

The sounds of movement behind the door intensified, coupled with heavy wheezing. Buster's voice, still strained, edged on breathless, "No, everything is fine."

I heard a large thud as something or someone fell hard. Buster's now far off voice complaining, "Crap, sonnava ..."

"I'm coming in!"

Grabbing the door handle, I pushed, the cheap panel flexing but not giving way. I backed up and kicked my heavy boot next to the knob. The door relented and flew inward, a small flurry of wood fragments showering the floor. I smiled grimly. There wasn't such a huge difference between Sutherland, USA and Jalalabad after all.

I wasn't overly surprised to see that the bathroom window had been broken out. When I stuck my head out, I saw the chubby frame of Buster Dowdy chugging down the alley. "Dowdy, stop! Dammit!"

The opening was a tight squeeze and I wondered how Dowdy had managed to get through. I dropped to the alley, twisting around to land on my feet. Dowdy was nowhere to be seen. By this time, my adrenaline was flowing, and I used it to fuel my sprint. Something about the urine-soaked alley, the broken-down cars, and chase caused a momentarily flashback. I had to stop for a moment to clear my head as I fought to focus on the here and now.

Shaking off my anxiety, I resumed the chase, running out of the alley and onto the street next to Dowdy's apartment. I scanned both directions and caught a glimpse of the chubby man half a block away.

He was losing steam. With both hands he pulled at the waistline of his pants, trying to keep the saggy material from completely falling off. Nearly tripping, he slowed to a walk and it wasn't much of a task to catch him.

"Hold on, Buster!" I called out when I was only a few yards away.

Dowdy recognized the futility of running and turned to face me. He lowered his flabby bulk into a wrestling stance with hands forward, ready to grapple.

"Are you serious? Come on Dowdy, we just need to take a ride down to County. Let's not do this!"

Dowdy growled between wheezy breaths, "Look, pissant. If you take me down, they're gonna lock me up." He reached into his pocket and pulled out a small six-inch blackjack shaped like a flattened bratwurst. A blackjack was like a baton, only smaller and easier to keep out of sight. In the hands of a pro, it was a dangerous weapon. Not so much with Dowdy.

"It doesn't have to go like this." I wasn't sure how to negotiate with him and didn't much want to end up in any sort of wrestling match if I could avoid it.

Buster Dowdy seemed to have a different plan and lunged. I saw his arm snap out from his body with speed I wouldn't have expected from a fat drunk guy. I slapped the hand away and slipped to the side. Having not made contact, he stumbled and fell forward, landing face-first on the walk.

I grabbed his shoulder and rolled him over. Once again, his speed surprised me as his hand darted toward my face, still holding the blackjack. I blocked the blow and resisted the instinct to follow through with a jab to his face. It was a mistake I immediately regretted as the end of the blackjack grazed along my cheek bone.

"Damn it," I growled, wrenching the blackjack from his hand and backing off. Ranger training had taught me to never relent when the enemy was on its heels. But I had a hard time seeing this drunk as my enemy and felt pity for him. "Get up." I demanded.

Dowdy struggled to his feet, but he was looking bad. His face was getting even redder and he appeared not to be able to catch his breath. He leaned over, rested his hands on his knees, and took short breaths as he tried to speak. "Look ... dumbass ... how about you take off ... and I won't have to beat your head in."

"Maybe we head to the emergency room. You don't look so good," I said.

He staggered as he tried to remain standing. "I don't feel so good." Dowdy was staring at the ground, sweat dripping from his face. I wondered if he might be having a heart attack.

Since I felt partially responsible for his condition, I stepped over to steady him.

He wrapped his arms around my shoulders and pulled me into an uncomfortable hug. It was at this point that I became aware of strange sounds emanating from deep within him. I caught the whiff of rancid apple cider mere seconds before the contents of Buster Dowdy's stomach were deposited onto my back, making a sickening splashing sound that would stay with me for quite a while.

I brought my arms up and jammed the heels of my hands hard into his middle. He let go and I backed up quickly, but not quite fast enough to avoid the unspeakable things he then spewed onto my front. Without my support, Buster Dowdy fell over in a heap where he continued to spew like a puke-filled balloon. I pulled off my tan camo jacket, which had taken the brunt of the assault, and threw it to the sidewalk, considering it a loss.

I held his blackjack in my hand and considered giving him a taste of his own medicine. But as revolted as I was, Dowdy was having a rough time of it.

"You gonna live?" I asked, settling onto my haunches.

He stared up at me but didn't respond until all at once, he pulled himself to a seated position. The purge of his stomach appeared to have done wonders for his color and I figured he'd live. I pulled out my one pair of cuffs.

"Put your hands behind your back," I said, hoping we wouldn't need to get into it again.

"Yeah, yeah, okay." The fight was gone from the man and he strained to bring his flabby arms behind his back. I moved behind him, locked the cuffs tightly onto his wrists, and helped him to his feet.

"You're pretty fast for an old guy," I said.

"I was a Marine in Desert Storm and I wrestled in high school," he said, although it sounded more like *rassled*. "I'd have put you down if I hadn't tied one on last night."

"Sure," I said, nudging him forward. I sighed. In the short time I'd been back, I'd seen too many ex-soldiers who couldn't find their way back into society. "Truck's around front."

I pushed Buster toward the front of the apartment complex where I'd parked my 1985 Ford F250 pickup. She was a classic without a spot of rust. My grandfather and I had just started to restore her when I'd signed up for the Army. While I'd been gone, he'd finished the job and presented her to me when I returned. The truck was about the only thing I owned in the world.

We hadn't yet turned the corner when I heard Diva, my German Shepherd, going ballistic. I'd locked her in the cab with the windows up just enough so she couldn't jump out. I wasn't particularly worried about someone reaching through the window. Her bark was more than enough to deter any idiot who approached.

What I hadn't considered, was that in this neighborhood, if all you could do was bark, you were just noise. When we rounded the corner, I saw two teen girls kneeling at the front of the truck, completely ignoring my furious dog. When I yelled, they jumped up and made a run for it, rolling four-hundred dollars' worth of tires and custom rims in front of them. I was all but broke, so I gave chase.

"Stay put," I yelled over my shoulder to Dowdy. He might make a break for it, but given his current condition, it was a risk worth taking.

The street we were running down was a mixture of single family houses in poor condition and small apartment buildings like the one Dowdy lived in. The kids had almost a block lead on me, but pushing tires was no easy feat and I easily closed the distance.

A block into the chase, I was almost on top of them. The taller of the two thieves was maybe fourteen years old, while the second was a couple of years younger. The older of the two took a quick turn and allowed the tire to roll away on its own. For me the chase was all about getting my stuff back, so I deflected the tire into a group of trash cans.

"Stop," I snapped, not breaking stride. I was no more than a meter from the smaller girl, who wasn't quite as willing to give up.

If she heard me, she gave no indication, but she was losing steam. I was still a regular runner and while I was gassing, I had plenty left in the tank. Pulling alongside, I planted my foot strategically on the inside of her stride.

I might have laughed aloud as the poor girl tripped and fell forward onto the rolling tire. Scrabbling for balance, her arms pinwheeled as she was pulled onto the ground, doing me a favor by knocking the tire onto its side. Lying there trying to catch her breath, she looked even smaller than when I'd given chase.

"What the fuck?" she asked in broken English. Her light-brown face was soiled and her dark hair had been cut short.

"Don't give me that crap," I said. "You took my tire."

She pushed against the tire that had trapped part of her coat. "Take it," she said, unable to move the weight.

"Who's gonna pay for the damage to my truck?"

"Not my problem," she said. "What shit-stain parks a nice ride down here?" Her words were a poor mix of Spanish and English, but she was communicating just fine.

"Watch your mouth," I said. "And it's definitely your problem." I tried to grab her wrist, but she jerked away, banging her elbow on the ground. If it hurt, she didn't give any indication.

"Get off, pervert," she said, even as I pulled at the tire, helping to free her.

"Ten bucks if you help me get the other tire back to the truck, otherwise I'm calling the police and handing you to them," I said.

She rolled her eyes hard at my offer, but when I extracted a ten from my jeans, she grabbed for it. "Si."

I snatched the money back and pushed it into my pocket. "When you get my tire back to the truck. What's your name?"

"Qué?" It appeared that her English skills were waning or just as likely she didn't want to tell me.

"Whatever," I said, starting to roll the tire back in the direction of Diva and my truck.

"Sue." She caught my eye and pushed the tire away from me, but still toward the truck.

It was my turn to roll my eyes. If she was Sue, I was Pappi Van Winkle. Fact was, I had too many things going on to push her on it. I ran off to where the other wheel had landed and started pushing it back to the truck. On the way back, I noticed a small white card and a flip phone on the ground, so I scooped them both up and stuffed them in a pocket.

When I arrived, I found Sue leaning against my truck, tire on the ground in front of her with her hand out. For a moment, I ignored her as I walked up to Diva and reached through the window to calm her. She whined while I ran my hand along her muzzle and scratched behind her ear.

"No dog... No dog...," Sue said, her face clouding with fear as I put my hand on the door handle.

"Her name is Diva," I said. "And unless I say, she wouldn't hurt a fly."

With the passenger door open, Diva jumped from the seat and eyed the small girl, sniffing but not advancing as the girl backed up.

"Nombre estúpido," Sue said.

I fished the card and phone from my pocket and Sue lunged for them, eliciting a deep throated warning growl from Diva.

"Glass houses, Amalia, " I said, reading her name from a YMCA ID that had her picture on it. Diva's warning was more than enough to back Amalia off, but to her credit, she didn't run. I flipped open her phone and dialed my own number. Once I felt the buzz in my pocket, I hung up.

"Mía," she pushed, looking at her belongings but this time not lunging for them.

I pulled a ten out and placed it on top of her phone and ID card. "Now, beat it." I handed the stack to her.

Without hesitation, Amalia grabbed the items and ran away. Diva lurched forward, loving a good chase, but I gave a quick reprimand and she settled.

"You alive over there?" I called to Dowdy, who was now lying face-up on the sidewalk where I'd left him.

"I'm not feeling right," he said, not bothering to get up.

"Could be the drinking." I crouched to inspect the damage that had been done. They'd pulled the front two wheels off, leaving one hub resting on the ground and the other still held up with an under-sized jack. The good news was, the old truck was plenty tough and I didn't find any real damage. Unfortunately, I could only find three lug nuts.

"That's just effing great!" I said.

"Yeah, tough neighborhood. Wouldn't catch me parking my ride here," Dowdy added unhelpfully.

"Yeah, thanks." I was in a pickle. I couldn't very well perp-walk Dowdy to an auto parts store, buy lug nuts, and walk him back. Unfortunately, there was a short list of people who would help me out. The most obvious person to call was my grandfather Lester Ploughman, who I called Pappi.

I pulled out my phone and thumbed the quick dial. I hated making the call. Growing up, Pappi might as well have been my dad, since I'd never known my bio-father and my mom had taken off when I was barely old enough to remember her. Pappi and Grandma Pearl had been my mother's foster parents and eventually adopted me after it was clear she wasn't coming back.

"Henry. How's it going, big man?" Pappi asked cheerfully.

"Heya, Papps! Thanks for picking up. Do you have a minute? I'm kind of in a bind."

"Just catching a baseball game. Turn it down, Pearl. It's Henry," Pappi voice was muffled as if his hand covered the telephone.

"I have a problem with the truck." I wasn't sure where to start.

"You need a lift? Darn it, I knew that battery was getting old."

I smiled. He was the king of maintenance.

"No. A couple of kids swiped my tires. I got 'em back, but they took my lug nuts."

"Where are you?"

"Sutherland," I said, reciting the address.

"Rough neighborhood," he said. Pappi had retired from the police force a year ago and knew the town well. "Need me to send a patrol car?"

"No, I'm good," I said. "I've got a skip and need to be the one to deliver him."

"Give me forty-five minutes," he said and hung up.

"Heel," I said and gave my left leg a quick slap. Diva looked at me intently and walked around to my left leg. "Good girl," I commended and walked over to Dowdy.

"Hey, you can't sic that thing on me. I have rights," he complained.

"Guard," I said, ignoring him. Diva locked eyes with Buster and growled menacingly. "You stay put and there won't be a problem."

I sat on the sidewalk a few feet away, not wanting to get any transfer of additional stink. To the average passerby, I suspected we looked and smelled equally bad, but I had some pride. My cheek felt like it was on fire when I gingerly brushed a finger across it. I couldn't detect any permanent damage, but what did I know?

It didn't take Dowdy long to give up on the staring match and divert his eyes. I decided to give him a break.

"Sit," I ordered.

Diva sat back and looked over to me, whining, clearly not impressed with my life choices.

Forty-five minutes later, almost to the minute, Pappi pulled up in his late eighties Suburban with Grandma Pearl seated next to him. I stood and gave them a friendly wave.

"Who've you got there?" Pappi asked, jumping out of the truck. "Is that your skip?"

"Buster Dowdy," I said.

Pappi was in excellent shape for being in his early sixties. He'd always been bigger than life when I was growing up. Retired now, he hadn't changed much except that his hair had gotten grayer and he had a tan from playing too much golf.

"Jack stands are in the back. Let's get her stable first," he said, rolling down the Suburban's back window.

I crossed around the front of the truck and stopped at Grandma's window to peck her on the cheek. "Heya, beautiful."

"He said I had to stay in the truck," she pouted and returned my kiss. Pearl was in equally good shape for her age because she spent time leading exercise classes at a fifties-plus senior living complex. "Oh, Biggs dear, you smell. What happened?"

"Trust me, you don't want to know," I said.

I joined Pappi at the truck where he was already lifting one side with a bottle jack he'd extracted from the toolbox behind the cab of my truck.

"What's the damage?" I asked.

"Twenty-five bucks, although Pearl said she'd trade for dinner this week," he said. "And she's right, you do have a smell going."

I chuckled and placed a stand in place. The pickup had been our project and we were comfortable working in amiable silence. Twenty minutes later, I finished tightening the last nut.

"Sorry to call you out, Pappi. I thought I had this handled."

"Most excitement I've had all week. Glad to help," he said, swinging into his Suburban.

I gave Grandma a final hug and waved as Pappi pulled away from the curb.

"Load up." I called to Diva, slapping the side of the truck with my hand. She bobbed her head once and ran at the truck, leaping easily into the bed. "Same to you Dowdy. And, *don't* make a mess in my truck. Got it?"

"Look, I gotta go, I don't think I can make it all the way down to county. I gotta pee," He sounded sincere and, in his defense, he had been sitting there for quite a while.

I considered him for a moment. "Don't push it, Buster, that didn't go so well for me last time. You're gonna need to hold it."

"I don't know if I can." He started to squirm.

I thought about it and then walked to the toolbox. I got a face full of dog tongue as I pulled a canvas tarp from under the jack I'd just replaced. "Sit on this," I said, opening it up and spreading it out on the seat and floorboard.

Dowdy looked disappointed but managed to wedge his body into the seat. The trip downtown was quiet; neither of us in a conversational mood. It was just getting dark when I pulled up to the county lockup.

"Good girl," I said as I clipped the leash attached to the truck bed onto Diva's harness. "No trouble, this is a police station."

She whined and sat on her haunches, clearly conveying that I was disappointing her. For a dog, she was ridiculously expressive.

Pulling Dowdy with me, I walked up to a dented steel door that had no handle, stepping over a suspicious pile on the sidewalk.

"You gotta ring the bell," Dowdy said, nodding at a button next to the door.

"Thanks." I pushed it and a few minutes later a uniformed officer opened the door and admitted us.

"Whew, you guys stink!" The officer, dressed in a neatly pressed uniform, waved his hand in front of his face.

"Yeah, thanks. I need to drop this guy off; he has a warrant." I looked at the officer expectantly.

"They'll take care of you at the window over there." The officer stood as far from us as he could and pointed across the empty foyer to where a female clerk sat behind a thick, plexi-glass pane.

"Stand over there," she said, handing me a receipt after finding Dowdy on her computer. I wasn't exactly sure where she meant, but guessed she was referring to the only other door in the room. It didn't have an exterior handle – apparently a common theme here. A few minutes later, two officers wearing rubber gloves stepped through and took control of Dowdy.

Once outside again, I let Diva off her leash. She jumped from the bed in through the open driver's side door, taking her preferred place in the passenger seat next to me.

I scrubbed the sides of her neck. "Good girl."

It wasn't a long drive to Sure Bond, although I wasn't sure if Finkle would still be there. As far as I knew, he owned the old, rundown brick building that housed his office and a couple of other struggling businesses. Plenty of on-street parking was available and I was pleased to see several lights on inside as I pulled up.

The front door was unlocked, so I pushed through to the small lobby. The layout was simple: an old beat-up desk, a few file cabinets, a dusty worn-down couch, and three unmatched chairs. Above the couch hung a black velvet painting with splashes of bright color that depicted a fat Elvis Presley in a white jumpsuit singing in a smoky lounge. Behind the empty desk was a short hallway with three office doors.

Vi, Finkle's assistant, was just coming out of one of the offices. "Got a call from Marge over at lockup," Vi said as I let the door slam. "Says you got taken out to lunch by Buster Dowdy. That right?"

"Pretty sure my coat will never be the same," I said, smiling. "He in?" I nodded at Finkle's closed door.

She nodded affirmatively. "You might have something in your hair."

Violet Brown was a somewhat overweight blonde in her mid-fifties. Her dress code tended toward bawdy and she spoke with an accent that had to come from the East Coast. While I wouldn't go so far as to say she was pretty, she got respect from me for working with what she had. We'd only met a couple of times, but I liked her attitude.

I knocked on Finkle's door and pushed through before he could answer. I found him reclining in his chair, feet propped up on the corner of his desk, intently reading through the contents of a folder. In contrast to Sure Bond's sparsely appointed lobby, every horizontal surface of Finkle's office was piled with stacks of papers, folders, and manila envelopes. Many of the stacks leaned against each other for support, giving the impression of a house of cards.

"You got Dowdy," he stated. "I told you it wouldn't be so hard, didn't I? You bring my cuffs back?"

My uncle, Chester Finkle, was in his late fifties or early sixties and wore a three-piece suit that had gone out of style at least twenty years ago. Even in the dim light, I could see what I suspected was a mustard stain on the brown-striped wool of his vest. Technically, he was a second cousin on my Mom's side, but I'd always known him as my uncle.

"Crap. No, they're still down at lockup."

"Well, they won't return them so you're out forty bucks. That brings your total to two hundred and sixty. Not a bad day's work. It's in the envelope there." I looked at his desk, noticed a white envelope and picked it up. Four fifties and three twenties. I frowned. How could he have known I'd forget the cuffs? Before I could ask, he continued. "If you're up for another one, come by in the morning."

"What time?"

Without bothering to look up from his file, he muttered, "Eleven thirty."

I shook my head at his definition of morning but took the clue and walked out.

"Henry," Vi said as I walked by. I turned to look at her. "Don't listen to that old fart. Marge has your cuffs. I already talked to her."

"Uh, thanks, Vi," I said. "How'd you know?

"She's a god-damned eavesdropper, that's how!" Finkle yelled from his office. "CIA's got nothing on her."

"Thin walls and cardboard doors. If the landlord wasn't so cheap, he'd have more privacy," Vi said with a raised voice. More quietly, she continued, "Marge will be on duty for another hour. Better hurry."

I gave her my warmest smile, the one I use to flirt with women who should know better. "You're all right, Vi."

She straightened her shoulders and smiled back at me as Finkle slammed something onto his desk. I took my cue and escaped out the front door. Back in the truck, I turned on the radio and hummed happily as Diva and I ran back to the station.

"You don't smell any better, you know." The officer was clearly enjoying himself. He was right, so there was really no reason to argue. I walked up to the clerk's window, this time noticing Marge's name-plate on the counter.

"Lucky Vi called when she did," Marge said, sliding the cuffs through the slot beneath the window.

"Thanks," I said.

"Skip recovery is a tough job, kid. Get out while you can. There are easier ways to make a buck," she offered unkindly.

3 / PROBATIONARY DICK

"Up for pizza tonight?"

My best friend, Snert – Alan Snerdly on his driver's license - was on the other end of the call. "No veggies."

Turns out, the pizza sat on the truck seat beside me. I knew well enough he didn't like anything but meat.

"I'm actually in your lot. Are you up or down?" I asked as I parked beside his dark blue electric Tesla two-door. I felt a pang of jealousy as I took care not to brush against the eighty-thousand-dollar vehicle.

Snert owned a hi-tech electronics repair shop a few blocks north of downtown Sutherland and lived on the top floors above the storefront. I punched a code into the panel at the back door and wound through the neatly organized storage room to the steps leading up to his apartment, Diva close on my heels. As expected, I found Snert hunched over his oversized desk nestled between tall windows at the front of the apartment. He waved a hand in front of his face, pushing away a thin, blue-gray trail of solder smoke.

"Smells good," he said, absently. "Just set it anywhere."

I found a rare open spot on the desk, flipped open the box, snagged a slice and set one aside to cool for Diva. I bent my own slice so as not to lose any of the grease in transport and dropped heavily into the couch that would likely be my bed for the night.

"Oh, hey." I leaned over and pulled my wallet out with my free hand. "I have your money ... well, some of it anyway." My running tab with Snert was up to six hundred dollars. It was something he insisted I didn't need to pay back, but no way would I let that stand.

He set the soldering iron into the ceramic insulated holder and kicked at the wooden floor, propelling his chair to the pizza. "Do you have time for a delivery tomorrow?" he asked, looking bug-eyed at me through the magnifying lenses mounted to a band around his forehead.

"I gotta run by Finkle's around noon, but I have time before that."

"Good. Needs to be there by ten. You'll never guess who I saw today."

"Who?"

"Bobby," he answered.

There was only one Bobby in our world who didn't need a last name and that was Bobby Dungalo.

Dungalo was Snert's kryptonite. Hearing his name brought back memories of the day Snert and I met. For some reason, when Snert turned twelve, his parents, who'd homeschooled him to that point, decided it was time to socialize him. They placed him into Sutherland Central Junior High. I still question that choice given Snert's short stature, chubby frame, and general nerdy outlook on life.

The class bully, Bobby Dungalo, had recognized that Snert was easy pickings the minute the poor kid walked in the front door. Bobby's daily routine soon consisted of shaking him down for money, food, and whatever else he found desirable. For weeks, Snert kept quiet and had even gone so far as to request additional money from his parents to keep Bobby happy.

One day, however, I happened to roll around the corner of a school hallway when I ran up on Bobby Dungalo, sitting squarely on top of Snert, his knee in Snert's back, and rifling through his backpack.

"Hey, get off him!" I'd said.

"Move on, dumbass. This bitch is mine." He'd used a racial slur, since Snert is black, but I prefer to tell the story without that part.

While addressing me, Bobby had turned slowly, leaving his knee on Snert's back. To his credit, Snert hadn't made a sound, but I will never forget the look of anguish on his face. That wasn't just physical pain, he was humiliated and terrified.

"Get off," I'd said. The phrase *in for a penny, in for a pound* had always resonated with me. If you looked at me now, you wouldn't think it, but at that time in my life, I was no match for Dungalo. But there I was and in a split second, I was fully committed.

"Last chance, bitch-lover, shove off or I'm-a gonna hand you a beating." Bobby Dungalo emphasized his point by pushing Snert's head into the floor.

And that was it. Something flipped a switch in my brain. I was no hero, but in that hallway, running onto Bobby Dungalo bullying a helpless kid half his weight, I knew what had to be done. Win or lose wasn't even part of my thinking.

Without another word, I took a step forward and kicked my foot into Bobby Dungalo's chest. The move caught him off guard. With a knee on Snert's back he was already off-balance. His bad luck was that a fire extinguisher hanging on the wall behind him was perfectly located to catch his head. Lights out for Bobby.

Initially, I'd thought I'd killed him. That notion was put to rest when he groaned a few seconds later. I knew exactly what had to be done next. You can't count on a lucky shot twice, so I helped Snert up off the floor and we sprinted down the hallway and out of the school, not stopping until we'd made it to my grandparent's house.

And that was that. Snert and I've been friends ever since. We were an odd couple. Snert excelled academically and helped me avoid flunking out, and I made it my responsibility to make sure he was invited to parties.

"Did you hear me?" Snert asked again.

"Yeah, you said you saw Bobby. Where'd you see him?"

Snert rolled his chair closer and handed me his oversized smart phone. His lock-screen showed an older Bobby Dungalo with wispy beard and balding head, wearing an orange vest while stabbing at a piece of garbage. I laughed and handed the phone back, taking an opportunity to grab another piece of pizza.

"You'll get a kick out of this." I pulled the sausage-shaped weapon from my pocket and set it on his desk.

"It's a blackjack," Snert said, turning his attention back to the small device he'd been working on when I arrived.

"I know. I've always wanted one," I said.

"Per municipal code, a weapon of this nature is illegal," Snert said.

"Damn effective, too," I said.

━━

The next morning I found a package on the desk next to the pizza box, with instructions that it needed to be delivered before ten o'clock. It was already nine thirty, so I grabbed a piece of cold pizza, and ran out the back door to the alley where Diva took care of the needful. Damn, I hated mornings.

We got lucky as traffic was lighter than usual. After dropping Snert's package off I drove to Sure Bond and pushed through the heavy glass door into the lobby. The sound of an argument between a strange man and Finkle filtered through paper-thin walls of the office. Vi was nowhere to be found, although the fact that she was in the office at eight the previous night suggested she might not work normal shifts.

I wasn't interested in breaking into the middle of a fight, so I flopped onto the couch, waving away a small cloud of dust that billowed up around me. I wasn't generally bothered by such things, so I pulled out my phone to catch up on the latest soccer games I'd missed.

Shortly after settling in, Finkle's door opened and an annoyed voice wafted out into the lobby. "Fact is, I got better things to do than babysit some rich old lady."

I hopped up off the couch and turned just in time to jump out of the way of a flabby, middle-aged man with a sagging face and greying hair. He wore a crumpled suit jacket over a dingy white shirt he hadn't bothered to tuck in. A wave of the same, sour smell I'd recently encountered with Buster Dowdy rolled by as he pushed past and barreled through the front door.

I looked back to Finkle whose face was flushed but showed no other sign of irritation. "Ben Tripper," Finkle matter-of-factly offered after the door closed. "Come on in." He turned and re-entered his office.

It took me a moment as I tried to figure out what had just occurred. I was impressed that Finkle didn't seem any more perturbed than he was.

Finkle, who had more than a small paunch lying over the top of his belt, exhaled and dropped into his chair, which immediately reclined under the assault of his bulk. He waved his hand at the only other open surface in the room: an uncomfortable looking wooden chair.

Behind his desk was another velvet Elvis painting, this one of the singer in a tropical setting. Distracted by the painting, I tripped on a small pile of documents leaning against the desk. Papers slid across the floor, cluttering my path to the chair. Half falling, I quickly twisted my way into the seat so as not to cause the pile to spread further. I bent over and tried unsuccessfully to tidy things.

"I wasn't sure I wanted to bring you on board, but Lester said you were in a spot and needed a job," he said, referring to Pappi.

I wasn't having any luck with the pile, so I let go and allowed the papers to disappear beneath my seat. Mention of Pappi got my attention. I knew he'd suggested that I talk to Finkle about the job, but didn't realize he'd spoken for me. The connection added a bit of pressure; I didn't want to disappoint either man.

He continued, "You did a good job with Buster Dowdy. Looks

like you even got a bit banged up. I wouldn't have expected that, but you never know in this business."

I appreciated the compliment. At least I wasn't sucking at this as bad as I'd feared.

"Since you're here, you must be ready for another job. Today is your lucky day. I have two for you. Well, really one and a half. First, I need you to run a file to the precinct for me."

He paused and stared over his reading glasses at me, obviously waiting for a response.

"Uh, sure. That sounds great."

"Get Henry a PI log book started," he shouted.

"On the desk," Vi's muffled voice responded.

"When'd she get here?" I asked.

"Ten-thirty," Vi called back through the open door.

"Right." Finkle hardly paused before continuing. "You need to log every hour you spend working for me. You need a thousand hours before you can sit for the voluntary licensure test for private investigations."

"Private investigator?"

"We get light investigation jobs periodically. It pays the bills and we can ask more if I say you're a probationary licensed private investigator."

I was impressed he got all those words out in a single breath. "Probationary is a thing?"

"No," he said. "But as I was saying, take this folder to Sergeant Williams at the second district. And this is the file on Marlin Creight. He's another skip. Try not getting him all fired up like you did Dowdy. This one can have an attitude. He used his mother's house as collateral, so I think he'll go easily enough. Just tell him what's on the line, I'm sure he'll go along. No real record of violence."

I started to protest the assertion that I'd mishandled Dowdy, but Finkle waved me off with his hand.

"Same deal, three hundred on delivery. Do you need another set of cuffs?"

"No. I got the cuffs back. And just so you know, Dowdy bolted on me. I didn't antagonize him *and* he smacked me with a blackjack." I didn't want to leave Finkle with an incorrect understanding of how things had gone down.

My words made no impression, though. "Williams takes an early lunch, you might want to get down there." He grabbed another file from his desk and turned in his chair, putting his back to me. My cue to leave.

"Leave the door open," he called as I exited the room.

Vi held up what I assumed was the logbook and the papers Finkle had referred to. A waft of overly sweet perfume hit me as I accepted the items from her.

"You smell nice," I said.

"Make sure you log yesterday, too," she said, smiling. "It adds up quickly."

One thousand hours seemed like a long time, but the idea of being a private investigator sounded interesting enough.

I loaded into the truck, set Sergeant William's folder onto the seat next to me and opened the file on Marlin Creight. I rolled my eyes at the picture of a muscular, bald, white guy with a swastika on his neck, wearing a wife beater t-shirt. What was it with the wife-beater shirts, already? This guy was not going to get a jump on me.

I flipped up his picture and read. Prior convictions for burglary, larceny, and even a few drug possession charges. He also had a couple of drunk and disorderlies along with resisting arrest. Despite his threatening appearance, there was nothing overtly violent in the file.

Creight's court date had passed and Finkle would have to put up twenty thousand dollars if he wasn't delivered to County within a week. I continued to read. Marlene Creight had guaranteed the bond, pledging her house.

I punched the police station's address into my phone. Twenty minutes later I arrived at a modern, single-story brick and glass building. The front doors opened into a tiled lobby and on the far end was a tall counter that had a transparent panel separating the public from officers working behind it.

In front of the counter on the tiled floor was a painted line. A sign next to the line read; "Stay behind line until called."

"Next." The officer looked up as I approached.

I stepped up, "I have a delivery for Sergeant Williams."

"Identification, please," he said.

I fumbled for my wallet and held out my driver's license.

"Have a seat. Someone will be down shortly," the officer said, nodding at a row of chairs that were bolted to the floor against the outside wall.

I walked over to the chairs. They had thick metal loops on the arms, which I imagined made it convenient for use with handcuffs. With that image in mind, I decided against sitting down.

Ten minutes later a uniformed female officer approached. I felt like I recognized her but couldn't quite place where. She was five-foot-six with jet-black hair pinned tightly in place. She was clearly wearing a vest beneath her black uniform and the holster on her utility belt lacked a weapon.

"Henry Biggston?" she asked with a flicker of recognition in her green eyes.

I had to remind myself that I was here for a purpose, which was not related to good-looking police women.

"Yes, ma'am," I replied.

"We went to high school together. Nala Swede." She held her hand out.

"Right. I was trying to figure out where I'd seen you before," I said, racking my brain. The name was familiar, the face was familiar, but something was off. But I took her hand, shaking it.

"Short hair. It gets everyone. You have something for Sergeant Williams?"

I held out the file from Finkle. "That's right."

"Great. Follow me," she said. "What have you been up to?"

She led me to a transparent door and waited for the officer who'd greeted me to buzz us through. We walked into a large open floor plan which was covered in desks, each with short cubicle walls separating them.

"Army after high school," I said. "I'm helping my uncle right now, he's a bail bondsman. How long have you been with the police?"

"Three years this week," she said. "After school I took a year off and then got an Associates in Criminology. It took longer than it should since I worked nights. Then I joined the force."

"Like it?" I asked.

"Most days," she said. "Changes your perspective on people, though."

As we walked, I began to recognize some level of organization to the open room. Tall glass barriers segregated working groups from each other, but there were no signs to help identify what the groupings might be. Nala stopped in front of a desk, where a middle-aged, powerfully-built man sat. The nameplate on his desk read *Sergeant Williams.*

"So, you want to be a Dick, Eh?" Williams had a slight paunch and his salt-and-pepper gray hair was cut short on his dark brown skin.

"What?" I asked.

"Finkle said you were green, but *work* with me," he said.

I looked to Nala for help.

"Private Investigator – Dick Tracy. It's his favorite joke," she said, smiling. "Finkle called earlier. Said you were coming. He and the sergeant go back."

"Finkle was a cop?"

"You have the file?" Williams ignored my question and nodded at my hand.

"Right." I said, handing him everything Finkle had given me.

"Word is you saw some action in the Sandbox," he said. "That right?"

"Seventy-Fifth Battalion, Afghanistan," I said.

"Damn, son. Ranger Battalion? Welcome back," he said. "Almost makes me feel bad about this next part."

"How's that?" I asked.

"Officer Swede, you know what Finkle calls his new Dick?" Williams asked, smiling.

"No, I don't," she said, shaking her head, clearly knowing exactly what was coming next.

"Probationary Private Eye," he said. "Wait for it ... that's right ... *Proby Dick.*"

"Nice, Sarge," Nala said, rolling her eyes.

"It's the small things, Swede." He leaned back, howling in laughter.

Nala walked back to the elevator with me and once the doors had closed behind us, she explained. "He's really a good guy. He just thinks his jokes are funny."

"I walked right into it," I said.

"You did ... and it made his day."

She led me back to the glass door by the front counter and let me out.

"It was nice to see you again, Biggs," she said.

I didn't miss the fact that she'd used my nickname.

"You too, Nala."

━━━

Creight's house wasn't far, assuming, that is, that he was still living with Mom. I figured the possibility was worth checking out.

I parked in front of the old two-story, brick house. The lawn was in shambles and weeds had grown up inside the rocked areas of the landscaping. From the street, the front door appeared weathered beyond repair. Leaving Diva in the cab, I hopped out and made my way up the walk.

I steeled myself. This guy wouldn't be quite the pushover Dowdy had been. I walked up the crumbling cement steps and across the sketchy porch to the front door. I wished I'd brought the blackjack with me.

I tried the doorbell but didn't hear anything. Maybe the ringer had just been turned down. I waited a few minutes and knocked.

"Mrs. Creight?" I called, raising my voice.

I heard shuffling on the other side of the door.

"Mrs. Creight, I need to talk to Marlin. I'm from Sure Bond and Marlin missed his court date. Your house is collateral and you could lose it if we can't get this worked out. I need you to open up."

I knocked again, this time a lot harder.

"Go away," an older woman's voice said from the other side of the door.

"Look, don't make this harder than it has to be. Marlin needs to make this right or you'll lose your house," I repeated.

The front door swung inward and a heavy-set, older woman with long stringy gray hair looked up at me, wearing a nightgown that did little to hide things that desperately needed hiding.

"You want this shit-hole. Take it," she said. She must have thought I was checking her out as she tilted her head and gave me a flirty look.

"Mrs. Creight, I don't want your house, but I do need to talk with Marlin," I said, doing my best to keep my expression neutral or, at a minimum, not gag. I looked over her shoulder into the rundown house. Her previous description of the house turned out to be accurate. In my peripheral I saw movement a few feet to my right. Things were about to get interesting.

"He's not here," she said.

A scrape on the porch and a sudden movement told me it was time to act and I turned just in time to block a blow from a wild-eyed man. I was in for a fight. The picture of Creight didn't do him justice. At six foot three, he was a nod taller than me and his muscles were puffed up like the Michelin Man – no doubt the result of steroids. I quickly decided to avoid any direct hits. Contrary to popular belief, muscle is muscle and he'd be a wrecking ball if given an open shot.

I'd boxed golden gloves as a kid and the fight started off pretty much as you'd expect. If you watch a man's mid-section, you know everything he's going to do. I raised my fists and easily slipped his first two strikes and returned fire with two quick jabs to his face that were designed to damage but not over commit me. I had no idea if Creight had any fighting experience and patience was called for.

I slapped away his next hit and followed through with a quick combination into his gut. I'd always been a blue-collar boxer, preferring to wear down my opponents by destroying their base instead of going for a quick kill. Against Creight, this was gold. I had caught him completely off guard, with his stomach muscles relaxed. He coughed and bent forward, stunned by my hits.

The next thing I knew, I heard a gunshot and felt heat along my ribs. I'd been shot before, so I recognized the sensation. I still didn't much like it. The impact of the bullet spun me away from Creight. I'll never forget the look of surprise on his mother's face as she watched me struggle for balance.

"Boom, bitch!" Creight cackled, taking advantage of the distraction.

A moment after I registered the pain along my ribs, I heard the meaty slap of Creight's fist and pain exploded on the side of my neck just below my chin. Desperately, I turned with the blow and brought an uppercut under his defenses. My aim was off and my fist grazed past his chin, scraping his ear. Without hesitation, Creight slammed his fist into my side where I'd been shot. The pain brought me to my knees.

"Stay down if you know what's good for you," Creight growled and kicked my head with a heavy work boot. His warning was unnecessary as I crumpled to the porch, the world fading around me. In that fleeting moment of consciousness, I recognized he was wearing no pants.

"MR. BIGGSTON, CAN YOU HEAR ME?" A man's insistent voice asked for the second or third time. In the background, Diva's frantic barking was incessant.

When I tried to open my mouth to respond, I found I couldn't. I opened my right eye slowly and looked at the speaker. He was wearing a white uniform shirt that had the blurry name of some company on it. About the only thing I could see clearly was a big blue X that had a vertical line through it.

"Mr. Biggston?" He asked again, giving me a minute to clear my head.

"Where... Who are you?" I asked.

"Emergency Medical Services," he said.

While I could only see through my left eye, my vision cleared sufficiently for me to get a look at the scene. An ambulance and two police cruisers were parked in front of and behind my truck. I was still on Creight's porch and had been raised into a seated position and propped against the rough brick wall. Sergeant Williams stood at the bottom of the stairs talking to another officer. I wondered if this meant that Nala was here, too, but I didn't have to wonder long as she strode up to speak to Williams.

"House is clear, Sarge. No sign of Creight or his mother," she said.

"Good work, Officer." He looked up at me and saw that I was watching the conversation. "I see our Mr. Biggston has regained consciousness. Why don't you take his statement?"

I appreciated that he was all business and had dropped the humorous references to my new career.

"Will do, Sarge," she said.

"Mr. Biggston, how are you feeling?" the paramedic asked, snapping his fingers in my field of vision, trying to get my attention back.

"My head is killing me," I said.

"You've been shot and it appears you've suffered blunt-force trauma to your head. You've all the symptoms of a concussion," he said. "We need to get you down to the hospital."

"Bullet. Is it still in me?" I asked, looking down at my bare chest, locating a thick bandage.

"No. It deflected off your rib," he said.

"Good," I said. "I'll be fine." It wasn't entirely bravado. I'd been shot more than once before. Ranger training had taught me to make honest assessments of my own and other's health status. There was nothing a hospital could do for me that I couldn't take care of on my own.

"It's protocol," he said.

I wasn't going to the hospital. "Seriously, back off a minute."

"Give us a minute, would you?" Nala asked. The EMS tech nodded assent and rolled from his knees and back onto his feet. Nala took his place, kneeling next to me. "Twice in a day. People are going to talk."

I laughed which caused me to wince. I'd need to take it easy for a few days. I definitely had a concussion.

"Would you mind telling me what happened? Sarge would like a statement."

"Not much to tell. Marlin Creight's a skip. Sure Bond has his paper. I was supposed to give him a ride down to County," I said.

"And he shot you?" she asked.

"Creight jumped me," I said. "His mom shot me."

The reference to the mother elicited a stifled laugh from Nala. "Wait. You got shot by an old lady and got a shiner from a drunk? All in two days?"

"That's about the size of it," I said.

"Can you tell me anything else?"

"Not much to tell," I said, but walked her through the short encounter.

When I finished, she changed the subject. "Are you still friends with Snert?"

That was unexpected, but I grinned. "Absolutely, we hang out all the time."

She smiled, and man, that got my attention. She had a beautiful smile. How had I forgotten this girl?

"I haven't kept in touch with him. We used to talk a lot in chemistry class," she said. "How's he doing?"

"He's amazing." I was proud of my best friend. He'd built his electronics business from nothing. "He finished engineering school early and started his own business."

"That's great," she said. "That just made my day."

"Are you turning down our services?" the EMS tech interrupted, recognizing our conversation had switched from official to personal.

"I am," I said.

Nala frowned at me. "Biggs, you sure? You don't look so great."

"I'm a combat medic," I said. "I can look after it."

"Your funeral," the EMS tech said, not impressed with my credentials.

"Swede, we've got another call," Sergeant Williams called from down the steps.

"Yes, Sarge," she said. "See ya around, Biggs."

"Shit, I hope not," I said. The look on her face was my first warning that my words could have been taken the wrong way. "I mean, not like this."

Her smile returned as she turned and jogged off after Williams.

I shook my head, then winced again as things swam in front of my eyes. I'd always been horrible around women. It was good to see that war hadn't changed everything.

A very worried Diva assaulted me when I gingerly climbed into the truck. Dog kisses and gunshot wounds don't mix well. She finally calmed and I started the engine to head for my grandparent's place. I needed to grab my medical kit and a fresh set of clothing. While I drew the line at living with them, if I hustled, I knew I could horn in on lunch.

There was something immediately relaxing about pulling off the highway and onto the familiar narrow asphalt. My grandparent's house was far from the closest neighbor, sitting on the last thirty acres of Pearl's father's old farm.

If there was a heaven for dogs, the farm was it and with a single glance over her shoulder, Diva ran off when I opened the door. I pulled on a crumpled shirt I'd left in the truck, covering my bandage. The swelling on my head and Dowdy's blackjack mark across my cheek wouldn't hide so well. Pearl met me, swinging open the screen door before I got there. She wore what she called a house dress. Not formal enough to go to church in, but good enough for working around the house. After a quick hug, she pulled back to look at my head. It had started bleeding again during the ride over.

"What happened to you?" she asked, worried. "Lester, come here and look at Bigg's face."

"Yes, Pearl, I'm coming," he said from out of sight. He'd be sitting in the living room, reading the news or catching up on a baseball game.

"Did you get in a fight? You're too old to be fighting, Henry," she scolded. "This bandage is soaked through."

"It's not that. I was on a job," I said.

"Come here and let's get that cleaned up," she said.

Pappi had made it into the hallway and she stopped the procession so he could examine my head.

"What happened?" I could see concern in his face as he watched me move slowly toward the kitchen. His eyes were sharp, but I knew he wouldn't want to worry his wife by voicing his suspicions about my injuries.

"Not here, Lester. Let's get him some lunch and then we can talk," she said.

He was scandalized. "But you called me out here!"

"Don't argue. Henry will you stay for lunch? I'll throw on another piece of chicken," she said.

"Grandma, you don't need to feed me," I said half-heartedly. "I just wanted to talk to Pappi for a few minutes."

"Nonsense," she said. "You can have your talk with Lester but let me clean up your face."

She pulled me into the powder room. The cool water on the cloth she used to wipe my face felt good, but pressure on the side of my head where Creight had kicked me caused new pain.

"There you go," she said, happy to have removed the grime. "Let's put an ice pack on that. You don't want it to swell. Now, are you sure you don't need to have that looked at?"

"Already did," I said. "I'll be fine."

She pursed her lips, not happy with my answer. "Lunch will be ready in fifteen minutes."

I walked through the family room and out to the deck where Pappi was setting another place.

"You're favoring your side. Were you shot?" he asked in a low voice. He'd been a policeman for most of his life. If anyone would understand my issues, he would.

"Just a graze," I said. "I was trying to pick up a skip."

"That him?" he asked, eyeing the folder.

I handed it to him.

Pearl bustled through the door, handing me a glass of water and setting a blue ice-pack next to a bottle of ibuprofen. "Drink this."

One didn't ignore the ministrations of Grandma Pearl. Not and stay out of trouble with the woman.

"Thanks, beautiful," I said.

Pappi was quiet while he flipped through the file. When she disappeared through the door, he gave his analysis. "Skinhead. Looks like a tweaker. How'd he get the jump on you?"

"His mother distracted me with a 9mm," I said.

"By shooting you?" he asked.

"Order of events is still a little fuzzy," I said. "The guy hit like a Mack truck."

"I guess I don't have to tell you that getting shot is an indication you're doing things the wrong way," he said. "I've always believed that the best lessons are the ones we learn the hard way. Tell me what you'd do differently."

"I was too tight on the door," I said. "Second time I've misjudged one of these guys."

"Good. Best to learn that lesson early. I'd say that's a good day's work. Were you packing?"

"No permit yet," I said.

"Surely you weren't planning on bringing this guy in alone, were you? These people aren't like us. Everything is a fight and it's never fair. Where was Diva?"

"In the truck," I said. He raised an eyebrow. For Pappi, he might as well have been yelling. "I know. Creight wouldn't have gotten within ten feet of me if I'd had Diva out."

"Would your CO have sent you to a house by yourself, looking for a guy like that, when you were in Afghanistan? I can tell you, no cop would walk up to that house unarmed or alone. Not with the possibility of a tweaker being there," he said. "I can't believe Finkle sent you on this job. I've got a mind to call him."

"No, don't do that. I've got to figure this out. I can't complain because he gives me a hard case. He'll never give me anything else," I said.

"Want to make it on your own, eh? I can understand that. And you learned something today. What else is on your mind?"

I could admit things to Pappi that I wouldn't tell anyone else. "I don't know where my balance is. I try not to come out swinging, but I'm getting my butt kicked."

"Lunch is ready." Pearl walked through the sliding glass door carrying a platter.

"Tomorrow, you go back to Finkle and tell him you need a second job. Tell him that Creight took off, but you've a line on him and you'll need a couple of days."

"But I don't have a line on him," I said.

"He'll go home in a day or two, they always do. The reason this Creight hasn't already been brought in is that he's a pain in the ass. Finkle doesn't have a lot of choices."

"Language, Lester," Pearl chided. "Now, that's enough shop talk."

"Just a second, Pearl," he said. "Start taking these jobs seriously. I assume you read Creight's jacket."

"Nothing in there about being violent," I said.

"You can't trust a jacket. Lawyers are good at getting charges reduced. I'll bet you knew this guy was trouble," he said.

"I did, but I didn't think ..."

He waved me off. "Your gut told you there was trouble. Don't ignore it next time. Now, what are you doing for lunch tomorrow, say noon?"

"Lunch? Sign me up," I said.

"Corner of Twelfth and Vine," he said. "You doing okay for cash?"

"I'm making it," I said.

5 / AN UNDERSTANDING

PEARL WOULD BE ANNOYED if I didn't leave my filthy clothing behind for her to wash, so when I got to the room they still thought of as mine, I tossed my rumpled shirt into the laundry and pulled on a fresh black t-shirt. I also grabbed my medical kit and my range bag that contained the 1911 Kimber 45-caliber that Pearl and Pappi had given me after my last tour. Pearl hadn't loved the gun as a gift idea, but it was a fantastic weapon.

Pearl followed me out to the truck. She eyed the bags and looked a little sad. "I wish you'd reconsider living with us, Henry. We love having you at the farm."

"Nothing's permanent," I said, tossing the bags into the back of the truck as Diva jumped into the cab.

"No more trouble. Okay?" she said, hugging me. I held my breath when her strong arms wrapped around my waist, but even if she didn't acknowledge the bandage she was gentle. When we released, she handed me a paper bag.

"I'll be careful," I said, opening the bag. Inside was a stack of sandwiches and a plastic bag of frozen cookies. "Thank you."

"Just remember where that comes from," she said, smiling slyly.

I hopped back in the truck without a clear idea of where to go next. I really didn't want to go to Snert's since he would just fuss about my face. So, like any self-respecting late twenty-something, I checked my phone and responded to the single message time-stamped a half hour ago.

SNERT: *Shop is swamped. You free?*

BIGGSTON: *Be there in twenty minutes.*

Thirty minutes later, I was parked in the back of his shop. Diva lazily got up and took a long stretch before she jumped down and followed me to the back entrance. I punched in the code on the security panel, opened the door and walked through the storage room. When I got to the stairwell, I released Diva and turned toward the shop. Diva was looking for a nap and raced up in search of her bed.

Snert was indeed busy, with one customer occupying his attention and two others milling around. They both looked at me expectantly when I entered.

"Who's next?" I asked.

A rotund woman in a gray business suit stepped forward, handing me a small box. "Our security system crashed. I was hoping Mr. Snerdly could figure out what's wrong with it."

"It will be a couple of days. He's currently working through a backlog," I responded. I had no idea if that was true but didn't want to pin Snert down with a promise he couldn't meet.

I turned the box over in my hand and noticed it had deep gouges on the back panel.

"Any idea what this is about?" I asked, pointing out the marks.

"I don't know. The employee who takes care of the system didn't come in today. Is there any way to expedite a service call?"

With a nod toward my friend, I finished writing a note. "Leave the box and I'll let Snert know it's a rush. He might have some flexibility in his schedule."

"Thank you." She sounded genuinely relieved.

Her response piqued my interest. "Are you having security issues otherwise?"

"I don't know. We've had irregular issues with our inventory. I don't know if it's bad accounting or theft," she said.

"If you want to wait, Snert will free up soon, or you can leave contact information and I'll have him look at the box and get back to you," I said.

"I'm in a bit of a rush." She handed me an embossed business card that read Lambert Textile Research. "Here's my card."

"What kind of work do you do at Lambert Textile Research?"

"Industrial research. Next generation textiles. I'm Penelope Lambert." A small smile accompanied her outstretched hand.

"The inventory you're missing, is it worth a lot?" I asked, accepting her hand.

"I'm not sure it's actually missing. I'm sorry, but how will this help with the repair?" she asked.

"Not sure. Snert might have recommendations for an upgraded security system, but the size of the space and value of what it's monitoring can make a difference. I'll pass your information along and either Snert or I will contact you tomorrow morning," I said.

"That will be fine."

Once she'd left, I finished scribbling notes about our conversation, taped it to the box, and slid it under the counter.

For the next two hours, the bell hanging over the front door kept dinging with a steady stream of customers. Some people were just looking for replacement items, although most were dropping off or picking up.

At six o'clock, Snert finally ushered the final customer out. By the look of things, I figured he had a full night of work ahead.

"Henry, what happened to your face?" he asked after he'd thrown the lock on the door.

"Disagreeable client. I had a paramedic look at it. I'm fine." I grabbed my medical bag from the supply room and followed him up to his apartment.

"Are you staying in tonight?" he asked as I filled the ice bag Pearl sent with me.

"If that's okay. Pearl sent cookies. Want one?" He wouldn't turn one down. I extracted four palm-sized cookies, handed two to him and set the other two on my ice bag.

"I'll never understand why you call her Pearl," he said, accepting the cookies. "She's your grandmother."

"Always been that way," I said.

"I was going to order Chinese, you up for some? My treat. You really bailed me out this afternoon," he said.

"That sounds fantastic," I stretched out on his couch and fired up the TV, looking for a game to watch. The cool of the ice bag felt wonderful as I placed it on my head.

"What happened to this security module?" Snert's question startled me awake. The smell of Chinese food caught my attention and I noticed the game I'd been watching was finished and a new one had started.

"The one from Lambert Textile?" I asked.

"Yes. Someone disabled it," he said.

"It's not broken?"

He frowned while holding the box up for me to see. "It needs minor repairs. They used a heavy metallic object to remove the control module from its casing. Worse yet, this is an older model that doesn't automatically upload to the cloud. Whoever removed it kept the temporary caching SIMM and broke the power supply. It's an easy fix, but this looks deliberate."

My eyes were drawn to the boxes of food on his desk. Those were mine. I loved moo shu and he was strictly a peanut butter chicken kind of guy. I wasn't in the mood to make the little tortillas, so I grabbed chopsticks, dumped the plum sauce on top and sat on a stool across from him, eating out of the box.

"Will you be able to fix it by tomorrow?"

"Need a part. It'll be the day after. You up for an install?" He glanced at me. "Pretty please? I'm buried. Change of season has everyone worked up."

How could I resist that face? And besides, I still owed him

money, even if he'd never hold me to it. "Sure. I don't have a lot going on. I can do it."

"I sent Mrs. Lambert an email. I'll work it out. You'll need the van."

Snert's van came complete with ladders and just about every tool necessary for installation of the various devices he serviced.

"Make sure to check for wi-fi signal wherever the core is stored," he said. "Otherwise we'll need to run a hard wire."

"Can do," I said, punching the additional instructions into my phone. "I'll talk to her about the upgrade. Any guess on cost?"

"Forty-five hundred installed. Comes with a five-year warranty, although it wouldn't cover this type of damage." He tapped the box.

"Got it. Just let me know."

"Have you ever considered just working with me?" Snert asked, growing serious. "We could be partners. You do the installation. I do the repairs. You're a natural salesman. People don't exactly look at me and think security."

I smiled. I loved where his heart was. "I don't bring enough to the plate, buddy. You need an employee, not a partner." Then my memory kicked in. "So, do you remember Nala Swede?"

"Nala? Of course. We were best friends. My *only* other friend. We met my junior year in high school," he said.

I had to work to remember what he considered his junior year. Snert had been on the fast-track and graduated early.

"Of course I remember her."

"I saw her today," I said. "She's a cop now."

"That's interesting," he mused.

"Yeah, I thought so too."

"No, not that." Snert was still fiddling with the security box. "Whoever removed this core missed the backup SIMM."

"Not following."

"This unit has a redundant cache that stores the last three hours of video," he said. "Whoever took it off the wall missed it."

"Give it to me," I said.

"I can't, Henry," he said. He only used my name when he was serious. "That's private customer data."

"Just put it someplace safe then," I said.

He shrugged. "I'm careful with all of my customer's data. So, do you feel like a movie? I've got a couple more hours of work, but I was feeling like something sci-fi."

Inwardly I groaned. I'd never gotten into science fiction, but it was Snert's house. "Yup, cue it up. I'll grab a beer."

"No beer, Biggs," he said firmly. "You're taking ibuprofen. It's dangerous." This time I wasn't as circumspect with my groan.

"Just one?" I begged, knowing I wasn't going to win the argument.

"Don't be a baby. You'll be asleep after the first twenty minutes."

I chuckled. He had me there.

―――

The next morning a warm tongue dragging across my face told me Diva needed to go out. The position of the sun on the buildings across the street told me it was about eight o'clock.

Sitting up, I gingerly felt my head. "Hold on, girl." It definitely felt like I'd been kicked in the head, but I was feeling better. I'd need to avoid further head trauma for at least a week, but then when wasn't that the objective? "Want to go out for a run?"

I immediately regretted my words. When I stood up, the bandage pulled across my skin and I was reminded of the bullet that had grazed my ribs. I was lucky. I didn't think the rib was broken, but the torn skin was tender. I pulled the bandage off and looked down at a nice trench, four inches long. Yeah, that probably should have been stitched up. I'd used a combination of steri-strips and skin glue to close it. The wound was too long for glue alone, but my patch had held overnight. Diva's patience ran out by the time I'd put on a fresh bandage, and she used her nose to prod me into action.

"One more second." A promise is a promise, so I changed into running shorts and shoes. She spun excitedly as I finally walked her to the stairs.

I would call the run a mixed success. It's always helpful to run off a young dog's excess energy and Diva would be easier to deal with today. One might think running shouldn't stress your obliques, but my wound was still fresh enough that even small twists and jars were painful. Like Diva, however, running cleared my mind and I felt better when we came back forty minutes later.

"Want some eggs?" Snert asked when I got out of the shower.

"Starving. Anything from Lambert?"

"She must be an early riser," he replied. "She's fine with a repair tomorrow if you're still up for it."

He really didn't understand that there wasn't anything I wouldn't do for him. "Count me in."

6 / BUDDIES

Buster Dowdy's blackjack was definitely going out with me today. I slid it into my pocket when Snert wasn't looking. He just didn't do illegal, no matter how minor. I had a couple of hours before meeting Pappi for lunch and decided to take a run by Marlin Creight's house. I wasn't sure if I should expect him home, but I was determined that he wouldn't get the drop on me a second time.

"Where are you headed?" Snert asked.

"A couple of appointments." Mentally, I face-palmed. I'd become such a fixture in his life that he wanted to know my schedule. While that might not be a problem for him, these days I got itchy when I didn't have a lot of space.

⸻

The clock on the dash said noon by the time I found a parking spot and snapped a leash on Diva. I was a little surprised to find that the address Pappi had given me for lunch ended up being a gun store.

I pushed through the front door and walked in. Diva alerted to the sound of muted gun fire; no doubt there was a range in the basement. In return, Diva was getting a cautionary look from an attractive woman standing near a case of rental handguns. Probably an employee, she was modeling a tight sleeveless tactical shirt. The woman approached slowly and the Glock holstered at her waist was obvious to both Diva and me.

"Can I help you?" she asked with a wary smile. "We're not supposed to have dogs on prem."

"Service dog," I said, as if that explained everything.

"She's a vet?" the woman asked, straightening her back. Something about her bearing made me suspect she was either active or ex-military.

"Army K-9," I said. "Got her ears blown out."

"Would she let me approach?"

"Diva, sit," I said, crouching beside Diva, letting her know the situation was safe. "Thanks for asking."

Diva was hit or miss with people. The woman must have worked for her, because Diva wiggled around like a puppy when the woman made contact.

"She's so well behaved. You her handler?"

"No, she was my buddy's," I said. I wasn't sure why I was willing to share with the woman. Maybe because I'd pegged her for ex-military. "You serve?" I deflected, though, not wanting her to ask the next question. Diva's handler, my buddy Angel, wasn't someone I was ready to talk about to anyone.

"Still do," she said. "Corporal, Army National Guard. Something I can help you with?"

"I'm meeting my grandfather here, although I thought he was inviting me for lunch," I said.

"Oh, you're here for the conceal carry course," she said. "I'm Mel Ramirez. I thought I'd been stood up."

I chuckled. I didn't think it was likely Mel got stood up very often. "Lester's not showing up, is he?"

"Been here and gone already. He and my dad are buddies from way back. Lester just told me to expect a student. On the bright side, he brought lunch for both of us," she said.

"He's been on me to get my conceal permit," I said. "I guess he resorted to clandestine means."

It was her turn to chuckle. "Well the good news is, while this is normally a full day course, we skip most of the gun-safety stuff with vets and I'd bet my Glock that you've served," she said.

"Two tours with the Seventy-Fifth," I said. "Sergeant Henry Biggston, reporting as ordered."

Her eyebrows raised. "Seventy-Fifth, no shit?" she said with deference. It was the kind of respect that only mattered to me when coming from another member of the service.

I pulled up my left t-shirt sleeve to expose my company tattoo.

"Damn proud to meet you," she said, holding out her hand.

"Hooah, Corporal," I said.

"Hooah, Sergeant," she replied.

The afternoon had flown by. I would have guessed two hours, but the clock said four thirty. Mel had an easy way about her, neither flirty nor self-conscious, and we'd covered a lot of material, most of which felt obvious. Our common background in the service had put both of us at ease.

"Do I pass muster?" I asked as she reviewed the test I'd filled out.

She chuckled. "Yes, but don't get a big head. I've only seen a couple of people fail." She stood up. "Give me a minute. Lester asked me to fax the course completion over to one of his buddies."

"Buddies?" I asked.

"Apparently he's good friends with Sheriff Lancaster."

"Bill?"

"You know William Lancaster?"

"Sure. But last I knew, he was a deputy," I said. "He used to come to the house for beers once in a while."

Mel raised her eyebrows. "That explains the fast-track. I'll be back in a second."

She left the door open, so I followed her out to get a look around the Thunder Alley store. Contrary to what one might expect, I hadn't spent much time in gun stores, most of my experience having been gained in the service.

"Looking for anything in particular?" A darkly-tanned, grey-haired man came up beside me as I scanned a glass case full of tactical shotguns. It was a good bet I was looking at Mel's father and the shop owner. Knowing that Pappi had pulled some strings here, it was also a good bet that Mel's father was one of Pappi's ex-cop friends. It was best to introduce myself either way.

"Henry Biggston," I said, offering my hand, sparing a look at Diva, who just sat next to me, wagging her tail happily.

The gesture earned me a smile. "Gabriel Ramirez. Friends call me G-Two, though. You're Lester's boy?" he asked, shaking my hand.

"Grandson. Yup," I answered. "I appreciate you making time for me this afternoon."

"Your grandfather is a good man," he said. "Are you just browsing or are you interested in the shotguns?" He pulled a key from his belt, unlocked the case, extracted an eighteen-hundred-dollar Benelli and handed it to me after opening the chamber. It was lighter than I'd expected, and I pulled it to my shoulder, sighting on the wall.

"Nice," I said, handing it back to him. "Probably just in dream mode, however. How much are you getting for those bean-bag rounds?"

"Four dollars apiece," he answered. "I could do twenty dollars for six, however."

I pulled out a twenty-dollar bill and handed it to him. I had an old twelve-gauge shotgun at the farm and non-lethal rounds seemed like a good idea if I got into trouble again. He plucked two packages of three rounds each from the display and handed them to me.

"Always the salesman," Mel said, joining us, placing a hand on her father's shoulder. "You're good to go, Henry."

"Call me Biggs," I said. "I owe you a cold one for getting me through all that. Want to grab a drink?"

"Sorry, Biggs. I've got the evening shift. Maybe another time." She didn't skip a beat.

I searched her face, trying to determine if I'd crossed a boundary. She seemed cool, so I nodded.

"Melinda." Her father's voice carried mild disapproval. "I do not believe Mister Biggston was asking for your hand in marriage. Go. Have a drink with him."

I raised my eyebrows and let my eyes flit between Mel and her father. My offer was being pushed very quickly and it suddenly occurred to me that Pappi's setup might have been for more than just my permit class. If so, Mel probably also suspected there was something going on.

She rolled her eyes as her cheeks flushed. Instead of responding to her father she grabbed my hand and pulled me toward the entrance. "Old men," she said with mock disgust.

Before we got outside, I needed Diva on a leash, so I stuffed the beanbag rounds in my pocket and bent to snap on her leash.

"Where would you like to go?" I asked, once we were outside. "My truck's only a couple of blocks away."

"Harry's is close," she said, pointing across the street. "He won't care about your dog."

We jaywalked, running across the street to a bar that had an awning across the front and outdoor seating cordoned off from the street by a low iron fence. A weathered sign above the entrance read 'Harry's Pub.' It wasn't exactly seedy, but we wouldn't get run over by suits either.

"You know, if you're not up for this, no sweat," I said as we walked in. There were a handful of people seated at a long, wooden bar. Only one of the dozen or so tables had a couple sitting at it.

"Veranda?" Mel called to the bartender who was looking in our direction. He nodded his head in acknowledgement and turned back to the glass he was filling. "You know Dad and Lester are trying to set us up, right?"

We went back out and I clipped Diva's leash to the railing next to a table. "Gathered that from the conversation."

We were interrupted by a waitress I hadn't seen inside. "Get you something to drink?"

"Anything light on tap," Mel answered.

"Make that two," I said.

"Light beer?" Mel looked at me scandalously. "I need light. You, not so much." She waved her hand to encompass her torso.

"Believe it or not, I like the taste," I said. "I don't like to get too filled up."

Mel laughed out loud. "You sure don't talk like any Ranger I've been around," she said.

"How many Rangers have you been around?" I asked.

"Plenty. I'm a 91F," she said, as if that explained everything, which it mostly did. Although a better description would have been 91 F Small Arms/Artillery Repairer.

"How many times you been over?" I asked.

"I started regular Army," she said. "In Iraq for two tours. After my gig was up, I moved to the National Guard so I could help Dad with the shop. Didn't exactly work out since I got deployed twice after that for a year each. I think I'm getting transferred in six months to another unit that's getting deployed. It'll finish out my four years if they do."

"You like it?" I asked.

"My last deployment, we were moving a bunch of equipment," she said, her face growing dark. "Truck in front of me got hit by an RPG. Killed everyone aboard. They had us pinned down for over an hour. I've never felt so helpless in my life. We didn't have anyone who had combat experience, least of all my Lieutenant."

I'd stilled as she'd started talking. To an outsider, the fact that she'd just jumped to the subject might have felt weird, but I got it. It was easy to get crap stuck in your head and sometimes it just came out.

The waitress, either through keen insight or a general lack of engagement, dropped our beers onto the table and left without speaking.

"Sorry. You don't need to hear this," she said, looking up at the waitress's back.

I picked up my beer and took a swig, mostly to show I wasn't perturbed by the conversation. "You had your service weapon?" I asked.

"For all the good it did me," she said. "We hid in the ditch while my CO called for help. I popped up a couple of times and one of those times, I took a hit. My jacket caught a lot of it, but it hurt like a sonnavabitch. To be honest, I just don't understand why they didn't come get us. They had us."

"You get a scar?" I asked.

She lifted her left arm and pulled at the ribbing of her tank top and the bra underneath. Any other time, I'd have had different thoughts, but she was baring her soul and I wasn't about to dishonor that. Mel revealed a large scar that ran just under her left breast and then back under her arm. It occurred to me that there was no possibility that breast hadn't been damaged as well.

"Pretty much wear one-piece swimsuits at this point," she said, smiling tightly. "Scars don't bother me, but people don't like them on women."

"I say fuck-em," I said. "You're a damn hero if you ask me, and you earned that scar. You should be wearing a bikini."

"Smooth," she said, grinning.

I probably blushed. "Oh. Right. Didn't really mean it that way."

"I know. You're the first man I've been out with who isn't put off by it. There's more damage, but we'd have to be better friends." She pulled hard on her own drink and sat back. "I've shown you mine, now you show me yours? You're favoring your side and it's clear someone tuned up your face. How long you been out?"

"This?" I asked, lifting my shirt and showing the bandage where Creight's mother had shot me. "No, I got shot by an old lady, and her deadbeat son stepped on my face."

She threw her head back and laughed. "Seriously? Give it up, Biggs. You going to have to tell me the whole story now."

The hour flew by, and I was disappointed when Mel finally stood and told me she had to get back to the shop.

"Do it again sometime?" I asked when we were standing on the street in front of her Dad's shop.

"Sure," Mel said. "Take it easy, Biggs."

On the way back to Snert's, my phone rang. I'd received a call from a number I didn't recognize while talking with Mel at the bar. I figured it was the same person, so I pulled out the phone and answered, not bothering to look at the number.

"Biggs," I said.

"Henry, it's Lester," Pappi said.

"You're a sneaky one," I said.

"It's worse than you think. I called in a favor from Sheriff Lancaster. You remember Bill, right?" he asked. "Your conceal carry was approved this afternoon."

"I didn't know he was sheriff. How's that possible? Mel just sent the papers in an hour ago," I said.

"Old and wizened. Bask in the glow already," he said. "What'd you think of Melinda Ramirez?"

I laughed. He was clearly enjoying himself. "Just had a drink with her. She's good people."

"Her dad, Gabriel, used to be on the job," Pappi said. "A lot of us go to Thunder Alley to get our weapons serviced."

"Don't I have to carry the permit?" I asked, suddenly realizing I didn't have any paper copy.

"Faxed it to Alan," he said. "I assume that's where you're staying?"

"Just temporarily," I said. I didn't feel like I was pulling my weight and I especially didn't like that I had to admit it to my grandfather.

"You'll get your footing soon enough, Henry," he said. "Pearl's calling. I gotta go."

"Thanks, Pappi," I said.

"Yup," he answered and hung up. He wasn't big on conversation.

When I got to the next stop light, I pulled up my missed calls. I had a voice mail from the number I'd missed while in the bar, so I hit play.

It was the cop, Nala. *"Hi Biggs – I was wondering if you wanted to grab dinner tonight?"*

Things were definitely taking a turn for the better. I'd spent the afternoon with Mel and now I was looking at an evening with Nala. I hadn't done much dating while in the service and suddenly, I was about to have two in the same day. I added her phone number to my contacts and fired back a message.

BIGGS: *Dinner sounds great. Tell me where and when.*

NALA: *I'll pick u up, 6:30. Where will u be? Dress warm.*

BIGGS: *Copy that. Snert's store. Dress warm?*

NALA: *Send address. Dress warm or be cold.*

Straight and to the point. I plucked an address card from my contacts and forwarded it to Nala's number. I smiled all the way back to the shop.

"What do you mean?" Evidently Snert wasn't fully prepared for my news. "Nala is coming over here? Now?" It was about six fifteen and though he'd closed up the shop, he was still working at his desk.

"She asked me out on a date," I said. "I can just meet her downstairs." He was more worried about this than I expected.

Snert followed me back to his spare room. "No. I want to see her."

I took down a dress shirt I'd left hanging there, did a body sniff check and decided it'd be smart to do a quick cleanup.

"She's not going to judge you," I said. "I was talking you up. She had no idea you were such a big deal nowadays."

"I'm not a big deal, Biggs." He picked up a large padded envelope from a table and handed it to me. "I got you something."

We weren't really in the gift exchange program. "What's this?"

The buzzer in the front room rang, alerting us to someone's presence at his street entrance, downstairs.

Chaos took over. Diva jumped and ran for the stairwell with a tentative woof and Snert looked around desperately, the package completely forgotten. "This place is a mess."

The buzzer sounded again.

I looked at him. "You want to let her up or should I meet her downstairs and just take off?"

"Ohhh. This place is a mess," he repeated.

"The door, Snert," I said. "Too late now."

He just stared down the hall at the open living area, frozen in confusion. It was left to me to take action, so I walked over to his computer desk, pushed the button on the wireless intercom device and talked in the general direction of Snert's computer monitor. "I'll be right down," I said. "Do you mind coming up? Snert would love to see you."

"Buzz me in. I'll run up," Nala replied.

I pushed the door release while looking over at Snert. "You have a little something on your ..." I pointed to his cheek. "No ... up a little. No ... you're not getting it. It's egg or something."

"I can't believe this is happening." The poor guy ran from the room in a panic.

I chuckled and jogged down the small landing at the bottom of the stairs just big enough to allow the door to swing inward. The portico outside was well lit and a good portion of the light made it through the thick translucent glass illuminating a woman's silhouette.

I pulled the door open and took in a short breath as I got a good look at Nala. I thought her hair had been cut short, but clearly she'd been wearing it up. Long silky waves of black hair cascaded over one shoulder and down her back. She wore a worn leather jacket, slim black pants, and held a motorcycle helmet. Nala grinned as she watched me take her in. I'll just say that her police uniform clearly didn't do her justice.

"Uh, hi, Nala."

"Hi yourself." She was still smiling, obviously appreciating my inarticulate moment. "Do you mind riding? I just got the hog." I followed her eyes to the street where a large, gunmetal gray motor-cycle sat.

"Hard to turn that down," I said, trying to sneak another look at her without being obvious. "Lot of bike there."

"Think I can't handle it?" she asked defensively, her eyebrows raised.

"I'm pretty sure last time we talked, I was the one laid out on the ground," I said. "I'll be honest, I was surprised to get your call."

"What? Because you got jumped by Creight?" she asked.

I tipped my head to the side and shrugged. "Not very macho of me. Did I mention he wasn't wearing any pants?"

The bark of laughter brightened her face. "No, you did not. While the cop in me believes you shouldn't have held any detail back, withholding that little nugget from Sergeant Williams was a good idea. He'd never let you live that down."

"Yeah, not sure why I told you just now," I said.

"Want to get going?" she asked.

"Yes. No. Wait! You want to see Snert first? He's just upstairs, he was asking about you."

"Think he remembers me?"

"He remembers."

I motioned upward, and she brushed past me, breaking into a jog on the stairs. I turned to follow and struggled not to gawk.

At the top of the stairs, Nala rounded the newel post to enter the living room and pulled up short. I caught up with her and while I wasn't surprised that Diva had come to check out the noise, I was surprised that she was growling, hackles straight up.

"Diva, down, " I said.

Diva stopped growling but refused to break eye contact with Nala.

"It's okay, girl," Nala said, trying to calm the dog, but Diva wasn't buying it and resumed growling.

I scooted around, placing myself between them. "Heel," I ordered. "Sorry, Nala. She's normally not like this."

Nala smiled. "Army K-9?"

"How'd you know?" I asked.

"I bet she smells gunpowder on my jacket. I'm no threat, Diva," she said, trying to sound reassuring. "Pretty young for discharge."

"Medical discharge. She's three."

"Nala!" Snert had changed clothing, and the smell of cologne preceded him as he ran over to give her a hug.

"Snert!" She returned his hug and lifted him off the ground. While Snert wasn't a large man, he was chubby. Her easy lift was impressive.

"How did I miss that you two were such good friends in high school?" I asked.

"You were too busy playing soccer, basketball, and whatever else let you out of school early. You seriously don't remember Snert and me sitting in the stands?" she asked.

"I guess I do. I just hadn't put it together," I lied. I didn't want to hurt her feelings, but I was completely blank. In my defense, I hadn't been all that interested in hanging out with girls in high school. If I had been, I would have remembered *her*.

"Would it help if I said I was three inches shorter and forty pounds heavier back then?" she asked.

A sudden, shocked feeling of understanding crashed through me. I would really have appreciated it if my epiphany hadn't hit my face like I was sure it had. But now I got it. She was the pudgy girl. If I'd known her name, I sure hadn't remembered it. And then it hit me.

"Ooooh. Nala, as in Panala. Damn, now I get it. Ugh. Yeah, I totally wasn't putting that together. Pretty shallow, right?" I said. "But, seriously. It's just ... you're all *this*, now." I gestured with one hand, sweeping from head to toe. I'd already buried myself, might as well be honest.

She rolled her eyes. "It's okay. I forgive you."

"I can assure you Henry is a compassionate friend. I would not say that his feelings towards his friends and acquaintances is lacking in depth," Snert said. I loved the little guy. He was first in line to tell me to shape up, but he was also first in line to defend me.

Nala gave Snert another hug and released him.

"Good. Because I'm feeling like Greek tonight and nobody eats Greek alone. That sound good to you, Biggs?" she asked.

"I'm game for anything."

"Do you have a jacket? It gets cold on the bike," she said.

She'd already seen me down for the count because of one skip. I didn't need to tell her the story about the other one. "No. Long story, but my jacket isn't usable anymore. I'll be fine," I said.

"I know of a great leather store. We could go there after dinner if you like," she said.

"We could at least look," I said. "I'm broke at the moment, so nothing too fancy."

"Place I'm thinking has used jackets if you don't mind that sort of thing. Gently used is nice with leather, because it's already broken in."

"Cool. Let's do it," I said.

"Nala. Do you have a helmet for Henry?" Snert asked.

"I do. I'll take good care of him."

He took a slow breath, unwilling to just let her leave again. "Please come by more often, Nala. I miss talking with you."

"I will."

I followed her down the stairs and out the front door. Her bike was an older Harley cruiser and it really did look like more than enough bike for her.

She swung a heavy boot over the seat and sat down, then looked back to where I was standing and handed me the helmet that had been strapped just behind the seat.

"Can you hear me all right?" The sound of her voice came through speakers in the helmet.

"Sure can."

"Good. Hop on and place your hands on my waist. When we turn, don't lean unless I do, and never more than me. If you get concerned, just lean into me, it actually makes us more stable," she said.

I climbed on, initially trying to give her some room, but the seat was designed to push me forward. I placed my hands on her hips and desperately tried to think of less interesting things.

"Ready?" she asked, firing up the engine.

"Sure."

With a roar, we were off. If I'd had any questions as to Nala's capability to handle the bike with me on it, they were soon put to rest. She maneuvered smoothly in and out of traffic. I did get cold, but Nala had warned me and there was nothing to do but survive.

"You doing okay back there?" she asked, sensing my discomfort. "You'd stay warmer if you got closer."

"First date," I said. "Don't want to walk home."

I felt the short laugh in her body. "Good call. Keep it PG and we'll be okay."

I slid into her as she slowed for the next stop and allowed my arms to wrap around her stomach. She had a narrow waist and I had difficulty reconciling my memory of Snert's chubby friend and the woman in front of me.

The restaurant was twenty minutes away and by the time we arrived I was fighting against my body's desire to shiver. Happily, I jumped off when she finally pulled to a stop.

"Just leave your helmet on the seat, " she said, strapping her own onto the seat before removing her leather jacket. She wore a simple blousy long-sleeved white dress shirt which was tucked into her leather pants. It was a nice look and highlighted her olive-toned skin.

"Aren't you worried about someone taking off with your gear?" I asked as she carefully draped her jacket over the bike.

"How much do you know about Sutherland?" she asked, giving me a knowing smile.

I wasn't sure what she was asking. I'd lived in the suburbs of Sutherland most of my life. The town was well known for its less-than-stellar crime rate. Personally, I wouldn't leave anything I cared about lying around and not under lock and key. "Well enough to know that, cop or not, someone's going to take that stuff."

"Not here they won't," she said, stepping onto the sidewalk.

Through the window, I saw that the restaurant was about half full. The patrons were generally well dressed and older.

I shrugged. I wasn't about to argue with her. "Come here often?" I asked, changing the subject.

That earned me a smile. "My uncle's place," she said, pulling the door open.

"Nala," a dark-haired, middle-aged woman exclaimed, standing up from where she'd been sitting at the bar. With arms wide open she pulled Nala in for an all-encompassing hug. After an awkward few moments, she released Nala and looked me up and down. "Tell me. Who is this dream boat?"

"Aunt Sophia, meet Henry Biggston," Nala said. "He's too young for you. Biggs and I went to high school together."

I held my hand out, but the woman pulled me in for a hug, too. I could have sworn both of her hands brushed my butt before she released me. "So nice to meet you, Henry Biggston. Anthony will be disappointed he missed you."

"Who's in the kitchen tonight?" Nala asked.

"Josephina and Ralph," she answered. "I see you took my advice with the shirt, dear. You're so pretty. Don't you think, Henry?"

"Absolutely," I agreed wholeheartedly. "She's a knockout."

My comment earned me a suspicious look from Sophia. Nala picked up on it and hooked her arm into my own.

"Any open table?" Nala queried.

"Yes. Of course. Red or white?" Sophia asked.

I felt like I was on a different planet as a lot more communication was going on around me than I was keeping up with.

"Wine preference, Biggs?" Nala asked, leading me to a table by the window.

"Seems like you have homefield advantage," I said. "Probably best if you make the choice."

"House white would be wonderful," Nala said. "I can get it."

"Nonsense," Sophia answered. "You brought Henry to our home for your first meal together. Today you sit and talk ... stare into each other's eyes. Let us work our magic."

After Sophia bustled away, Nala held a hand up to her mouth

and whispered. "She can be a little much. We can leave if you're uncomfortable."

"Are you kidding? She's great," I said. "Let me guess, you worked here before joining the force?"

"Still does sometimes," Sophia answered for her and gracefully turned over wineglasses that were already on the table and poured a deep-burgundy-colored wine into each.

This time I waited until Sophia left, humming to herself. "I may not know wines, but this doesn't look white," I said as low as I could.

"Red wine is the drink of passion," Sophia said, startling me. She was back with a basket of cut bread that she set on the table. Nala rolled her eyes.

"You really do look nice," I said, picking up the basket of bread. "I'm not sure what I said to annoy her, though. You want some?"

"You caught that? No bread for me."

"Hard to miss," I said.

"I'm glad the swelling is down on your face. It's too pretty to get messed up," she said.

As expected, the date was awkward as we tested subjects and tried to find things we had in common. Toward the end, however, we slipped into a comfortable rhythm. Nala's mother was Persian, and her dad was Australian. They'd met in Florida when they were young. Nala had been a police officer for a couple of years and liked working with her partner, Williams, who was still her senior and had originally been her training officer. As the night wore on, I could also tell she was edging around a conversation she didn't want to have.

"I didn't know your dad had been on the job," she said.

"Grandfather. Dad's never been in the picture. Pappi retired a year ago. Sounded like Williams knew him."

"I thought that was your dad. Sorry," she said.

"Don't be. I never knew my father."

"You want to get out of here?"

"Sure. I'll settle up. Have you seen the waiter?" I asked.

"Already taken care of. I invited you to my family's restaurant, it's my treat."

"Do I get to pay when I invite you and pick the place?" I asked.

Her surprise was evident. "Are you saying you want to go out again?"

"Who wouldn't?" I asked. It was my turn to show genuine surprise.

She sighed. "I feel like you're not getting it."

That comment brought my eyebrows up. "What's to get? Seriously, you're gorgeous, fun to talk to, and you're probably packing heat," I said.

"My uncle's connected," she said. "The reason I can leave my helmet on the bike is because people are afraid of him."

"But you're a cop," I said. "How's that work?"

"I love my uncle, so there are some things we don't talk about. By the way, the reason I'm wearing a long-sleeved shirt is because of this." Nala unbuttoned her shirt.

I looked around the restaurant. There weren't quite as many patrons here now, but still, this was weird. "Whoa, hold on there. I don't think we need to..." I cut short as she tugged the tails of the white shirt out of her pants and undid the cuffs, finally pulling it off. Beneath the shirt she wore a white undershirt with thin straps. "What are you doing, Nala?"

"Putting it all on the table," she said, folding the shirt into her lap. My eyes traced over her muscular shoulders and down her shapely arms sleeved with tattoos. As far as I could tell, the tattoos stopped at her collar bone on the front but continued around her back.

"Damn, girl," I said, impressed. In the Army, I'd done my fair share of weight lifting and I never had anywhere near the kind of definition she had. "Do you ever eat carbs?"

"That's it?" she asked in a voice gilded with anger and disbelief. "I tell you I'm an Iranian weight-lifting dirty cop covered with gang tats and you want to know if I eat carbs?"

I tipped my head to the side and shrugged. "Just selfish, I guess."

She was hot and pushed abruptly back from the table. "I'll call you a cab. You're an asshole."

"True statement," I agreed with a small smile. I could see why she didn't have a lot of success on first dates. "I'm not going anywhere, though."

"What are you doing?" she asked, narrowing her eyes. She'd gotten to her feet and was leaning on the table, her faces inches from mine. With a hiss, she asked, "Are you mocking me?"

"Good guess," I said. "We have a nice dinner together and just when I think things are going good, you fucking turn into Doctor Jekyll."

"Mr. Hyde," she corrected.

"Does that ever work for you?" I asked. "*Are* you a dirty cop? *Are* you a gangster? *Are* you a jihadist?"

"No," she said in a small voice, anger draining from her face.

I stood up, walked slowly around the table, placed one hand behind her neck and the other on her small waist and pulled her to me. She didn't offer much resistance, melted into my body, and looked up into my eyes.

"That's all I need," I said and leaned in, kissing her while breathing in her light perfume.

It was after midnight when we finally decided to call it a night. We'd left the restaurant after it became obvious Sophia wanted to close and moved on to an all-night donut shop. We'd forgotten all about finding me a jacket and the ride back was cold enough to cause me to draw in close to Nala. If she minded, she didn't say anything.

"Biggs. Something's going on at the shop. There are cruisers out front," she said. I hadn't been paying attention as we approached. Nala swung to the side of the street and parked almost a block away.

I pulled out my phone and dialed Snert.

"Hi, Henry. Are you having a nice time with Nala?" he asked.

"Yes. What's going on? There are police cruisers out front."

"I didn't want to worry you, but I had a break-in."

"Were you hurt?" I asked. That was one of my greatest fears. Snert wasn't well-suited to defending himself.

"No, Henry. I received a timely warning and placed Diva and myself in the safe room."

"Good. Okay, we're here. Are you upstairs or in the shop?"

"I'm still in the safe room."

"Understood."

"What's going on?" Nala asked.

"Break-in, but Snert's okay," I said.

"Let me find out who's in charge and see what's going on," she said.

I followed Nala to a policeman who initially held his hand up to stop us. He dropped it when Nala got close enough for him to recognize her.

"Looking good, Swede," he said, with a quick waggle of his eyebrows.

"Who's got the scene, Billy?" Nala ignored his bad behavior.

"Sergeant Gowan. She's in the shop trying to locate the owner."

Nala nodded her head and walked through the shop's open front door.

"What are you doing here, Swede?" a thickset woman asked.

"Hi, Sarge. Dropping off a friend. Saw you had a gig," she said.

"You live around here?" The woman, who I assumed was Sergeant Gowan, asked then shifted her attention to me.

"I live upstairs with the owner, Alan Snerdly," It wasn't technically accurate, I considered myself to be between homes.

"Do you know where we can find Mr. Snerdly? We're responding to an alarm and haven't been able to locate him," Gowan said.

"He's locked in a safe room," I said. "He's worried things aren't safe."

The shop looked like a hurricane had hit the place. Parts and tools were scattered everywhere and the safe had been ripped out of the wall and lay open on the floor.

"Whoever did this was looking for something. We'd like to know if he has any idea what that was," she said.

"Did they get into his apartment?" I asked.

"I don't know."

"He does a lot of his work up there. The interior staircase in the back is easy to miss."

She gave a sharp nod. "Stay here."

Nala leaned down and pulled a pistol from where it was hidden beneath the hem of her leather pants. I watched as she followed Sergeant Gowan and another officer into the back of the shop. With instructions from me, they found the door and worked their way up the stairs.

I waited for the group to make it up the stairs, then followed. Gowan gave me a dirty look as I appeared inside the apartment, but at least she didn't order me to go away. The apartment only had four rooms if you counted the bathroom, and they cleared it quickly. The apartment was just as trashed as the shop had been.

"You're saying there's a safe room?" Gowan asked.

"Yup. If you don't mind waiting on the stairs, I'll let him know it's safe. I don't think he wants anyone to know where it's located."

"Seriously?" she asked, annoyed.

"Sorry," I said.

She complied and walked back to the stairs, ordering the other officer, Jenkins, to go back down and finish a survey of the shop.

I knew Snert was listening to the entire conversation so I knocked on a wooden panel in the hallway that led back to the bedroom and bathroom. The wall slid back silently and Snert stepped out of what was effectively a dumbwaiter that served as a pass-through to a hidden room. Diva jumped through the opening after him and gave a quick bark, warning me that Gowan was standing in the hallway.

"You okay, buddy?" I knelt and grabbed Diva by the collar. Between the break-in and now cops, it was best to keep direct control of her.

"Oh, yes. I received a warning about the break-in at seven twenty-four."

Snert's emotions were tricky. He was always quick to answer a literal question, but his emotions weren't so easy to identify.

I frowned. "You were in the safe room for a long time before you called the cops."

"I didn't want anyone to get hurt," Snert answered. "So I waited until they were gone."

"The police have some questions for you. Are you up for it?"

"Is Nala still here?" he asked.

"She's downstairs. She won't leave without talking to you first," I said.

"I'm good," Snert replied.

We spent another hour talking to Gowan and in the end, Snert promised to compile his security footage as well as a complete list of all missing and damaged items. As expected, he had no idea why anyone would break into his shop, or what they could be looking for.

It was three o'clock in the morning when the police finally left. Nala had to report for her regular shift in a few hours. She was in for a long day. Even worse, since she was technically working, she felt awkward about saying goodbye in front of the other officers, so I had to settle for a peck on the cheek.

"HENRY. WAKE UP," Snert's insistent voice finally broke through.

Through bleary eyes, I looked at the clock. It read eight o'clock. Snert was, if anything, punctual.

He was standing in front of the couch holding a cup of orange juice and a banana. "Do you need breakfast before you go out to Lambert Textile? I believe Penelope is expecting you to reinstall their system core this morning."

I sat up and accepted both. "Their box wasn't damaged or stolen last night?"

"No. I was working on the unit, so I took it to the safe room. Don't forget to mention the upgrades," he said.

"What about that backup SIMM?"

He fished around in his pocket and produced a small plastic case not a lot larger than my thumbnail. "Maybe you should hold on to this," he said, handing me the small container.

"Agreed," I said. "Send the address to my phone?"

"Yes, and please survey the location where the core was installed. It's likely the wall will need repair. The van has a fresh supply of that epoxy you like."

"Good. I guess I'd better get going, I've a lot going on this morning," I said.

"Will you be seeing Nala Swede again? I like her very much."

"Are you looking to take a run at her?" I asked, joking.

"Me?" he squeaked. "No. No. Henry, you misunderstand. I was wondering if your date was satisfactory – enough so that you would have a second? Nala wanted to date you in high school. I'd never get in her way."

I loved this guy. He made me smile. "You're a good man."

Snert held out a small, padded black bag. "You know, I have plenty of work like this if you would like to supplement your bounty-hunter income."

"Private investigator," I corrected, accepting the bag. "Sounds better."

I didn't want to talk about my career decisions, so I made for the back stairs. Diva, not to be left behind, jumped up and followed. Snert and I had an understanding. If we didn't feel like talking about something, we didn't. I hated the idea of charity, which is what a job working for Snert would feel like. Today, I was just helping a friend, and besides I still owed him.

Snert's van was in the alley. I popped open the back doors and did a quick survey of tools, placing the bag in a recessed well in the top of the portable workbench. The van, like Snert's Tesla, was top-of-the-line. A Mercedes Benz Sprinter, it had a customized interior that resembled a mad-scientist's lab. All work vans wanted to grow up to be this van. At six-two, I had to hunch to walk inside, but it was so neatly organized, that hardly mattered. Truth was, I enjoyed driving it.

I whistled, and Diva raced behind me, jumping into the passenger seat. I guess she liked the van as much as I did. I pulled the back doors closed and punched the power button on the integrated laptop attached to the work surface. It would take a minute or so to start up, but once going, it provided mobile internet and I'd be able to communicate with Snert from the jobsite if I needed help.

I slipped into the driver's-side seat and started her up, enjoying the purr of the diesel engine. Not unexpectedly, Snert had already programmed Lambert Textiles' address into the nav system. Lambert was an easy drive, only twenty minutes from downtown to a warehouse district.

A short bark alerted me to the fact that Diva wanted the window down. Her tail turned into a dangerous weapon as I struggled to comply.

The building was older with a brick façade on the front and was deep enough that I suspected it had originally been some sort of factory. As I drove past, I noticed a wide ramp down to two loading docks that ended up being roughly at ground level – a sure sign of an older building retrofit. I had no problem finding a parking spot and since Diva was staying in the van, I switched on the A/C and set out of a water bowl.

"I'm giving you a break on the whole *truck tire debacle*. You couldn't have stopped those kids," I said. "But this is Snert's van. I don't want to be changing tires today. You got it?"

She whined and twisted her head at me as if she understood what I was saying. Sometimes she did, but I didn't think this was one of those moments.

The cement walk up to the front of Lambert's had a small tract of grass on each side with an even larger grassy area in front of the building's old casement windows to the left. That would be where management's offices were located. A flag pole sat in the middle of the small lawn and sported a limp, tattered American flag. I frowned. I wasn't big on etiquette, but the flag actually meant something to me. Seeing the symbol in sad shape was my personal issue, but it still bugged me.

I pushed the thought from my head, walked through the double glass doors, and stepped into a nondescript foyer. The receptionist was seated at a utilitarian desk, typing on her computer. She stopped and looked up when I approached.

"May I help you?" she asked.

"Yes. I'm here from Snerdly Electronics to see Penelope Lambert. She's expecting me," I said.

"Certainly." She pressed a button on an ancient office phone. "Mrs. Lambert. There's a gentleman here to see you. He says you're expecting him."

"Thanks, Madge. Send him back, please."

The woman stood and gave me a polite smile. She was wearing a light green sweater over a shapeless grey skirt. Her bright-red lipstick seemed out of place for her otherwise frumpy outfit.

"This way." She walked down the hallway, swinging her hips more than I thought was necessary, then stopped just past a door, motioning for me to go inside.

Lambert's office wasn't fancy. She sat behind a metal desk with two sturdy guest chairs. The office did indeed look over the small lawn and flagpole.

"Thank you, Madge." Lambert stood up from her desk and held her hand out to me. "I'm sorry, I don't recall your name."

"Henry Biggston. Most people call me Biggs," I said and accepted her hand.

"Was Mr. Snerdly able to repair the security device?"

"He was. He also suggested that your system should have recorded whoever damaged the core. It's common practice to have one of the video feeds monitoring the system core. There's probably a computer in a closet somewhere."

"I wouldn't know about that. We could talk to Tom, my night-shift manager, about it. He's responsible for the system."

"If I recall, he missed a day of work?" I said. "He's back?"

"Haven't heard from him, but that's not unusual," she replied. "He comes in at four, he's always on time."

"You might bring it up with him. If you'll show me where the system is located, I'll get this installed." I pulled the core out of my shoulder bag.

Lambert led me out of her office. We walked down the hallway, turning just before the lobby. She pushed open a heavy steel door that led into the warehouse. Along the right side, separated from the main space by a glass wall was a laboratory. The other three walls in the room were stark white. Along each were long black counters filled with equipment, beakers, and all sorts of things I associated with chemistry class.

"It's just inside here," she said, walking to a glass door into the lab. She punched in a code on a security panel, not bothering to hide the keystrokes as she entered them. I mentally shrugged. Perhaps security wasn't as big a thing as she'd made it seem. To our right was a countertop with a sink on one end and cabinets both below and above. The setup looked like an industrial break room, although I doubted the cabinets held food.

"How many people have access to the lab?"

"Maybe a dozen."

She opened the middle cabinet door, exposing a Bontel 3000 security system. There wasn't a lot to this type of system. A cradle was mounted on the wall with tamperproof bolts. Wires ran down to a bank of hard-drives. I couldn't help but notice that, out of four storage drives, only one remained. When I held the core up next to the cradle, the scrapes on the core matched gouges in the wall.

I ran my finger over the gouges. "Not very subtle."

"How long will it take to install?" she asked, sounding almost bored.

"I need to drill out the cradle and replace it. Whoever removed the core broke the cradle at the same time. It'll take twenty or thirty minutes, I'd guess. Did you know you're missing storage devices?" I pointed at the open bays.

"That's odd," she said. "But look, there's one in there. Maybe that's all we have."

I'd spent enough time around the systems Snert worked with to know how they operated. The drive bays were redundant and required a minimum of two drives for recoverable operation. "Probably not the best setup," I said. "This system would have originally come with three drives, even though it will operate with just one.

There should still be logs on the drive that's left. I can get Snert to look at them. He'd be able to tell us when the other drives were removed."

"Would that cost a lot?" she asked.

"I doubt he'd charge for looking," I said. "Even then, the extra drives aren't expensive. A hundred bucks a piece or so."

"Have him take a look then, but don't install anything. I'll be in my office. Don't leave the lab. If you do, you'll need me to get you back in," she said.

"Might take a couple of trips."

With a sigh, she kicked a triangular piece of wood across the white floor so it sat next to the door. "Just prop the door open in that case. We're not running any sequences right now, so it'll be fine. Now, if you don't need anything else?"

"Nope, we'll get you fixed up," I leaned down and propped the door open.

Lambert nodded and left.

I put my shoulder bag on the nearby countertop and pulled out the drill. The only way to remove a security bolt was to drill it out completely. The drill bit Snert provided perfectly centered itself on the bolt, which was designed with a small flaw in the dead center that could be drilled out with the precisely correct bit. Aside from the small flaw, the bolt was made of a nearly impervious material. If you didn't hit the softer material directly, the bit would just slide off. As it was, the tool was suited to the job and I drilled out the four bolts.

With the cradle removed from the wall, it was an easy matter to install the new cradle. I had to fill the old holes with an epoxy and then slip the new security bolts in. I pushed the repaired core into the cradle and started the system. It would take a minute or two, so I walked back to the van to grab a diagnostic cable and Snert's portable computer. Once I was back in the lab, I called him on my cell.

"How is your installation proceeding, Henry?" Snert asked after picking up on the first ring.

"Standard wall mount," I said. "I'm letting the resin cure right now, but I ran into something I need your help with."

"Yes? How can I help?" he asked.

"There's only a single drive in the RAID enclosure," I said. "I was wondering if you could look at the system logs and figure out when the other drives were removed."

"That should not be difficult," he said. "I will need you to take the Bontel diagnostic cable and laptop into the space. Do you believe you will have trouble connecting to the Sprinter's network?"

"We're already connected," I said. "You should be able to see it now."

"Oh," Snert said. "Very good, Henry, I do see it. I'm downloading the logs now. Umm ... That's very interesting. This drive has a new installation of the system software. The logs were initialized on the morning when Mrs. Lambert came to my store. This is very suspicious, Henry. Also, two of the video feeds appear to have been disabled. We are not receiving signals."

"Which video feeds aren't working?"

"The loading dock and the east end of the lab. If you look at the wall, you will see it," he said.

"Are you looking at me?"

"Yes, I am able to see you through the west camera," he said.

"And how do you know it's on the west?"

"It is labeled 'Laboratory West End.'"

Ask a stupid question, I thought to myself and rolled my eyes. "Okay, I'll let Mrs. Lambert know. Do we have cameras that would work if she asks? And is everything else working okay?"

"Yes, the system is fully operational," Snert said. "I strongly recommend against a single drive RAID configuration, though."

"I know. I'll talk to her about cloud storage and the cameras."

I collected my tools and swept up the small amount of debris I'd generated. After closing the cabinet, I retraced my steps back to Lambert's office. She'd left her door open, so I knocked on the door frame and leaned in.

"Come on in. Any problems?" she asked.

I walked into her office and stood in front of her desk. "A couple. First the good news. Snert has the system operational again."

"And the bad?"

"Two things," I said. "Were you aware that two of your video feeds have been damaged?"

"Which ones?" she asked.

"East wall of the lab and loading dock," I said.

"They're broken?"

"I haven't been outside to inspect the loading dock, but the camera in the lab has been removed from the mounting bracket."

"Is that something you can fix?" she asked.

"I don't have any cameras with me, but Snert has them in storage. Would you like me to check into it?"

"How much would that cost?" she asked.

"I'll have Snert send you a quote along with the invoice for today."

"Very well. Anything else?"

"Your system was reinitialized yesterday morning," I said. "I was searching through the logs to find out when your redundant drives were removed, but initialization means there's no remaining log. In security systems, this is generally considered a no-no."

She gave me a small frown. "You think someone is tampering with the system on purpose?"

"Not for me to judge," I said, "but the core was forcibly removed from the wall, the system was reinitialized, making it impossible to perform any forensics, and two cameras aren't working. It could all be coincidence ..."

"But you don't think so," she finished for me.

"What Snert and I think isn't pertinent. People install security systems for different reasons. If you're worried about theft, industrial espionage, or other things a video security system is particularly good at identifying, then I'd say this is a good warning. If you want people to think you have security so they're not tempted, but you're not particularly interested in the effort of maintaining a system, I'd say you're probably okay. Get the right tool for the right job is my advice."

"It's not that what we do here isn't critical," she said. "There is potential for industrial espionage."

"Would a loss cost you more than forty-five hundred dollars?" I asked.

"Forty-five hundred?" she asked, wincing. "On top of what you did today?"

"That's right," I said. "State-of-the-art cloud upload with backup cellular alerts. We'd tie into your existing physical alarm system. If someone tries to disable the system, we'll know about it right when it happens. I noticed you're using ACME for door alarms. We work with them all the time."

"I'll let you know by the end of the day," she said. "Thank you for coming out so quickly."

"I'll get out of your hair." I pushed off the door jam and headed back down the hallway.

When I walked past Madge's desk, she was on the phone and looked up at me questioningly. I pointed to the front door and she nodded with understanding.

Diva had been penned up long enough that I was tempted to let her run on the grass, but I thought better of it and fired up the engine. The asphalt pavement was broken up so I drove slowly around to the loading bay. There were a bunch of empty barrels and wooden pallets stacked against the building and it didn't look like there'd been a delivery for quite a while.

I pulled up close and it only took a couple of seconds to locate the camera. Or rather, the remains of the camera. The brick façade of the old building didn't extend to the loading dock and the cinder block wall around the camera's mount was heavily pitted, as if someone had shot at it. The camera housing hung loosely about fifteen feet from the ground, twenty if I had to put my ladder at the bottom of the ramp. I didn't have anywhere to be right away, so I pulled the extension ladder from beneath the floor of the van where it was neatly hidden away and climbed up.

Heights had never bothered me and Snert's ladder was sturdy, so I leaned back and took a couple pictures of the camera housing and surrounding wall damage with my phone. If Lambert needed any prodding to get a new system from Snert, the bullet holes in the steel housing and in her building would probably do the job.

A few minutes later, I had the ladder loaded back up and the broken camera in a bin for Snert to look at later. I dialed Snert on the truck phone as we headed out of the parking lot.

"You get those pictures?" I asked before he could greet me.

"What am I looking at?" he asked. "I think that's a broken camera."

"That's right. Someone shot out Lambert's video camera, the one outside over the loading dock," I said.

"Can you tell from where?" he asked.

"Angle looked sharp. Probably stood below and shot up," I said. "They didn't appear to be a very good shot."

"Wouldn't someone hear gunshots?"

"Probably not out here," I said. "Industrial parks have lots of loud noises. Gunshot monitoring wouldn't work very well."

———

Driving back to Snert's, I had a lot to think about. We'd stepped into something. That much I was sure of.

Snerdly Electronics Shop apparently wasn't that busy, although it was still late morning and things didn't tend to heat up until afternoon. I found Snert in the supply room, still cleaning up from the break-in.

I set the bin containing the camera pieces from Lambert's on the counter. "Here's that camera housing."

"Did you put gas in the Sprinter?" he asked.

"Still over three quarters," I said. "I think I have Lambert sold on your new system. If that didn't do it, those bullet holes probably will."

"That's very concerning, Henry," he said. "I don't want you involved in a dangerous environment. I did not like your choice to join the Army. I worried for you the entire time you were there." He slid the padded envelope over to me. "You didn't open the present I got for you."

"What is it, already?" I asked, filling Diva's water dish.

Snert couldn't wait any longer and opened the package himself. He pulled out a thick white t-shirt and handed it to me. It was oddly bulky and not like any shirt I'd ever worn.

"It's body armor," he said. "The newest stuff on the market. It'll stop anything short of a .357 magnum or a .44. It's level IIIA if that means anything to you."

I looked at the shirt with newfound respect. "Now, that's something."

"Also, your grandfather faxed a permit over and dropped off this box this morning." He pointed to a small plastic box at the end of his work table.

"Busy day for me." I recognized the box style and flipped up the plastic tabs. Inside was a small 9mm Walther pistol and an ankle strap holster. A transfer of ownership from Pappi to me was included along with a box of premium hollow points.

"It seems we all want to keep you safe," Snert said. "Tell me you'll wear the shirt."

"I know you care, buddy," I said, giving him a side hug. "I'll wear your shirt."

"But you aren't going to change your behavior." He already knew the answer.

"I can't," I said. "Besides, I think bullets were merely a convenient way to remove that camera."

"That doesn't change the fact that Marlene Creight shot you," he said.

"Marlene is Marlin's mother?" I asked.

"Yes. She is currently a fugitive," he said.

"I'm not worried about her," I said. "She was scared and defending her son."

"I don't like it."

"That's why you sell first-rate security systems," I said, "and Penelope Lambert needs your help."

"You realize the commission on such a sale, in combination with the other jobs you've recently done for me, will eliminate your debt. Although I'd be more than happy to apply only a small portion of it if you'd prefer the money."

"Nope. Debts come first," I said. "Pappi always said that a man who had no debts was truly free. I like being free."

"You do not need to owe me," he said, taking a serious tone.

"I know. But Pappi also said a man pays his own way."

"I understand," he said, looking down. "I never wanted this to get between us."

"No worries. You're stuck with me," I said. "Change of subject. If someone were looking for Lambert's system core in your shop last night, what would they have gotten? The storage units were taken, and the system was reinitialized."

"Besides the cache you have? Nothing."

"You can't recover data from the RAID drive?" I asked.

"No. Security systems are very good at scrubbing the drives during initialization," he said. "That's different from normal laptops. See, the files on your computer are broken into bunches of little pieces. It's really the directory service that does all the hard work because it knows where to find all the parts. Most attempts to erase or format the computer result in those directory pointers getting lost, but the data stays put. Clever folks with the right tools can go in and find those old pieces and put them back together."

I might or might not have followed the entire conversation, recognizing it as Snert techno babble. "So, we do or do not need to get that hard drive?"

"Wouldn't have anything on it. Good security systems will write data on top of all those little pieces. The drive would be unrecover-able," he said.

"What about the cache. Why wouldn't that have been initialized?"

"Just not how it works," he said.

"So, whoever initialized it and tore it off the wall didn't know what they were doing?"

"It's not obvious," he said. "But any competent technician would have known to look for the cache."

"I guess we'll know more when Lambert's night manager shows up. I was thinking about dropping by there tomorrow to see if I can get some answers," I said. "Hey, where did that fax go, the one you said came in today?"

"It's a conceal carry permit," he said, picking up a card from the bench. "I laminated it for you."

"You're too good to me," I said, stuffing the permit into my wallet. "You feel like pizza tonight?"

THE NEXT MORNING, I snuck out of Snert's apartment while he was still asleep. Before talking to Uncle Chester, I wanted to take another run at Creight. And this time, I wouldn't leave Diva in the truck.

With a bag of breakfast muffins, I parked the truck a block from Creight's house and settled back, tossing a muffin to Diva and opening a large coffee for me. I wished I had binoculars, but it wasn't yet seven thirty. If Marlin was home, I doubted he'd be up and rolling yet.

What became clear was that not much around the house had changed since I'd been shot by his mother. From my vantage point, I could make out blood stains still on the porch. The screen door, which had been broken in the scuffle, hung awkwardly from a single hinge and screeched when the wind caught it. If Marlin were inside, he'd at least have torn the door off. The noise was well past annoying.

The neighborhood, while rundown, wasn't without activity. As I sat there, I started to get a feeling for Marlin's neighbors. On the north side, a rundown pickup truck sat in the driveway of a small house. Dark stains on the cement were a good indication of a persistent oil leak. The truck was fitted with ladder hooks, although there were no ladders in view. I suspected the truck owner worked construction, which was currently depressed in Sutherland.

On the other side of Marlene's was a sign advertising a rental. The house on that lot was small and in equally poor condition, with overgrown weeds and a broken window over the front door. I doubted the landlord would find a tenant any time soon. Since I had nothing better to do, I dialed the number on the sign. I wasn't surprised when a recording prompted me to leave the address of the property I was interested in and my phone number; I would receive a call within two business days. Why not? I complied.

Across the street and adjacent to where I'd parked was a slightly better cared-for property, in that the lawn was mowed and the two cars in the driveway were newer. Kid's toys spilled out of buckets, but someone had made an attempt to pick them up. And finally, directly across from Creight's was a dark brown brick two-story with a couple of newspapers on the porch. The property wasn't in terrible shape, but the paint on the porch was starting to peel. From what I could see, Creight's and the rental were in competition for biggest losers.

A whine from Diva reminded me that she needed to do her business. I grabbed a plastic grocery bag, her leash and let her out of the truck. One thing I appreciated about having her along was that she gave me cover when I needed to nose around. Without being too conspicuous, I walked up the sidewalk opposite Creight's house.

Being aware and being cautious were two things the Rangers drilled into me. Just because you can't see someone, doesn't mean they're not watching. I didn't believe Creight was up yet, but it was likely that at least one neighbor had seen us out walking. Turning around, I walked back to the house with the toys and jay-walked directly to the rental.

I made a show of inspecting the house, which wasn't necessarily just acting. I wanted a place of my own, and a fixer upper might be my only chance. I walked up the cracked sidewalk to the front door and peered inside. Diva did her business, which I quickly bagged.

Nothing would get people's attention faster than leaving dog crap behind.

What I could see of the house's interior was just what one might expect: old hardwood floors that hadn't seen a new finish in years, arched openings into dusty little rooms and a smattering of broken furniture that had been left behind. The house had nice bones but was a wreck inside.

I sighed, walked back to the sidewalk and continued past Creight's house, trying not to look like I was scoping it out. Of course, that's exactly what I was doing. Up close, I saw nothing that suggested he was home. I urged Diva along and smiled at construction-man who was just exiting his home, wearing a paint-stained shirt, carrying a toolbox, and whistling. He gave me a friendly wave and climbed into his truck as I passed behind it.

At the corner, I crossed over and started walking back toward my truck. Best I could tell, Creight wasn't home. I'd toyed with the idea of knocking on his door, but after the last incident, I couldn't imagine he'd answer and I didn't want to spook him.

I was almost to my truck when I heard a cough behind me. The sound was twenty feet or more away, so I continued, planning to ignore whoever it was. An older man called out, "You looking to rent the old Peabody place?"

I turned and saw an old, white-haired man leaning on the porch railing at the corner of the brick two-story and staring at me. I waved. The guy had to be eighty and life hadn't been kind. His arm shook as he feebly lifted it to return my wave.

"Thinking about it," I gave Diva a tug so that we headed his way. "Looks pretty rough. Think it's okay?"

"Bullshit," he said, not quite under his breath. "I seen you before. Marlene shot you on her porch two days back."

"Think you have the wrong guy," I said. "I wouldn't be up and running around if I'd been shot, would I?"

He chuckled, trembling as he stepped onto the rotting wooden steps at the edge of his porch. He wasn't a big man. Baggy clothes hung on his stooped frame and suspenders were the only thing holding his pants in place.

"That Marlin's always been a bad kid. Apple doesn't fall far from the tree. Marlene's as mean as an alley cat in a bathtub full of water." He sat on the top step and held his shaking arms out for Diva. I unsnapped her leash and let her make the decision. Quick as she could move, she wiggled up between his legs and pushed her long snout under his chin.

"What gave me away?" I'd caught sight of a Marine tattoo on his forearm and made a decision not to BS him.

"You know what an old guy does for entertainment?"

"Golf?" I asked.

"Not bloody likely. Now that's a good girl." He chuckled as he brushed Diva's back. "Always loved dogs. They got a sense about people, you know. She's the one who gave you away. I watched her go all kinds of crazy when Marlene shot you the other day. That's what I love about dogs. You never have to question their loyalty. Now, what were we talking about?"

"What old guys do," I prompted.

"Oh. Right," he said. "I sit right there." He pointed at the front window of his home. It was partially blocked by the porch, but I could see a recliner that sat in front of the window. "And I watch. You must have driven up when I was napping the other day. It was the yelling that woke me up. I was the one who called 911. Marlene must not have hit you too bad."

I pulled up my shirt to show my bandage. The skin had started to stitch together with aid of more glue and Steri-Strips. "I've had worse, but it's not the sort of thing you get used to," I said.

Trembling fingers pulled at his collared cotton shirt and the t-shirt underneath. Just below his collar bone was an old bullet wound. "Got that in Nam," he said. "Hurt like a sonnavabitch. Where'd you serve?"

"Army. Seventy-Fifth Regiment. Afghanistan," I said. "Call me Biggs."

"Jonesy. I won't hold Army against you, especially since we both bled for her, my brother," he said, placing a shaking hand onto my arm.

"How'd you know I got shot in the service?" I asked.

"A man my age knows these things," he said. "So, what do you want so bad with Marlene that you'd come back after she shot you?"

"I'm not after her," I said. "Marlin skipped bail. I was trying to take him downtown."

"He ain't there."

"Has he been back since his mom shot me?" I asked.

"Was here last night. You want to be careful with that one, though," he said. "I've seen him beat a man half-to-death in his yard. You got a card?"

"Card?"

"Don't be dense, son. I know you're a ground pounder and all, but a man in your line of work surely has a business card," he said.

"Sorry, I'm just getting started."

"Well get your pen out and give me your phone number. I'll give you a call if he comes back," he said.

I pulled a pen out and wrote my phone number on the back of a receipt I found tucked in a different pocket. I also made a mental note to get some business cards, or to at least carry a better supply of paper.

"I'd appreciate that, Mr. Jonesy. I need to get going, but can I help you back up?" I held my hand out.

Jonesy turned his head and spat under the railing. "Day this Marine needs help from the Army is the day they put me six feet under. But I'd shake your hand." He didn't relinquish his grip, and with great effort, pulled against the handshake until he reached a standing position. He grinned and then turned abruptly and walked up the stairs.

"Let's go, girl," I said, slapping my thigh. Diva gave a quick bark, still watching Jonesy, and then turned away and followed me back to the truck.

I looked at my watch. It was nine thirty and I wanted to get down to Sure Bond and try to get more work. As I played it out in my head, the most likely scenario was that Finkle would fire me on the spot since I'd let Creight get the better of me. If he didn't, because of Jonesy, I might actually have a shot at bringing Creight in.

THE LOBBY of Sure Bond was as empty as it was grimy, but Finkle's door was open so I knocked on the frame to get his attention.

"What do you need, Biggston?" he asked.

Mentally, I steeled myself. "Another job."

"You get Creight?" he asked.

"No. I missed him. I need something else while I'm working on him, something that doesn't involve getting shot or having my head bashed in." Acknowledging my failure out loud was irritating.

"I heard about your dust-up. I thought you were some sort of a badass war hero. Why should I give you something else if you can't get Creight?"

Acid poured into my stomach. My uncle had never served. He had no right to toss my service record in my face. I didn't normally have a short fuse, but I knew the warning signs. I also knew he needed to get stepped back.

"Rangers go in hot and with a team. You weren't straight with me about Creight. He's got tons of priors. You sent me in there with no warning and it got my head caved in. Pull that shit again and we'll settle up nice and clean. You copy?" I growled.

Instead of barking back, Finkle looked up, setting papers onto his lap. "Now, there's the man I thought I was hiring. If I give you another job, you'll still get Creight?"

"Not for three hundred bucks."

"Six hundred if you have him by the end of next week. Otherwise they're going to call in his bond and I'm going to be out ten thousand. I do have another matter you could look into, though."

"Twelve hundred," I said.

He frowned, peered at me, and then nodded. "A thousand and don't make a habit of renegotiating."

"The other job?"

He handed me the file on his lap. "This one came out of the blue, but's it's not the sort of thing I'm interested in, so do with it what you want."

I tried not to let triumph reach my eyes as I accepted the file. Inside was a picture of an elegant middle-aged blonde woman and single sheet of paper with only an address typed neatly at the top.

"What's with her?" I asked. I recognized the general location for the address: a nice neighborhood near one of Sutherland's many golf-courses.

"She's the client. Probably wants you to take pictures of a cheating spouse."

"What's it pay?"

"That's between the two of you. Like I said, I don't want any part of it."

"I thought you were interested in investigative work," I said.

"Take it or leave it. Just make sure you bring Creight in by next Friday."

My bullshit detector was going off, but I couldn't put my finger on exactly what was bothering me. The fact that Finkle didn't want any part of what seemed to be a typical PI job made me suspicious.

"Understood. Thanks." I used the file to give him a mock salute and walked out. He wasn't one for long conversations, but frankly I didn't enjoy being around him either.

"Don't thank me, kid. Just do your job," he said as a parting shot. He was definitely a get-the-last-word-in type of guy.

I let it go.

⸺

I rarely feel out of place, but the guard shack of Belmont Estates looked like it probably cost as much as my grandparent's farm. The immaculately manicured center island was covered with blooming flowers and thick iron rolling gates had been pulled behind tall brick walls that ran for as far as my eye could see.

"Purpose of your visit?" A middle-aged man with a donut belly, a Glock 9mm on his hip, and holding some sort of computer tablet, leaned out of the building. Over his shoulder, I saw a row of AR style long guns. They looked very similar to the M4 I used to carry. And while difficult to procure, I suspected these were not the civilian versions.

"Here to visit DeLovely Manning," I said.

"Name?" he asked, annoyed. He looked past me to Diva, who seemed completely uninterested.

"Henry Biggston."

"Wait for me to lower the tire traps. The Manning estate is Number Fourteen. You will drive eight tenths of a mile forward, turn right and drive another quarter of a mile. You will see the number fourteen on a bright white post. Turn in when you see the post," he said. "Do not vary from these instructions."

I nodded. I'd seen the traps in the pavement ahead and I'd also noticed the traps raised behind me. Belmont Estates took their security seriously. A few moments after entering the shack, both traps lowered into the pavement and the man waved me through.

It was as if I'd entered an entirely different world. For the first quarter of a mile, there were no homes at all. Instead, I passed through lightly-forested, beautifully-maintained green spaces. The first home that came into view was monstrous, sprawling in every conceivable direction, each wing attempting to outdo the next.

I passed four estates before I finally arrived at the white post that had a bold #14 emblazoned on it. I turned off the main road, curious to see the type of structure someone named DeLovely Manning would choose to live in. Apparently, the further down the road you went in Belmont Estates, the more valuable and elaborate the houses were. The Manning house was enormous, with a façade of sandstone, huge arched openings and Juliet balconies. I rolled closer, the road turning into a wide brick driveway that led to the home's soaring entryway.

When I pulled beneath the covered, pillared section of the drive, a man appeared from behind one of the shrubs, carrying hedge clippers, shouting and waving his hands. "No park. No park," he said in broken English. "Go side for delivery."

I turned off the truck and jumped out. I wasn't about to go to the side entrance, so I waved him off and walked up to the front door. For a moment, I was stumped, seeing neither an obvious knocker nor a doorbell on the massive doors, hand-carved from solid pieces of some exotic wood. I was saved from my confusion when the door was opened by an older man, wearing a brown suit.

"Ah, Mr. Biggston. We were told to expect your visit this late morning," he said with a stuffy English accent. "Madame has retired to the receiving room. Would you follow me?"

"Sure." I couldn't help myself and stared as I attempted to take in the grand entrance, complete with a wide melodramatic staircase, dark hardwood floors, and miles of wall paneling which stretched all the way to the back of the house. If light hadn't been flooding in from a full bank of windows, the look would have been too dark. As it was, the entry felt airy and expansive.

"Welcome to Manning Manor, Mr. Biggston." DeLovely Manning was more beautiful and yet older than the picture in her file. She wore a light-green business suit with matching skirt and a beige blouse. A single string of pearls adorned her neck, knotted low so they settled between heavy breasts. She paused, allowing me a moment to take her in.

Idly, I wondered if the pause was planned for affect or if it was something she'd been forced to adopt after years of dealing with the responses of people who met her for the first time.

"Tea. Coffee. A biscuit?" Like the man who'd answered the door and was standing only a few feet behind me, she spoke with an English accent, although less pronounced.

"No, I'm fine," I said. Something about her demeanor put me at ease, as if I, in my tactical boots, jeans, and black t-shirt, was an ordinary fixture in this mega-multi-million-dollar estate.

"You are indeed a fine specimen," she purred, closing on me. Her smile reminded me of a cat watching a mouse just before pouncing for a final, killing stroke. "Chester Finkle said you were a hero. He did not mention your broad shoulders."

I was proud of myself for not jumping when she reached over and traced a finger along my shoulder and down my chest.

"He said you had a job for me," I said, not sure what to do about her hand.

"Is it true you were a Ranger? That you killed for our country?" she asked.

The question immediately removed all of the oxygen from the room and her playfulness was no longer cute.

"Fuck off." I turned and walked toward the door.

"Oh, don't pout," she called from behind me, as brown-suit stepped into my path.

"Move, or lose a testicle," I growled quietly.

"Madame desires to speak with you," he said and drew a telescoping baton from his pocket.

I'd had enough. My quota had been filled this week when it came to giving people the benefit of the doubt. I stepped forward and rabbit punched him in the solar plexus. The move caught him off guard as he exhaled sharply. Before he could drop his baton, I ripped it from his hand, flicked it open, and snapped it across his shin. If I had swung it full force, I could have inflicted real damage. As it was, he yelped, grabbed his knee, and hopped away.

"Mr. Biggston. Henry. Please," DeLovely said. "I'm sorry for our bad manners."

I walked purposefully out the front door and around to the driver's side of the truck. Diva's excitement and the sound of clattering heels warned of DeLovely's approach. I was starting to cool off as I turned the key and the engine sputtered to life.

"Diva, lie down," I ordered. While I wasn't thrilled with Manning, I didn't want Diva causing her any grief. Diva whined but settled onto the seat.

"Please, Mr. Biggston, I need your help," the woman said, leaning onto the open window of the passenger-side door. "I don't even know what I did wrong."

Diva's growl probably wasn't audible to the woman, but she pulled back when she looked through and saw the dog there on the seat.

"War isn't a game, Mrs. Manning," I said.

"I know. I know," she said. "Please. Just hear me out. Finkle said you needed the job. Don't let your pride get in your way."

It was the perfect thing to say, as Grandma Pearl had often chided me with those same words. According to her, I allowed people to get my goat. It was an odd saying that never made sense to me. But according to Pearl, it was my greatest fault.

"I'll give you a couple of days," I said. "But I can't make any promises."

"You don't even know what the job is," she said.

I rolled my eyes and spoke as mockingly as I dared. "You want me to follow your husband around and take pictures of him with his mistress."

"Finkle was to keep that to himself. My husband is a dangerous man."

"A thousand a day plus expenses," I said. "And I can't start until tomorrow at the earliest."

It felt like a ridiculous number, but she didn't blink as she pulled two banded stacks of bills from her purse and set the money on the passenger seat next to Diva. It was a gutsy move and I was proud of Diva for not snapping at her.

"I'll pay five hundred a day. That's two thousand there. I want pictures with timestamps and locations. I also expect daily updates." She pulled a phone from her purse and set it next to the money. "Use only this phone to contact me. Send a single text message and I'll return your call when I can. The phone number is already programmed into it. Do you have a camera?"

"No," I said.

"Go to Bucky's Big Box and buy a Canon Rebel with a 300mm zoom," she said, dropping two more stacks of bills onto the seat. "Keep receipts for equipment purchased."

"If your husband is dangerous, why are you doing this?" I asked.

"Manning isn't my maiden name," she said, as if that explained everything.

I leaned over and opened the glove box and threw the wads of money and phone into it. Pretty cavalier, eh? "You've bought yourself four days," I said. "Where can I find him?"

She smiled and reached between her breasts, pulling out a thumbnail sized USB drive. "This is the information my last PI gathered. See if you can do better."

I probably should have turned her down right then. Even I knew that this was in over my head, but the fact was, I wanted the money. Even more, I wanted to prove that I could make it in this business.

"What happened to your last PI?" I asked.

"Lost his nerve."

"Right." I pulled the gear shift down, placing the truck into drive. "I'll call when I have something."

"Updates every day, Mr. Biggston," she said, stepping back.

"Copy that." I drove off. A quick glance in the rearview mirror and I saw that she stood and watched my truck until I turned the corner. Interesting woman, that.

11 / SPREAD 'EM

My first stop was Bucky's Big Box. I pulled two thin stacks of hundreds from the glove compartment. I was starting at zero and needed more equipment than her two-thousand-dollar allowance would provide, but it would be a good start.

The security guard who sat by the large glass doors wearing a pastel blue Bucky's shirt looked uncomfortable on the stool and didn't give me a second look when I passed through the security scanners. I knew the scanners were there to detect RFID tags and wondered if they'd pick up on the Walther I had strapped to my ankle. If they did, the big man wasn't even remotely interested. My first stop wasn't to look at cameras but instead I headed to the computer section.

"Can I help you?" The nerdy kid who approached couldn't have been older than sixteen, but my friendship with Snert had removed any preconceived notions regarding physical appearance and knowledge of computers.

"Do you have ruggedized laptops? I don't need a lot of power but I'm hard on things," I said.

"What kind of battery life do you need?" he asked, not missing a beat.

"Longer is better," I said. "But I'd rather have light weight."

"Yeah, see that's a problem," he said in a high, nasally voice. "Rugged and long battery life means heavy."

"Rugged is first priority. After that, weight," I said.

He led me to a display that had two computers with Vietnam War era camouflage on their cases. "That's easy."

I wondered if anyone had told the manufacturer that US forces spent the majority of their time in deserts nowadays and not jungles.

"This one's on sale for twenty-nine hundred dollars. Fully ruggedized to military specifications."

"Damn," I said. "I need to spend more like a thousand."

He nodded and moved off from the jungle display. "This one is considered semi-rugged. It has a stronger case, is shock resistant and temperature adaptive. It costs thirteen hundred. You mind me asking what you're doing with it?"

"Photographer," I said. "I need something for the field. USB, SIMMs, Bluetooth, that sort of thing."

"Photo editing?" he asked.

"No, I just need to browse the internet, read emails, connect to a camera, that sort of thing," I said.

"You don't want a laptop then," he said. "Follow me."

I felt a little awkward traipsing behind the nerd as we wound our way to an adjacent portion of the store. I marveled at his ability to look past the myriad devices and pluck a pad from its hiding place behind extra inventory at the back of a shelf.

"This little baby meets military spec 810G," he said proudly. Being ex-military, I wasn't quite as impressed by his pronouncement. The Army had specs for everything, it didn't mean the equipment was any good. "The only complaint is, it can get hot if you run it for very long. Standard Android OS so you can add a keyboard and all that."

"USB and Bluetooth?" I asked.

"Of course. Everything is Bluetooth," He shook his head, disappointed by my question. "Charge and data transfer on a standard micro-USB. If you need a full-spec USB, it comes with a dongle. And best of all, this little baby is only eight hundred bucks."

He continued on and on. I figured the familiar nerd-buzzing in my ears was a good thing, however, I had just about zero interest in the full details.

"Do you work on commission?" I asked.

"Not supposed to say, but yes" He looked around nervously as he answered.

"Good, pack that up. I need a camera and a bag to hold them both," I said.

"I have just the thing," he said, smiling.

Eighteen hundred dollars lighter, I finally exited the store with a new backpack filled with electronics and optics. With an hour to kill before Lambert's night manager would arrive, I unpacked everything, set aside the manuals, separated the packaging and ran the trash over to a can near the store's front entrance.

One of the downsides to my beautiful old truck is that there's exactly one cigarette lighter, which meant I'd need to make sure I kept the rechargeables topped off. The tablet had a third of a charge, so it should be plugged in first.

"Diva, want to take a quick run to the farm?" Even with ears damaged by explosives in Afghanistan, Diva heard better than most humans and she gave me a happy look. I thought there was a good chance I'd be spending the night in the truck and figured I could pick up the topper and sleeping roll I used for camping.

In the middle of the afternoon, traffic was light, so I made good time. Instead of stopping at the house, I drove straight out to the barn. Pappi's and Pearl's vehicles were both gone, which was just as well as I needed to keep moving.

The white camper shell wasn't anything special aside from the fact that it converted the truck bed into an enclosed space. Grandma Pearl had sewn flowery curtains for the windows on each side, and while it wasn't exactly the look I was after, they provided a good visual block.

Installing a camper shell isn't a one-man job, although it can be done. I backed the truck up next to the sawhorses where the shell sat and parked. As soon as I opened the driver's side door, Diva jumped over me, setting off on her rounds.

"I'll just get this by myself," I called after her. The next few minutes weren't going to be easy.

I squatted as low as I could get and duckwalked under the shell, which was open on one end. I positioned myself roughly in the center and turned awkwardly, putting my hands on the ceiling and rising up. The shell was plenty heavy, and I strained to lift it. Luckily, I didn't need to go far. With a burst of just about everything I had, I heaved one end up onto the truck's bed rails. I blew out a heavy breath and pushed the topper forward in small, controlled lifts until the open end rested against the truck's cab. Opening the tailgate, I slid in and tightened the clamps that would hold it into place. It was better that I ignore the pull in my side. No sense worrying when there wasn't anything I could do about it.

The next item I needed was the wooden frame Pappi and I had built. The frame's only goal was to hold two plywood sheets fourteen inches off the truck's bed. This would give me underneath storage and a nice, flat surface for a bed roll.

I whistled for Diva and grabbed my water bottle, taking a long drink. The whole job hadn't taken more than forty minutes but was completely anaerobic and I was winded. Diva ran back to the truck. She was happier here at the farm than anywhere else, but she preferred human company. I suppose I wasn't much different.

Having the camper shell gave the two of us a few more options, one of which was that I could open the rear window of the truck to the bed. With all of my new gear, the cab had become cluttered and Diva was short on space. She wasn't about to give up her spot, so I slid equipment through the window and onto the platform, keeping the electronics within reach.

I drove straight to Lambert Textile, not arriving until a shade past four o'clock. I didn't actually have a good excuse for showing up, but curiosity had gotten the better of me. Something in my gut told me Lambert was mixed up in something she shouldn't be. What I didn't know was if she was involved or just an innocent bystander. I pulled my new tablet out and plugged in the card reader, loading up the cached data from Lambert's security system. I'd told Snert I wouldn't look at the images unless my need to know became critical. I'll admit, even as the words left my mouth, I knew I'd be watching the recordings.

The card had five MPEG files on it. The naming conventions weren't obvious, but it didn't take much imagination to assume they contained footage from the five installed cameras on the property. Opening the first file, I recognized the view from the front of the building. I might need to get back to that but for the moment, I just wrote down the filename, identified the camera and closed the window. The second file was the camera in the hallway where the company execs had their offices. I added the information to my list and moved on.

The third camera view was of the loading dock. I was finally getting somewhere. Three hours. The smartest approach would be to skip through, stopping every five or ten minutes to see if the scene changed. An hour into watching, I noticed a truck enter the camera's field of view. I wrote down the timecode and scanned forward, going more slowly. The truck swung around and backed into the neighbor's loading dock. The bay door opened and light poured out.

"Well, hello there."

Two men stood on the loading dock, backlit, with what I was sure were pistols in their hands. The camera's resolution wasn't great, but I'd seen enough guns in my life to be relatively sure. A forklift appeared, mostly disappeared into the back of the vehicle, and then slowly backed out with a large crate.

Even with poor resolution and distance, it was clear the crate was heavier than the forklift was capable of safely carrying. As the operator backed up, the crate swayed back and forth alarmingly and the two men holding the guns started yelling angrily. I couldn't make out what they were saying, but I could make some pretty good guesses. Plus, I figured Snert could get better audio and visual playback later with his professional equipment.

Abruptly, the forklift stopped, which turned out to be a critical mistake. The unbalanced crate tipped back, banging against it. If the operator had stopped right then, he would probably have been okay, but there was a lot of shouting and he apparently panicked. He chose that moment to start backing again. At that point, there was nothing more he could do as the crate tipped forward, toppling off.

The crate smashed onto the cement floor and broke open. I was shocked when several small bodies writhed around amongst the broken wood of the crate. Without hesitation, one of the armed men grabbed for the chain to pull down the heavy bay door, trapping most of the debris inside and cutting off the light. What images the camera could pick up were drastically reduced. I continued to watch, my heart racing as I considered what I'd just witnessed. Were those really people in that crate? What were they doing in there?

Movement caught my eye in the dim light escaping from the warehouse. Apparently, someone had fallen off the dock to the ground. The figure ran toward the Lambert building, the image quickly resolving into a young girl, maybe early teens. Her age was hard to guess because she was thin and moving fast. She disappeared from the camera's view, heading to the front of the Lambert building.

I hit pause and noted the time, closed the video, and opened the front camera view, moving to that timecode. For a moment, there was nothing. I was just about to start scanning when the now frantic girl appeared, running up to pound on the front door.

My heart sank as I recognized her face. Unbelievable. It was the street punk who'd stolen one of my tires. I blanked on her name, but my heart hammered in my chest. It was hard to see the girl, once full of bravado, terrified and running for her life. A moment later, a man appeared in the dim front hallway as he ran to open the front door. I'd never seen a picture of Tom Lampkin, the night supervisor, but I was sure that's who this was.

A warning bark from Diva broke my fixation on the computer screen. I looked up to see Mrs. Lambert running toward the truck, shouting unintelligibly.

"Easy girl." I tried calming Diva as I pulled the card from its socket and jammed it into my pocket. Lambert's timing was terrible, but she was in full-blown panic mode. I jumped out and hadn't even fully rounded the front of the truck when she started yelling again.

"Mr. Biggston. Oh, thank God!" Unlike our previous encounters, the woman was completely disheveled. Strands of her straight hair had pulled out of the bun she typically wore, and mascara was smudged on her cheeks like she'd been crying and wiping at her eyes.

"Mrs. Lambert. What going on?" I asked.

"It's Tom. I can't reach him. He's not answering his home or cell phones. I sent Madge over to his house and no one answered, *and* his car is gone," she said. "The police say it's too early for a missing person's report and that there was nothing illegal about not showing up to work. Then I told them about the security system. They said I could come down and file a report, but the officer said that he didn't think there was anything they could do. I sent everyone home. And just now I heard noises coming from the lab. I thought it might be Tom, but when I looked, it was someone else. I just ran."

I placed my hands on her arms, anchoring her. "Slow down, Mrs. Lambert," I said.

"Penelope," she said, looking up at me. Gone was the confident business woman.

"Penelope," I repeated. "When did this happen?"

"Just now," she said. "They're back there now."

"Got it." I whistled and Diva bounded out of the truck, coming up next to me.

"My purse," she said. "What if he takes it?"

"You get a new one," I said. "If someone is here, they're not looking for your purse."

"But it has my car keys and house keys."

"Stop, Penelope," I pulled her around to the other side of the truck. "Here's what we're going to do. These are my truck keys. You're going to sit in it with the doors locked. If you see anything bad, you're going to drive off and call the cops."

"What about you?"

"Ma'am, I'm a former Army Ranger," I said. "If anyone gets past me, you'll have bigger things to worry about. Now repeat what I just said."

"If I see anything bad I'm to call the police," she said and hastily added, "but I'm to drive away first."

"That's right." I reached behind the seat, pulled out my Kimber 1911 and an extra magazine, which I stuffed into my pocket. "Now get in and don't be a hero."

"Be careful," she said, looking between me and my handgun, phone wobbling in her trembling hand.

"Copy that," I said and ran back toward the building, racking a round into the chamber. "Diva. Hunt 'em up."

Diva's entire demeanor shifted in an instant. Her normally wagging tail and floppy ears transformed to pointed ears and tail between her legs. She'd been trained to locate explosives as well as interdiction of hostile forces and she took her job seriously. My heart hammered in my chest. I hadn't had a gun in my hand with intent to do harm since I'd left the Army. There's nothing to miss about people shooting at you, but I'd be a liar if I said I didn't miss the action. There's something elemental about combat. At its core, it's as real as it gets.

"Heel," I ordered, my voice low and harsh as we pushed through the front door. A good handler would have Diva on a leash and focus on controlling her through the chaos. I was alone on this one and needed all my focus on the mission, plus I didn't have the training. That said, I felt I had something even better, which was that Diva and I understood each other. She settled in next to my left leg, alert and ready for anything.

Working a building solo is a bit of a trick. The last thing I wanted was to be surprised from behind. Lambert had said she'd seen someone in the lab, but they could be anywhere, especially if they were looking for something. Using corners as cover, I moved through the inside of the building and down to Lambert's office. It looked untouched, so I turned around and headed back the way I'd come.

There were closed doors on both sides of the hallway. With a team, I'd have cleared each one of them, but I wanted to get to the lab and if Diva didn't smell or hear people behind a door, I wasn't about to waste my time.

"Hold," I ordered when we arrived at the door to the warehouse. The lab was on the right and we'd be visible from most of the wide-open warehouse. Placing my shoulder against the swinging door on the right, I pushed it open slightly, giving myself a view of the left side toward the front. With the door open, I heard the muted sound of someone moving equipment, likely in the lab. I allowed the door to close and switched to the other side.

When I pushed the swinging door in, it suddenly flew away, causing me to stumble, as I'd unbalanced myself just a bit to push it open. A large hand grabbed me and pulled me through, flinging me to the ground. Instinctively, I pushed off with my legs, doubling the man's force to give me the wherewithal to roll on my shoulder and back onto my feet. In his other hand, he held a gun.

"Jack, we got trouble," he shouted, not expecting me to make it back up so quickly. The only problem was, his pistol was pointed right at me. Even an accidental discharge would end up in another gunshot wound for me.

Of course, what the man didn't know was that I'd come with backup. Like a blur, Diva charged and jumped, latching onto his gun arm. He screamed, firing, only the gun no longer pointed at me.

A second gunshot exploded to my right, missing both me and the man, who Diva had brought to the ground. "Dammit! Jack! Get this dog off me!"

Diva shook her head, still attached to the struggling man. Looking across to the laboratory, I found the elusive Jack, apparently trying to aim at Diva. I returned fire, intentionally missing. Most people have difficulty returning fire when they've been fired upon and Jack was no exception. His next shot went wild and I fired two more rounds into the wall next to him.

That was all Jack could take and he bolted across the open warehouse floor. For a moment, I tracked him in my sights. At eight yards, he'd have been an easy shot, but I wasn't about to shoot a fleeing man.

"Diva, heel," I ordered. "Diva!"

When Diva released, the man curled into a fetal position, cradling his arm. The sound of an engine starting and the squeal of tires told the rest of the story. Jack wasn't sticking around.

"Arms to your side," I said, leveling my gun at the man on the floor.

"Fuck you. Your dog tore up my arm," he said.

"I'll put her on your nut sack next," I said, kicking his gun away, still pointing mine at him.

"Fuck off."

Right. I should have gone for something more believable. Still, he wasn't moving and while he was beefy, his wound and the potential for more were probably sufficient deterrent. I threw on the safety and slid my pistol into the back of my pants. The heat of the barrel warmed my butt and I winced. I needed to start carrying a holster. I was also glad I hadn't fired more than four shots. I pulled handcuffs from my back pocket, pushed my knee into the man's back and wrenched his good arm around. He started to resist, but I brought his arm up past the point of comfort. He released a howl he'd apparently been holding onto.

"What are you, a cop?" he asked.

"Concerned citizen."

I grabbed his wounded arm and pulled it back. When the man tightened his muscles and arched back, Diva growled, approaching so they were nose to nose. Whatever fight he'd had dissipated and I locked the other wrist into a cuff.

"You're fucking dead. You know that? Dead," he said.

"Up." I took my knee off his back and helped him up.

I nodded. "Not today." I pulled out my phone and one-handedly dialed Nala.

"Heya, Biggs, miss me already?" she asked, her voice low but sassy.

"Sure do," I said. "But I got a problem."

"What kind of problem?"

"Break-in at Lambert Textile, out here in the industrial park," I said.

"Is that where you were putting that security system?"

"That's right. Good memory."

"Snert sure got that system repaired fast. Shouldn't you just let the alarm company handle it?" she said, not seeming to understand that I was on-site.

"There were two men, one got away. He lobbed a few shots at me," I said. "I have the other one in custody. He pulled a gun, but Diva took him down."

In a split second, she was all business. "Sarge, we have a 10-30, 10-34 at Lambert Textile. Biggs, take cover, we're on the way."

I was already pushing the guy ahead of me toward the front of the building. "Shit. Okay,"

By the time we'd exited the front door, I heard multiple sirens – probably some as close as a half mile away. I shoved my prisoner toward the truck. Whatever code Nala gave had Sutherland's finest in an uproar and I wasn't about to let Diva get shot. I pushed the man to the ground and opened the back of the truck. Diva looked at me like I'd grown a second nose, but finally jumped in.

"What's going on, Mr. Biggston?" Penelope called from the truck's partially-opened window.

"I'm about to get arrested," I said as two patrol cars skidded into the parking lot. "Would you call Snert and let him know?"

I made a show of turning toward the cars and holding my gun with two fingers. I placed it on the ground and backed away. My prisoner took the opportunity to roll over and make a run for it. I let him go and just watched as one of the two patrol cars accelerated in his direction.

"Hands over your head!" a woman's amplified voice ordered. My hands were already raised, but the officer's adrenaline was pumping, and she was moving through a training sequence. "Turn around and back slowly to my vehicle."

This next part was going to suck. I'd already shown a weapon and they wouldn't go easy on me.

AFTER WARNING the officer who was taking me down about my ankle holster, I'd expected to be flattened to the pavement and roughed up some. I provided no resistance and while I'd been nicely pinned with a knee across my back, once the cuffs were on I was allowed to rest my back against the vehicle while four officers took control of the man that wore my cuffs. He did not go quite so easily and it took all of them to load him into a vehicle where he continued to yell insults.

"Now, don't give me any trouble," a male officer said, approaching me after the tussle. "I'm going to help you up. Do you have anything in your pockets that we need to be worried about? They won't be as forgiving as I am downtown."

I'd already been patted down for more weapons, but the first officer had gone over me fast. "Personal items," I said. "Wallet. Cards. USB stick. That sort of thing." He grabbed my arm and helped me to my feet.

"Do you mind if I turn them out?" he asked.

"No, sir," I answered.

"What happened to your face?" he asked. "Those bruises look a few days old."

"I work for Sure Bond. I had a skip tune me up a bit," I said.

"You're a big boy. Must have been quite a skip."

"Actually, his mom shot me first," I said.

"Ooh. I heard about that. Marlin Creight?"

"That's the guy."

"What are you doing out here at Lambert, loaded for bear, no less?" he asked.

"I've been doing some work for Mrs. Lambert. Her security system was disabled a few days back. I was here to check on her."

"She'll say that?"

"I'm sure she will."

"Your gun smells like it was fired," he said. "You have a permit to carry?"

"In the wallet," I answered. While we'd been talking, he'd emptied my pockets into a plastic bag.

"You're going to need to come downtown," he said. "Looks like things are on the up and up, but with weapons being discharged, the brass will want it all documented." He pushed me toward the back of the vehicle and started opening the back door when Penelope Lambert made it over to us.

"What are you doing?" she demanded. "This man saved my life." It was an exaggeration, but I appreciated where her heart was.

"Ma'am, I need you to step back," he said. Another officer saw the problem and hustled to his side, taking control of me.

"It's okay, Mrs. Lambert. They're just doing their job. Call Snert. Have him come get Diva," I said.

"Are you sure? I can call my lawyer. I'm sure she can get you out of this."

The officer who'd been trying to put me in the car was starting to lose patience. "Ma'am." His tone was more forceful as he crowded her, trying to get her to back off.

"Call Snert," I said. I slid down into the back of the patrol car, hoping to end the conversation before Lambert got herself into real trouble. The female officer, picking up on my strategy, slammed the door behind me.

Lambert looked annoyed, but backed away, taking out her phone.

⸻

My reception wasn't much better when I arrived at the police station. I was led into a small room that had a video camera in it and was left to sit for three hours. Finally, a man and a woman, both wearing inexpensive suits entered. The woman sported an empty holster on her hip beneath a short jacket.

"Henry Biggston," the woman said. "Not sure if you know this, but Sutherland takes a dim view of its citizens shooting up warehouses. We feel the same way when it comes to dogs attacking our good citizens. Fortunately for your dog, no good citizen was attacked."

She pulled up a chair and sat across from me. Her partner didn't move much past the door and just stood there, observing me.

"Am I under arrest?" I asked.

"I'm Detective Sandy Chessen and you're being held for questioning," she said dryly, as if it were a routine matter.

"Okay."

"Why were you at Lambert Textile this afternoon?" she started.

I didn't have anything to hide, so I walked the two of them through an abbreviated sequence of events.

"And you were just there to check on this night shift manager who's apparently missing?"

"Tom Lampkin," I said. "He was supposed to show up for work after four o'clock. I wanted to ask him about the damaged security system."

"You were strapped pretty heavy," the man by the door interjected.

"Mrs. Lambert came running out to the parking lot and asked for help. I had the 1911 in my truck, so I grabbed it. My carry weapon isn't all that accurate, three-inch barrel and all."

He nodded and waited as his partner pulled out the bag containing my personal items, including DeLovely's USB stick as well as the SIMM memory from Lambert's security system.

"Want to tell us about what's on the USB drive?" Detective Chessen asked. "It appears to be encrypted."

I wrinkled my eyebrows. DeLovely hadn't said anything about encryption. "You'll be more interested in the SIMM. There's something hinky going on next door to Lambert's and I think Tom Lampkin might be in trouble. Also, I watched part of the video and it shows a girl that looked like she was in trouble."

"This?" Chessen asked, pulling the SIMM card from the bag. "Our techs say it's empty."

The door opened and a sharply-dressed suit walked in. "And that would be illegal search and seizure," he said. "Mr. Biggston, stop talking and stand up. You're free to go."

"Hey. Look here!" Chessen's partner stepped forward and placed a meaty hand on the man's chest. "You can't bust into an interrogation like this."

"You will kindly remove your grimy hand from my chest, Detective Grumby," the man said. "You're illegally holding this man and have executed an illegal search. Would you like to add assault?"

"Let's go, Dave," Detective Chessen said, standing. "He's lawyered up."

"I'm not letting this pissant push me around!" The detective removed his hand, but squared up on the lawyer, blocking his path further into the room.

"Dave, it's not worth it," Chessen said, her calm voice trying to de-escalate the man. "We got nothing on Biggston."

The two left the room while I looked from the lawyer to the retreating forms of the two detectives. "Who are you?" I asked, finally, emptying the bag and putting things back into my pockets.

"Jacks Pendleton. Your lawyer," he said.

"Did Alan Snerdly hire you?" I asked.

"DeLovely Manning. I strongly urge you not to discuss this matter further with the police," he said.

"How did she know I was here?"

"Ms. Manning is well informed," he said. "Now, shall we go, or have you found this room to your liking?"

I followed Pendleton, hoping to make a hasty exit, but I noticed Nala talking to another officer on the far side of the room. The officer seemed perturbed. He was shaking his head and nodding in my direction. Nala turned and raised her eyebrows, tipping her head in acknowledgement.

"Hey, I'm good," I said, touching Pendleton on the sleeve.

Pendleton turned and looked at where I'd touched him, grimacing. "Don't forget what I said. Keep your mouth shut." And with that he spun on his heel and was gone.

"What's going on, Biggs?" Nala asked. "How are you hooked up with Pendleton?"

"You know that guy?"

"Uh, *yeah*. He's a high-powered criminal lawyer. I wouldn't have thought he was in your price range," she said.

"You working?" I asked.

"Nah, I'm done for the day," she said. "Want to grab some coffee and decompress?"

"Sure, I just need to make a couple of calls first," I said.

"That works, I need to change. Give me ten minutes and meet me in the lobby."

The atrium of the Second Precinct was large, with marble floors and extra seating. A myriad of city and county government offices shared the entrance, but it was getting late and the atrium was mostly empty.

My first call was to Snert.

"Henry, are you okay?" Snert asked. "I met with some very unpleasant police who wanted to take Diva to animal control."

"Did they?" I asked.

"They were about to, but Mrs. Lambert convinced them to let us bring her home," Snert said. "What's going on, Henry? I'm very worried."

"We'll have to talk about it later," I said.

"Where did that Android tablet in your truck come from?" Snert asked, sounding more peevish than I'd have expected.

"I'm working a job," I said. "I needed a tablet to connect to the camera."

"I could have helped with that," he said.

"Is it a bad tablet?"

"It is not the best, but it's functional."

"Sorry, buddy. I probably should have asked, but I rely on you too much already," I said.

"Well, expect to talk about that later," Snert said. "I'm starting to believe there's a relationship between the break-in at my office and Penelope's security system."

"King of the understatement," I said. "I'll catch you up in the morning."

"You're not coming home?" he asked. I winced. He was definitely getting too used to me living at his place. I loved Snert as a brother, but things were getting a little too close.

Best to just ignore his question for now. "What about Diva and the truck?"

"Lester came for Diva. He said it'd be best if she wasn't in town. Your truck is still at Lambert Textile. I made sure it was locked up," he said. "I didn't have any way to bring it home."

"Understood," I said. "I'll get a ride over there. Hey, I gotta go."

"Be careful, Henry," he said.

My next call was to Pappi.

"They're going to keep your piece for a while," he said after I explained the events. I kept back the details of the girl I'd seen running in the video. It didn't seem like the sort of thing I wanted to discuss in an open area, much less on a cell phone.

"How long?"

"A month, maybe longer," he said. "The detectives need to close things out. You should be able to get your Walther back, though."

"Where?" I asked.

"You're at the Second Precinct?"

"Yeah," I answered.

"Talk to the property clerk, they'll get you squared away. Henry, you've had a hard run here these last few days. You need to de-escalate. Might be time to hand over that Lambert job to another security company."

"I hear you Pappi, but there's more going on here than I can talk about on the phone," I said.

"Even more reason to back down," he said. "You don't have your team, Henry. You can't carry the weight of the world on your shoulders. Let Sutherland PD take care of this. You need to let this go."

"I gotta go, Pappi," I said.

"Understood, Henry. Just think about what I said."

"Copy that." I hung up the phone and stared at it. Pappi wouldn't back down, but I couldn't tell him what was going on. Not yet.

"You ready?" Nala asked. She'd changed into tight jeans and a sweatshirt.

"Where's the property clerk?"

"Why?" she asked, knitting her eyebrows. "Didn't Chessen give you your stuff back?"

I pulled out the receipt I'd received for my Walther and held it out to her.

"I didn't know you carried," she said, giving me an appraising look.

"Don't call it conceal for nothing," I said.

———

"You want to tell me what happened today?" Nala asked. I found it ironic that she'd chosen an all-night donut shop to grab our coffee. "Rumor is you were throwing lead with a couple of burglars in the warehouse district. And then you pull Pendleton out of your back pocket. Everyone knows he's connected."

"Like you?" I asked.

"No. Not like me," she said, her mouth turning into a pout. "I can't help who my family is."

"You want to hear the whole story?" I asked. I was tired of repeating it, but at the same time I'd gotten good at identifying the salient parts. For Nala, I didn't skip the part where I watched the video, nor what I felt had happened. As I recounted the story, I recalled the girl's name, Amalia Rouca. That, I didn't share.

"That's insane," she said, her eyebrows raised in alarm. "Did you tell the detectives about the girl and the video?"

"Not really," I said. "I was starting to get into it when that lawyer showed up and told me to shut up."

"I hate to say it, but that's probably the best advice you'll receive," she said. "I know Chessen. If she's got you in her sights, you don't want to give her any ammo."

"But a girl might have been kidnapped, or worse," I said.

"And you can prove what?" Nala asked. "Trust me, they'll think you're part of it. Until you have something, you don't want to go throwing accusations around."

"That video is pretty telling. It explains why Tom Lampkin is missing," I said. "If he helped that girl and those thugs figured it out, that'd be trouble for him."

Suddenly, Nala stood. "Shit. You might get your chance," she whispered harshly. "Remember what I said."

I turned and saw that Chessen herself had just entered the donut shop. She scanned the booths and since we were nearly the only customers in the restaurant, she saw us immediately. Apparently, we were exactly who she was looking for and she stalked angrily toward us.

I turned back to the table, mentally doing a face palm. My luck could not be beat today. I picked up my fork and took a bite of the banana cream pie the waitress had left with our coffee. The pie tasted like it'd been made fresh that morning and I realized just how hungry I was.

"Hey. Save some of that for me," Nala whispered, looking exasperated as she sat back in the booth.

"Snooze, you lose," I said, grabbing another bite. I completely ignored Chessen as she thumped both hands down on the edge of the table.

"Detective Chessen," Nala said, scooting over to make room.

"Officer Swede." Chessen ignored the invitation and leaned onto the table, invading my personal space. The move was a flagrant attempt at intimidation and probably served her well during interrogations. "Look Biggston. I know you think you got away with something today, but you didn't. I'll figure out what you're into and I'll put you down."

I pulled the SIMM from my pocket and held it up for her to see. "Right back at you," I said. "This card had video on it before you got your hands on it."

"Techs say it was blank. If that's what they said, then that's the truth," she growled. "You have something to do with Lampkin going missing? You stealing from Lambert? You should come clean, Biggston. If you had even a sliver of the honor your grandfather does, you would."

Well, that wasn't how to handle me. I looked her straight in the face now. "How can you be so sure I'm on the wrong side of this?" I asked. "From my seat, someone's covering something up. If not you, then who?"

"*You* had a chance to clear all this up at the station an hour ago. *You* lawyered up with a shark. It's *you* who hasn't been forthcoming here, Biggston," she snarled. "Something's going on in that warehouse and you're mixed up in it."

"I'm not saying anything to you while you're up in my face."

The waitress chose that moment to inconspicuously slide a second piece of pie onto the table. She slunk away.

Chessen rolled her eyes but relented, pushed off the table with her fists and sat next to Nala. To show her contempt, however, she grabbed a clean fork from the table and speared a chunk of my pie. "Sue me," she said, when I looked at her with raised eyebrows. "I missed dinner."

I pushed the plate in her direction and leaned forward so I wouldn't have to talk too loudly. "The videos on that SIMM were from Lambert Textile's five security cameras," I started. "The time-stamps were all from three nights ago when someone vandalized their system. A camera on the loading dock was shot at and destroyed. Another camera in the lab area as well as the system core were ripped out of the wall. Interesting thing is, before the core went offline, someone reinitialized the entire security system."

"There's more to this than a vandalized security system," Chessen stated flatly. "And if the system was initialized, what good is that card?"

"That's what I thought that too," I said. "Turns out, Lambert's system had a cache on this SIMM card. We got lucky. The system was disabled when they pulled it off the wall, after they initialized the long-term storage. By disabling, they ended up keeping that last three hours from each camera."

"And that's what was on this card you've been waving around," she said.

"That's right and I'll prove it when I get back to a computer that works," I said.

"Last time I'll tell you. That card is empty. Our techs are good at what they do. What was in the video?" she asked.

"I didn't get a chance to watch all of it," I said. "I was in the process of going through the files while parked at Lambert's waiting to talk with Lampkin. That's when Penelope Lambert came running out and told me someone was in her warehouse."

"Tell me again why you were at Lambert's tonight? I always get stuck on that part," she said.

This was wearisome. I wasn't changing my story. I told her again.

"Tom Lampkin, Lambert's night shift supervisor was supposed to show up for work tonight. I had some questions for him."

"Because you're a thoughtful bail bondsman? You see why I'm having trouble with this?"

"I was hired by Snerdly Electronics to reinstall Lambert's repaired security system. Which I did," I said. "I guess I just wanted to know how the system had been damaged."

"That's a bit outside your expertise, wouldn't you say?" she asked.

"What? You never get a hunch?" I asked. "Something felt off and I wanted to talk to Lampkin. I got there early so I figured I'd run through the video footage. Do you want to know what was on the video?"

"Sure," she said patronizingly. "Tell me what's on this video."

I'd locked eyes with Chessen and was surprised when I felt a hand on my arm. I looked over to Nala, who was giving me a warning look. Her action caught Chessen's attention as well.

"Officer Swede, do you have something to add?" she asked. "Because if you fuck up my interview, I'll have you on road construction detail for the rest of your career."

"No, ma'am," she answered. "I just know this is a sensitive subject for Biggs."

Chessen looked back to me. "And?"

"I'm going to get my buddy to look at this card and see if he can recover the data. That is, *if* it's really missing," I said.

"I can't figure you out, Biggston. First impression, I think you're trash. Next, I start to think maybe you're on the level. But, now you're back to asshole mode," she said, finishing off the pie and standing up. "You should know. Those boys you were tossing lead at aren't real nice. So, if you're actually innocent in all this, it might be time to pick a side."

"Thank you, Detective," Nala said.

"You need to get clear of this, Swede," Chessen said and stalked off, no happier than she'd been when she'd entered.

"Shit," I said, when Chessen finally exited the shop. "What's her problem?"

"Being a cop, people yank you around all day. She's just keeping professional distance," she said.

"Yeah. Some people might confuse that with being a jackass."

Nala chuckled nervously. "Right. So, we're probably going to need to cool it for a while. Chessen is going to make trouble for me if she sees us together."

"Think we could do the cooling off after you run me out to Lambert Textile to get my truck?" I asked.

"Sure," Nala said. "I have an early shift tomorrow, so I'll probably need to head home after that."

The night air was cold as I rode on the back of Nala's bike, but I was fired up enough that it barely registered. The ride took twenty minutes and I felt no small amount of relief when I caught sight of my truck in Lambert's parking lot.

"You have a key?" Nala asked, setting her helmet on the motor-cycle seat.

"Hide-a-key," I said. "I'm good."

She smiled and leaned in, kissing me lightly on the cheek. "You're a good guy, Biggs."

"Thanks for the ride," I said as she pulled her helmet back on. She waved and was off.

A couple of lights in the Lambert parking lot were broken, but there was enough illumination to make me think the truck was in good shape. I circled around, making sure the tires were still on and nothing else had changed since I'd been dragged off by the police. I fished my hand under the rear fender, searching for the magnetic key holder I'd hidden there. Instead of the metal box, my fingers ran across an unfamiliar object.

I shook my head in disgust, I should have had Nala wait until I had the key before I let her take off. I pulled the phone out of my pocket, turned on the flashlight and stuck my head down next to the wheel, peering up where I was certain the key should be. A fast-blinking LED caught my attention and my eyes fell on a hunk of moldable explosive the size of a deck of cards sitting right where my key had been.

I was screwed.

Instinct took over and I turned and sprinted from the truck, frantically searching for cover. The only breaks in the flat parking lot were the tapered cement posts that served as the base of each light pole. The nearest three-foot-high plinth wasn't much cover but there was no question in my mind I had only moments before I'd be a fine pink mist. A beep emanated from the wheel well and I was out of time. I dove for the nearest post and scrunched as much of my body as I could behind the cement as hellfire erupted from my beloved truck.

I HEARD familiar rhythmic beeping and someone whispering nearby. I fought to open my eyes, but I couldn't. It didn't matter. I drifted back to sleep.

What seemed like seconds later, I awoke to more beeping, only this time I was cognizant of the fact that where ever I was, it was bright, loud, and the sounds were annoying. I just wanted to sleep. I was so tired, I was unable to open my eyes. The smell of antiseptic hit me and my reality snapped into place. I was in a hospital. Even so, I couldn't bring myself to care and drifted back into unconsciousness.

I'm not sure how often I fought against the forces that held me to the bed. It felt like forever and yet, it felt like no time at all.

"I think he's starting to wake." The woman's voice was familiar, although I wasn't sure why I'd be familiar with any of the Army nurses.

A dull ache spread throughout my body, reminding me of the explosion that had blown up half my team. I'd seen the grenade bounce along the floor. I thought my time had come, only, at the last second, I was knocked to the ground by my buddy, Angel. Of course, that wasn't the name his mother had given him. He'd earned the name after his Army basic training haircut had started to grow out.

The more his hair tried to grow back, the more comical he looked. Prematurely thinning anyway, Angel had been left with peach fuzz except for an area of curly brown hair around his bald-spot, giving him a look that was more like a halo than a flat top. Maybe we should have called him Saint, but if you'd known him, that wouldn't have been your first choice.

"Angel," I tried to call out. The hospital had disappeared and I was back in the earthen building, the explosion still ringing in my ears. I pushed Angel's massive bulk off the top of me and discovered that he was a bloody mess. His uniform had been burned away and in its place was an unrecognizable mass of gore.

Someone pulled at my arms as I tried to reach my friend. I had to stop the bleeding or he would bleed out in minutes. I fought against whoever was holding me, desperately trying to save Angel. My vision clouded as blood ran into my eyes. I tried to wipe it away but couldn't.

"Clear the way," a voice of authority boomed.

"Angel's down," I called out. Whoever was coming would help him. I had to get the man's attention.

"I've got him, son." I couldn't get a good look at the dark figure, but his confidence gave me hope and I relaxed. I felt a small prick on my arm and sank into blackness.

Some time later, I started to wake.

"Henry, it's Grandma Pearl."

I smiled. I couldn't imagine what she was doing all the way over here in Afghanistan, but it felt like a huge weight had been lifted.

"Hey, beautiful," I said, trying to force my eyes open.

She squeezed my hand and patted it. I smelled her faint perfume and felt a light kiss on my cheek, just like she'd done when putting me to bed all those years ago.

"Henry, you're safe," she said. "You're in the Sutherland General Hospital."

"Where's Angel?" I asked. "He's hurt."

"Henry." It was Pappi's voice. "Angel didn't make it. You and your team tried to save him, but he died shielding you and Tommy from a grenade. That was three years ago. You've been in a coma. Doctor said it was the best way to reduce the swelling in your brain caused by the explosion."

"I've been in a coma for three years?" I asked, trying to push myself upright.

"No, dear," Pearl answered, brushing a cool hand across my forehead. "Doctor said you'd be confused. Your brain is trying to put two events together and Lester needs to hush. You just need to know you are safe right now and you're waking up because the doctor is bringing you off the medicine."

I managed to get an eye open. The light was insanely bright and I winced. "Can we turn down the lights?"

Pearl brought her hand over my forehead and shaded my eyes. "Lester, get the lights."

"I want to sit up," I said.

"Take it slow, Henry," she said.

I pushed against the mattress and tried to sit up just about the time the lights turned off. My head hurt like the dickens and I had a difficult time feeling just about anything else. No doubt I was on some heavy meds. With a whirring of motors, the bed lifted, slowly elevating my back.

I became aware of a tube in my nose and reached for it.

"Nurse," Pearl said excitedly, trying to move my hand away from the tube. "Nurse!"

I gave the tube a good yank and a long pull, then gagged as I discovered it was in a lot deeper than expected. I also wasn't one to give up on a good idea and just about the time the overhead lights flicked on again, I'd completely removed it.

"Mr. Biggston," a man in scrubs admonished. "Are we going to have problems with you?"

"Sorry, Doc," I said. "Didn't feel right."

"Nurse Garry," the man said. "Lester, Pearl, could I have the room for a moment?"

"Seriously, they can stay," I said. "I'm all done."

"Seriously," he mimicked. "I sincerely doubt that."

I looked over just in time to see Pappi's backside as if he couldn't scoot out of the room fast enough.

"I can stay with you, Henry." Pearl tried to calm me down. "You have more than one tube. It's nothing to be ashamed of. I'll close my eyes."

Adrenaline is a fantastic way to dump morphine from your body. My eyes flew open as I looked from Pearl to the sheet that covered my torso and then up to Nurse Garry. The look on his face was somewhere between sarcastic and compassionate as he nodded agreement.

"Only takes a second and you'll just feel a small pinch," he said.

His speech might have worked on someone who'd never had a catheter removed before, but I knew exactly what was coming. "Damnit," I said. "You couldn't get that out while I was still under?"

"No," he answered. "We prefer to share this little joy with the patients. We call it a bonding moment."

"Bonding?" I asked, pushing back in my bed. Where I thought I was going, I have no idea. There was no escaping the man.

"I could get someone else if you're uncomfortable," he said, a twinkle in his eye.

"Pearl. Maybe you should give us a minute," I said.

"Okay, Henry," she said. "I'll be right outside."

"I feel like it helps to hum something," Garry said as he snapped on sterile gloves.

I shook my head. I was in the hands of a sadist. To his credit, however, he didn't waste any time and while it wasn't a particularly comfortable procedure, it was over in a moment.

"Aside from the obvious, Henry, how are you feeling? Can you rate your pain on a scale from one to ten?" Garry asked.

"Three," I said. "I've a killer headache coming but otherwise I'm doing good."

Garry's eyes grew serious. "Don't be a hero here, Henry. We can manage pain. I know you're feeling more than three."

"Not really," I said. "It's all relative, right?"

"You have a number of old wounds," he said. "Did you serve?"

"Army," I said. "A couple of tours. You?"

"Sandbox," he said. "Medic. Way I hear it, you were Seventy-Fifth."

"That's right."

"Seventy-Fifth saw a lot of action and I patched a lot of guys like you up. Thank you for what you did over there, Henry." His voice was warm and his eyes had lost the sarcasm.

"Call me Biggs," I said. "And thank you, Garry. Without you guys, I'd have lost a lot more buddies."

"See?" Garry said, humor returning to his eyes. "We bonded. And not just because I was holding your go-go stick."

I smiled. "I generally expect dinner first."

"Do you, now?" he said with a grin. "Doc says you're clear for broth and Jell-O shots, less the tequila. Once you keep that down for a couple of hours, we'll upgrade you to cottage cheese. Yum. Any of that sound good?"

"Water," I said.

He turned his back on me, walked a couple feet over to the sink and poured water into a plastic cup. He had a hitch in his walk and my eyes fell to his artificial leg.

<hr />

A knock sounded on the door of my new room. I'd been awake for a full day and that had qualified me for an upgrade – meaning a move out of intensive care. I'd sent Pappi and Pearl home once I learned they'd been at the hospital almost non-stop for the last five days. Pearl promised to return in the morning, but I saw the fatigue in her eyes.

"Come in," I said.

A small flower arrangement held by a heavily tattooed arm preceded Nala into the room. "Biggs! I thought you were dead." She rushed over and leaned in for an awkward hug. "I had my music blasting and never even heard the explosion. When I saw the emergency response headed your way, I just knew you were in trouble."

"Things are still a bit fuzzy." I was a little surprised. Her eyes were rimmed red and her cheeks puffy. It looked like she'd been crying. "I'm glad you weren't hurt."

"How fuzzy?" she asked, her eyebrows knitted together in concern.

"I don't know what I was doing out at Lambert," I said. "Last thing I remember was being questioned by Detective Chessen and some suit releasing me."

"You don't remember having pie afterward?" she asked, her face relaxing.

I shook my head. "Doc says I might get some of it back, but he wasn't that hopeful."

"Things are getting pretty heavy, Biggs," she said, grabbing my hand as she sat in the chair next to me. "You need to leave this Lambert thing alone."

"Alone?" I asked. "All I've done is install a security system and get shot at."

She lowered her voice and leaned in. "You were talking crazy – like you'd seen video of a girl and this missing guy, Lampkin."

Her mentioning the video brought back details. I *had* seen a video of a girl running for her life.

As if summoned by our conversation, Detective Chessen lightly knocked and stuck her head in the room. I'd only seen her once before, during an interrogation at the police station. She'd been across the table from me in pit-bull mode. She was a solid, middle-aged woman, not entirely unpleasant looking, although she looked severe in her dark gray suit with a shoulder holster peeking out.

Nala squeezed my hand and whispered. "I need to go. I can't be seen with you."

"Have a minute?" Chessen asked, raising her eyebrows. I suspect she was going for *not-an-asshole*, but wasn't sure it was a look she'd yet mastered.

I shrugged. "Sure."

"I was just leaving," Nala said, keeping her head down as she scooted past Chessen.

"What's that all about?" Chessen asked, looking after Nala as she left.

"Just stopped by with some flowers. Figured it was from all of you down at the station," I said.

"Right," Chessen said flatly. "You get a look at who rigged your truck?"

"My truck? Seriously?" I asked. "How bad?"

"I think they're still picking up pieces in Kansas. Funny what you find after an explosion, though." She carried a large brown paper bag over to the bed. Pulling out a plastic zip-lock, she held it up so I could see its contents: three small, wrapped bundles of cash, DeLovely's burner phone and my handcuffs. "Never believe who answered the only number on the phone."

I wasn't about to bite. If she was fishing, she needed better bait. "Who?"

She tilted her head and gave me an appraising look. "Can't quite figure you, Biggston. What are you up to?"

"Appreciate the cuffs. Didn't think I was getting them back," I said. "Is there anything illegal about carrying cash and a phone?"

"Not a bit. I figured you'd want it back," she tossed the bag onto my legs. "Want to explain this?" she pulled out a second, larger, clear evidence bag. Inside was a piece of black-stained white material.

"Got me," I said.

She opened the bag and pulled out the torn remains of the t-shirt Snert had given me. There were three holes in the top layer – just where my heart would have been. Someone had shot me. Instinctively, my hand went to my chest. I thought the soreness I felt had been caused by the explosion.

"What the hell?" I asked.

She nodded. "Twenty-two caliber rounds. Ask me, it looks like a hit. I'm thinking whoever it was must have been interrupted."

"I'm not following."

"Pros will finish with a headshot, just to make sure," she said. "Let me spell it out for you. Whoever you pissed off blew up your truck and when that didn't do it, they circled back to finish the job. I told you before, it's time to pick a side in this, Biggston. Come clean and we'll do what we can to keep you safe."

"I don't know a thing," I said. "Aside from seeing that girl on the video."

"What girl?" Chessen asked. "What video?"

I shook my head in disbelief. "The video on the memory stick from the god-damn security system."

"Don't bark at me, Biggston. This is the first I'm hearing about any girl," she said. "That memory stick was clean when we got it."

"Bullshit," I said. "Where are my things?" I pushed my legs around, setting the bag of money and the phone on my table.

"Hey, hold on there," she said. "Tell me what you're looking for. I can help."

"I'm fine." I brushed her off and walked over to where my wallet and phone were sitting inside a bag the hospital had supplied. I brought the bag back and dumped it on the bed. "Fuck. It's not here."

Chessen shrugged. "I'm telling you it was empty. Now tell me about the girl."

"How do I know you're not part of this?" I asked. "That card had video on it when I got taken into custody. Why would I make that up?"

"Yeah. Dirty cop. That's always the go-to," she said, annoyed. "Your grandfather was on the force. You should know better."

"The video showed a bunch of girls in a big crate that broke open inside a warehouse. There were men with guns. One of the girls escaped and ran over to the Lambert building. I saw Lampkin in the video. I think he was trying to help that girl," I said.

She pulled out her notepad. "Slow down and repeat what you just told me."

"You believe me?" I asked.

"It's not a matter of believing you. If you saw something, I need to get it recorded. Now, how many girls and when did this happen?" she asked.

"The explosion," I said, suddenly remembering. "I reinstalled that security system. There should be video."

Chessen shook her head. "Nope. Those boys who were shooting at you took the entire system this time. We already talked to Mr. Snerdly. Apparently, Penelope Lambert hadn't made a decision about upgrading."

I slammed my fist into the bed and my voice broke as I exclaimed, "Damn it!"

"What's this matter to you, Biggston? You don't know Lampkin or that girl," she said.

"You didn't see her," I said. "She was terrified. She was clawing at that door."

"You have time to look at some pictures?"

"Now?" I asked.

"No. But I could have someone down here tomorrow. When are you getting out?" she asked.

I found it intriguing how easily she slipped between accusing me and enlisting my help.

"Doc said day after tomorrow."

"Hang on," she said. "I'll be back in a couple minutes."

I looked at the personal belongings I'd dumped out onto my bed and started putting everything back into the bag, along with the cash and burner DeLovely Manning had given me. I still had DeLovely's USB drive, my pocket knife and about twenty-five hundred bucks. It occurred to me that, aside from Diva and the clothing I had either at the farm or Snert's, I was looking at everything I owned in the world. I could hardly believe I'd lost the truck Pappi and I had worked so hard on together.

"You up for some company, Biggs?" Snert asked from the hallway. Pearl had told me that Snert had stayed the first two days, not leaving my side. He'd only been convinced to leave when the doctor had convinced him I was doing well. I'd been expecting to see him this evening now that his shop was closed.

"Sure," I said, setting the bag aside.

"I'm sorry I got you involved in this," Snert started. "It's all my fault. I should have known that Lambert's security system damage was more than vandalism."

"Buddy, your gift saved my life," I said, reaching for and mussing up his hair, something he especially hated. His tight curls typically sat close to his head until they were mussed and then they stuck up oddly.

Despite it all, he smiled. "That brand has a really good rating. I bought you two more. They should be here tomorrow or the next day."

Chessen cleared her throat. Snert spun toward the doorway, his eyes wide as he caught sight of her holstered gun.

"Hang on a sec, Snert. Detective Chessen was just leaving," I said.

"Not really," Chessen said. "You ever see this girl?" She walked past Snert and held her phone out to me. The picture on the phone was of a dead teen lying next to a dumpster. Her clothing was filthy and torn, her body no better. I heard the blood rushing in my ears, but it wasn't Amalia.

"Not her," I said, pushing the phone away.

"Hold on," Chessen said, flipping to another picture. The scene was similar, probably the same alley. My heart sank. It was Amalia's older sister. She had fresh bruises on her face and her lip had been torn open, blood caked on her cheek. She looked so tiny and helpless lying in a fetal position against the crumbling brick of the building.

I clenched my teeth. "Where is this picture from?" I asked. I felt responsible. If I'd done something about that video the girl might still be alive.

"Is it her?" Chessen pressed.

"No, it's the girl's sister. Where did you find the bodies?"

"Probably shouldn't tell you this. These two were found near

Fourth and Durango. It's a rough area. They were moved there, however."

"When?" I asked.

"The bodies were discovered the morning after Lambert's security system was vandalized. Guatemalan illegals. Probably shipped over the border for sex trafficking. There's evidence of abuse."

"Her sister's name is Amalia Rouca," I said, my voice pinched with emotion. "Did you find any other girls?"

Chessen reared back. "Any more? How do you know this girl? What the hell, Biggston?"

I shook my head. "I don't know her. Not really. I caught the two of them stealing tires from my truck. The younger one, Amalia, dropped an ID card."

"This could be huge," Chessen said. "We've never had a name before. They've always been Jane Does. Listen closely. You need to stop talking to Swede about this."

"Why?"

"This is the first lead we've had on these bastards in eighteen months. I don't need word getting out," she said. "You tell Swede, she'll tell her boss and you know how it goes: pretty soon everyone knows. So far, all I've got is a name and a guy with a flakey memory."

"There were four other girls in that crate," I said.

"You're not getting it. There are always more," Chessen said. "We need to cut the head off the snake."

"And save those girls," I pushed back.

"Okay, hero," she said. "I'd like that. But just so we're clear, if you get anywhere near this case, I'll have you up on obstruction. I've already got the feds up my ass and I don't need Johnny hero fucking things up."

"WHAT DID SHE WANT?" Snert asked, once Chessen had left.

"Questions about that SIMM card from Lambert's security system," I said. "Somehow it disappeared in the explosion."

I was having trouble getting the picture of Amalia's sister out of my head. From the timeline, I knew she was already dead by the time we'd gotten the video, but she had to have been abducted right after I caught her stealing my tires.

"I brought you a get-well gift," he said, reaching into a desert-sand-colored backpack.

"I think you saved my life with that armored t-shirt, buddy. You don't owe me. I owe *you*," I said. Something important pushed at my subconscious, but I couldn't work through it as we talked.

Snert beamed at the praise. "The shirt manufacturer says they're effective against shrapnel. I guess you proved that."

"Sure enough," I said, leaning back and folding my arms behind me. Telling him about the gunshots would only upset him, so I decided not to mention it. Whatever had been nipping at my subconscious slipped away.

From the pack, he pulled out an electronic tablet and handed it to me. The entire thing was about an inch thick and looked to have an eight-inch screen. The hard case around the outside had an Army camo pattern on it.

"The screen is kind of a pain. It's covered by a tungsten-alloy plate. You have to flip it around," he said.

I rolled my eyes. "I think I can figure it out," I said dryly, flipping the device open. "I got blown up. No brains actually leaked out."

Snert ignored me and continued. "USB ports and cellular service. I hooked it up to my business account for now. I figure you're sort of part of the company, so it's a reasonable expense."

I touched the internet browser and was surprised at how quickly the app fired up. "It's fast," I said, admiringly. "Must have been expensive."

"Speed is all about battery consumption. Since the housing is a little bigger, we could get more battery – so it's fast," he said.

"That's a pretty big get-well gift," I said.

"Well," he said, digging in the backpack to retrieve the mangled remains of the camera and tablet I'd bought only a couple days before. "Apparently, you need a bit more than *ruggedized*." Snert made air-quotes as he said it.

"I also threw in one of my cameras," he said. "You can borrow it for as long as you need. You know, if you have a receipt from Bucky's, your insurance should cover your tablet and the camera."

"Receipt was in the truck. Besides, I paid cash," I said.

"Yeah. You're screwed. How much was the truck insured for?"

"Not sure," I said. "It was on Pappi's insurance. Mostly, it was his truck. He paid for most of the parts."

"Who was on the title?"

"I was. But that's because he wanted me to feel a sense of owner-ship. All part of getting me to take charge of my life," I said. I dropped my eyes. "Which I'm doing a bang-up job of."

"I doubt he sees it that way," Snert said. "You have three jobs. You're not lazy. You're just finding your own way."

"Three?"

"Working for me, Sure Bond, and that investigative job you got the camera for," he said.

"Why is it so hard to get going on any of those jobs?" I asked. "Well, not the installs. That's not hard, but the other stuff?"

"Be patient. You'll get the hang of it, Biggs." He pulled a rectangular bottle from the pack. It was a green fruit and veggie smoothie he knew I enjoyed. I was so tired of dull hospital food that my mouth watered upon seeing it.

"Oh man, I could hug you right now," I said, opening the bottle.

"I have two more. I bet the nurses would put 'em in the fridge if I ask. Oh, and the backpack is yours, too. I didn't know what you liked, but I figured you lost a few in the explosion and this looked, well, you know, soldiery," he said.

Our conversation was interrupted by another knock on the door. I was starting to run out of people I knew and was surprised when Mel Ramirez stuck her head in the door. "Mind if I come in?" she asked.

Instead of the tight para-military style clothing she'd worn at her father's gun shop, she had on a white summer dress with large blue tropical flowers on it. Not overly tall, but full-figured in just the right places, she was quite a sight. Her long silky hair was loose and trailing down her back in waves.

I must have been staring, because she looked a little awkward as she stepped gingerly into the room, glancing from Snert to me and back again.

Fortunately, Snert recovered before I did. "I was just going. I'll come by tomorrow. Don't forget, I left that camera in the pack for you."

"Sorry, Mel," I said. "It's just ... you didn't look like you."

"I'll take that as a compliment," she said and turned to Snert. "You don't need to leave on my account. You must be Alan."

Snert looked from Mel to me, confusion apparent on his face.

"Mel manages her dad's gun-range downtown," I said. "We had

drinks a couple days ago after my conceal carry class. I might have mentioned you."

"Isn't that the night you ..."

I cut him off, as I was certain he was about to mention my date with Nala. "The night your store was broken into," I finished for him.

"You didn't say she was pretty," Snert whispered.

"I wasn't wearing a dress at the shop," Mel said, not even pretending that she didn't hear him. "I just came from church with my family, but I heard you were up and around, so I wanted to stop in."

"It's Saturday night," Snert said. "Who goes to church on Saturday?"

Mel smiled. "It's a big congregation. There's a group of us who go on Saturdays so there's more room on Sunday. You know us Latinos. Big families." She stretched her arms out wide for emphasis.

"Isn't that a stereotype?" Snert asked innocently.

"Maybe," she answered. "But I have a brother, two sisters and ten cousins. Most of whom are married and have kids. Trust me, there are a lot of us."

"I didn't know your family was so big," I said.

"I don't lead with it. Some men find it intimidating," she said. "So, how are you feeling? Still have ringing in your ears?"

"Yeah. Sometimes when I move, things don't feel like they're completely sync'd with reality," I said.

"You didn't tell me that," Snert complained.

"Mel was in the service," I said, as if that explained everything.

"Still in the reserves," she said, sitting on the edge of the bed. "Hey, I can't stay long. I just wanted to check on you and invite you to a picnic."

"Like on a date?" Snert asked. Trust him to make awkward my reality.

"Why not?" Mel asked. "It's casual – a family thing – so there's no pressure. And besides, your grandparents will be there."

"At your picnic?" I asked.

"The event has gotten out of control. It's like a really big church pot-luck out at my uncle's farm," she said. "Alan, you could come too. Every family brings a dish. There's always way too much food, so you really wouldn't need to bring anything."

"Ooh, I could fire up the smoker. I've been dying to try a new pork rub recipe," Snert said. "And you should call me Snert. Everyone does."

"That's a funny name, but so is Mel." She jumped off the bed. "And with that, I need to get going. My sister is waiting in the car." She turned back to me, leaned in and gave me a quick peck on the cheek. "Give me a call. I'd love to see you next Sunday."

"Can do," I said.

"I'll walk out with you. Can't be too careful nowadays" Snert said. "Besides, Biggs needs his rest."

I smiled. It was a surprising move on Snert's part and I had to give him credit for it.

"My hero." Mel hooked her arm through Snert's and gave me a little wave over her shoulder.

"Wait, I don't have your number," I called as the two disappeared through the door.

"I'll get it," Snert called back.

I shook my head in disbelief. Maybe my head injury was worse than I thought.

"How's our patient doing?" The doctor's voice preceded his entrance. If there was something I disliked the most about hospitals, it would be that there was never a quiet moment.

"Ready to leave," I said.

"Still have that swimmy feeling?" he asked, shining a bright light into my eyes.

"Nope. I'm one hundred percent," I lied. "You need to discharge me."

He nodded. "Insurance company says the same thing. If you keep making progress, I don't see why you can't leave tomorrow. You're going to have to take it easy. You've had substantial head trauma.

Another hit like the one you experienced could lead to permanent brain damage."

"Is all this necessary?" I waved to the IV line and sensors.

"I'll take the IV line out in the morning when I stop by for rounds. How's the pain?" he asked, looking up from the clipboard. "It looks like you've been refusing pain management."

"I'm fine," I said. It wasn't a big lie. I'd always had a high threshold for pain. "I've seen a lot of friends get hooked on pain meds. I don't have any room for that."

"I'll order ibuprofen," he said. "Same stuff you buy at the grocery store. I need you to take six-hundred milligrams, three times a day for at least a week. I'm interested in reducing the swelling more than pain management."

"Copy that," I said.

"Good." He patted my leg. "Tomorrow then."

My room was finally empty. I grinned ironically to myself as my phone buzzed on the counter. Someone had turned off the ringer. In all the activity, I hadn't had a moment to even look at it, although I didn't generally get a lot of calls beyond the people who knew I was in the hospital. It was probably Snert sending me Mel's phone number.

With an IV and sensor leads attached, getting out of bed was something of a process. I'd already learned how to turn off the alarms so I could drag the bottle along with me to the bathroom. I grabbed the backpack Snert had left, both phones and the cash, and dumped it all in a pile on my bed before sitting back down. There's something about being in a hospital that always made me feel like I'd lost control of my life.

"You okay in here?" The male voice no doubt belonged to one of a myriad of nurses that worked the floor. I stuffed the items into the bag, not feeling like the nurse needed to see the cash and phones.

"Yup," I said. "All good."

A man in scrubs stepped in with a reassuring smile. "Your leads must have slipped off," he said, closing the door behind him. Something in his manner set me on edge. Whether it was his already-gloved hands or perhaps the wide gold necklace, he didn't feel like a nurse to me.

"Just had to get up for a minute," I said, surreptitiously wrapping my hands around the straps of my backpack.

"Good," he said. "I just need to get the alarms taken care of."

The guy was good. He didn't break character as he closed the distance between us. That said, in my peripheral vision, I saw his left arm tucked into his side with his hand hidden by his leg.

There was a flicker of understanding in his eyes as they landed on my hand, now clenching the backpack straps. In slow motion, his left arm swung away from his leg and a small silenced pistol became visible in his hand. In a single fluid move, I flipped one leg off the side of the bed and swung the backpack around. The bag itself was cushioned, but it was also weighted down with Snert's camera, my two phones, and the rugged notebook.

A muffled gunshot sounded as the pack made contact with the man's shoulder and skipped up over his head. My arm exploded in pain as the movement tore out the IV, pulling the stand over with a crash. I didn't dare stop. By taking the initiative, I'd raised my odds of surviving, but not by much. The pack – or more likely, the effects I was still experiencing from the concussion – had caused me to over-rotate and I grabbed for the bed. I felt a powerful blow to my back as the man somehow came back with an elbow. I fell to the ground. It was a terrible place to be with a man standing over me holding a pistol.

I struck out with the only attack I had available, which was to kick out my leg into the man's groin. Chunks of floor ricocheted into my face as the gun fired again. It turns out, however, that a full heel-kick to the groin is about as effective a way to bring down a man as any other attack ever invented. The man crumpled, firing wildly a third time and falling to a knee.

I wasted no time. Twisting, I brought my other leg around and braced with my hands to execute a front-snap kick. Unsuccessfully, he attempted to cover his face as I made contact with his head. He fell sideways and then into a heap on the floor.

"Hey, what's going on in here?" A woman's voice came from the doorway.

"911," I called back as I brought my legs back under me and sprang forward, dragging along instruments still connected to my chest.

"Mr. Biggston. Get off. You're hurting him," the woman called back. From her perspective, I was pounding on one of the other nurses, but I wasn't about to stop.

"Call 911," I shouted and brought my fist down onto the man's neck. I'd been aiming for his head, but he was squirming about, trying to recover from my other attacks. His hand shot out and grabbed at the pistol on the floor. His finger must have caught the trigger as there was fresh gunfire.

The nurse who'd been arguing with me squeaked in fear and darted from the room, yelling, "Nine One One!"

Going for the gun had been a mistake. He'd had to stretch for it, allowing me to completely control the fight. Now, in his defense, he couldn't have known that I had boxing experience. It wasn't as if I was currently a fighter, but there are some things you just don't forget. Landing a good hit was one of them. With my knees under me, I drove my fist once again into the side of his head, this time with a lot more power. My fist landed on his ear and made a satisfying crunching sound and, more importantly, rotated his head. In a smooth motion, I swung my shoulders over and drove my other fist into his perfectly-lined-up face. I felt his lights turn off as my fist made contact.

"Get off!" a man ordered as I stood. I looked over. A security guard was aiming a can of pepper spray at me.

"Nice timing." I reached down and grabbed the pistol from my would-be assassin's hand.

"I'll shoot," he said.

I ignored him and ejected the magazine. I pulled the gun's slide back and unloaded the chambered round. The weapon was a newer Ruger 22 caliber. It was trivial to remove the barrel, so I did and tossed the collection of parts into a waste basket.

"Settle down," I ordered, making eye contact. "I was just attacked. Have you called the police?"

"You attacked a nurse," he argued, leveling the spray at me. A second security guard showed up behind him.

"Do you have any cuffs or zip ties?"

"That man doesn't work here." The nurse who'd run out screaming 911 had come back into the room. She was being careful to stay behind the guard's shoulder.

"Look. He's going to wake up and I suspect he'll be pissed when he does. Cuffs?"

The guard gave me a bewildered look. I shook my head and picked up my backpack, withdrawing my cuffs. Unkindly, I rolled the fake nurse over and dragged him to the bed, placing the cuffs on his wrists, but not until I'd looped them through the steel frame of the bed. I grabbed a marker from the white-board on the wall and tore the man's sleeve open. I wrote 'Cuffs belong to Henry Biggston.' I didn't think I'd see them again, but it was worth a try.

The nurse pushed past the guard. "Your arm is bleeding. You tore out your IV."

"Can you get some gauze?" I asked, pulling at the drawers and discovering there was nothing useful in them.

"Put your hands on your head." The guard had finally recovered enough to speak intelligently. "Police are on their way."

"No," I said.

I was a little surprised when the nurse got in the guard's face and placed her hands on his chest, pushing him backward. "This man is our patient. Can't you see he was attacked? Wait outside."

I picked up the waste bin that had the gun pieces in it. "Cops are going to want this." I leaned around the nurse to hand it to the useless guard. "You'll want to give Detective Chessen at the Second Precinct a call."

The nurse left to find bandages and a new IV but by the time she returned, I'd pulled on my pants, removed the hospital gown and was searching through the drawers for a shirt. I wasn't even remotely surprised when I found a clean and folded shirt, obviously left behind by Pearl.

"What are you doing, Mr. Biggston?" she asked. "Police are on the way."

"Finding a new place to sleep," I said. "It's impossible to get any rest around here."

I THREW THE BACKPACK ON, slipping both arms through to give me maximum mobility. The nurse just looked from me to the man on the floor, confused about her priorities. When I tried to exit the room, I wasn't a bit surprised when the older of the two guards placed a hand on my chest to stop me.

"Police are on the way. You need to stick around," he said, giving me his best attempt at intimidation. I had him at two hundred forty and five ten, which meant I gave up almost fifty pounds, but had at least three inches on him. I also doubted the fifty pounds I gave up were in muscle.

I looked at his hand and then slowly back up into his face with my best don't-mess-with-me stare. The old guy was clearly doing what he thought was the right thing and I wasn't about to hurt him for that. That said, I wasn't sticking around for round two of the shit-show circus I'd somehow stumbled into.

"Cops already have my info," I said. "Wouldn't your time be better served making sure that guy doesn't get loose?" I angled my head in the general direction of my would-be assassin, who was starting to move.

Concern flashed across his face as he glanced into the room. I took the opportunity, turned sideways and slipped past him, annoyed that my backpack got caught on the doorframe.

"You need to stop right there," he ordered.

It was too late, as I was already a dozen feet down the hallway with my hand on the door to the stairs. I didn't bother responding. The guy had made an effort and could report that to the cops and his superiors when asked. I was certain that would be the end of his pursuit. I started down the stairs, slowly at first. The movement felt good and with each step my body seemed to come more alive. I still had a low-level headache, but it wasn't anything I couldn't manage.

When I reached the first level, I had a choice - either enter the lobby or exit the building. There was an alarm on the outside exit, a simple device that would make a piercing wail until someone came and turned it off. If the cops were coming, the siren might draw their attention. I gambled. The reports of shots fired and a handcuffed suspect would surely draw them up to my room first.

I chuckled to myself as the siren made no noise when I exited into the night air. Thunder crackled above me as I jogged up a flight of stairs and across the pavement. Three police cruisers with flashing lights but no sirens cruised into the hospital parking lot and I slowed. They would certainly detain me if they figured out who I was, but I believed I was a few minutes ahead of the information of my departure.

As soon as they passed, I broke into an easy jog. It was the sort of pace I'd been trained to keep for hours, although I wasn't in top shape like I had been a couple of years back, especially after living through a truck explosion and a gunshot wound to my torso. I chose to be glad that I was upright at all. The night air, light sprinkles of rain, and blessed quiet were just what I needed to clear my head. The antiseptic smell of the hospital combined with the machines, alarms and constant checks by the staff made it impossible to think.

I needed a safe place that wasn't near family. So far, I'd been the sole target and planned to keep it that way. The rain increased so I pulled out my phone and checked the weather. It was sixty degrees and likely to continue to rain for the next six hours with the temperature dropping to the low fifties. If I kept moving, I wouldn't be in immediate danger of hypothermia, but those conditions drove home the point that I needed cover. Across the street I noticed a small park and more importantly, a picnic shelter. Such a public area wouldn't work as a place to sleep, but it would provide momentary respite.

I made it to the shelter just as the rain increased to a deluge. I shivered. Even with exertion, I was cold. I had zero anxiety, however, as I'd been a lot colder and in much worse conditions. The rain sheeted off the roof as I pulled out DeLovely Manning's burner phone. Either she didn't know the number or she was patient beyond expectation, as there were still no missed calls logged on the phone. I pulled up the single contact on the phone and formed a text message:

BIGGS: *I've run into unexpected complications. Thank you for assist at police station. I plan to start surveillance tomorrow.*

I didn't expect an immediate response, so I put the phone down and pulled out my personal phone. I hadn't had time to look at it since I'd been in the hospital, mostly because I'd seen everyone who would want to call me.

I was surprised to see I had missed ten calls and five waiting voicemails. The sound of the rain on the roof was loud enough that I had difficulty hearing, but I caught most of it. The first three were all from three days ago and from the same number.

"Hey, Army. *That asshat is home. You might want to get over here and take out the trash.*"

"Damnit, Army. *You gonna do something today? Looks like Creight's about to pack up. Get yer ass over here!*"

"Day late and a dollar short. *You missed him, Army.*"

The voice belonged to Jonesy, the old man who lived across from Creight's house. I looked at the time. It was ten thirty and probably too late to call. Creight was a lower priority right now, but I didn't want Jonesy to stop giving me information, so I hit the call back.

I was just about to hang up when he answered. "Damn, Army, thought you wanted that Creight fella."

I had to wait as he coughed wetly for the next thirty seconds. He followed up the attack by spitting and finally clearing his throat.

"Heya, Jonesy," I said. "I had some problems. Wish I hadn't missed your call."

DeLovely's burner phone buzzed while I was talking and I opened it as I waited for Jonesy's response.

DELOVELY: Where are you?

BIGGS: Nowhere. How'd you know to send the lawyer?

DELOVELY: I'm keeping tabs. You need to watch the USB.

BIGGS: How do you know I haven't?

DELOVELY: Password is your unit number. Be careful. You're attracting a lot of heat.

BIGGS: From who?

"Army, you still there?" Jonesy asked. I'd tuned him out as I was texting with DeLovely. Fortunately, I'd paid enough attention to know that he hadn't done much more than complain about the noise on my side of the call.

"Sorry. I lost my ride and it's raining like a bitch here," I said.

"Lost how?" he asked. "You weren't part of that thing over in the industrial park, were you?"

"Best if we don't talk about it," I said.

"What are you doing outside at this time of night? You need a place to crash?" he asked. "I got this big house."

"No can do, Jonesy," I said. "I can't bring more folks into this mess."

"Look, Army," he said. "I ain't afraid of nothing. You can even take the Crown Vic out for a ride. That is, if you'll change the oil and put gas in her."

DELOVELY: Look at the USB.

I erased the messages from the phone and closed it. She wasn't going to say anything else.

"Maybe just for tonight," I said.

"Where are you at?" he asked. "I'll come get you."

There was no doubt in my mind that Jonesy could hardly make it down the steps of his house. He definitely had no business driving a car.

"I'm close," I lied. "See you in forty minutes."

"Back door is open." He started coughing again and hung up.

I opened a car-service app and plugged in Creight's address since I didn't know Jonesy's off the top of my head. I was in luck as a car was only two minutes away. I waited until I saw headlights approaching and then ran out to wave the car down as it slowed.

For a moment, it was touch and go as the driver attempted to determine if I was a crazy or a drunk or some combination. An elderly black man rolled down the passenger window about half way.

"You call for a ride?" he asked.

I tried the door handle and found that it was locked.

"That's me," I answered. "Can you unlock?"

"You been drinking?" he asked, warily. "Just so you know, I can defend myself."

"No drinking," I answered. "I just got caught out in this rain."

He unlocked the doors. "Get in back."

I slid in, glad to be out of the rain.

"You know the police are looking for an escapee from the hospital."

"That so?" I asked. "How'd you hear that?"

"We get updates," he said, pointing to his phone which was attached to a holder in the air-conditioner vent.

"Is he dangerous?" I asked.

"They didn't say," the man answered, pulling away from the curb. There was virtually no traffic as he drove back toward the hospital. "But you might want to take off that wristband."

I looked down at my wrist. I was indeed wearing the hospital band. "Why'd you stop?" I asked.

"I got a boy your age," he said. "No good thing ever came from getting questioned by the police."

I nodded my head. "Thanks."

I'd heard the same sentiment from Angel. Before he died, we had several late-night talks about police and the community. With Pappi being a cop, I'd started out as an ardent defender. I knew for a fact that Pappi cared enough to get things right. Angel, however, had a much different perspective. For him and his family, the police got things wrong often enough that trust had been broken. Like most things, there didn't seem to be a perfect answer. Tonight, however, I was glad for my driver's perspective.

After passing the hospital, I finally looked at my phone again. I had two more voicemails from another unknown number. The voice-to-text translation showed that it was a callback on the overgrown house rental next to Creight. The translation was obviously wrong. It read that the asking price was three-fifty a month, with first and last due up front. Even though it was late, I dialed the number.

I'd expected the call to go to voicemail and was surprised when a man's voice answered. "Hello?" he asked groggily.

"I'm returning your call about the house on Sycamore Street," I said.

"It's kind of late," the man answered.

"I thought I'd get your voicemail."

"What can I tell you about it?" he asked.

"I didn't quite catch the rent."

"Have you been there?" he asked, the interest in his voice pushing the sleep away.

"I looked through the windows," I said. "It could use some work."

"Seven hundred for first and last," he answered. "You gotta mow and keep snow off the walks. Air conditioning doesn't work, but it heats okay."

"I don't have a steady job," I said, "but I can pay in cash."

"You into drugs?"

"My grandfather is a cop," I said, looking into the mirror at my driver. If he was listening, he didn't seem to care. "That wouldn't fly."

"Oh? Cop you say?" he asked, suddenly interested. "How 'bout you meet me out there tomorrow morning."

"Eight o'clock?" I asked.

"Bring your cash," he said and hung up.

From my backpack, I pulled out the tablet and camera Snert had given me. I'd used the pack as a club and was worried I'd broken the camera. Pulling it out, I inspected it for damage. In the dark vehicle, it didn't seem any the worse for wear. I turned it on and sighted out the window through the lens. It was working and had good clarity even through the dark, rainy night. I replaced the lens cap, pushed it back into the pack, and retrieved DeLovely's USB stick. I had to search around for an adaptor cable, but soon I had the stick hanging out the side of the rugged notebook.

When I attempted to open the drive, I was prompted for a password. I'd had at least six unit numbers while in the Army. Most of my action had been while part of Bravo Company, so I typed that on the virtual keyboard. The drive opened and showed a hierarchy of folders. My eyes were drawn immediately to the one labeled with my name - Biggston.

I poked at the folder icon, my heart beating faster. What in the heck was Manning doing with pictures of me in a file about her cheating husband? There were dozens of pictures, starting with me in Snert's work van at Lambert's. I'd never even seen anyone nearby, yet the series of photos chronicled all of my outside activities, including my inspection of the broken video camera over the loading dock. Several pictures showed a shadowy figure standing at the corner of the adjacent building, also watching me. I zoomed in and recognized the face of one of the men I'd traded shots with in Lambert's warehouse. He was the man who'd gotten away.

In addition to the pictures of me, I found a startling amount of personal detail about my life. Documents mentioned my father, who had left when I was two, and my mother, who'd disappeared only a few years after that. Then I read details about Pearl and Pappi, including their estimated net worth, ages, social security numbers, and even their parent's names.

"We're here," my driver announced, grabbing my attention.

"Thanks for the ride," I said, sliding out. The rain had stopped and I saw no lights on in Creight's house.

"Stay safe," he called as he drove off.

I immediately noticed how dark the street was as he pulled away. There were a few light poles, but none of the lights were working. Several of the houses on the other side of the street had exterior lights but none were lit on Creight's side. I'd once heard a conversation about how a single broken window in one house in a neighborhood could cause the failure of the entire neighborhood. It felt like an exaggeration, but the concept wasn't lost on me. Creight's house was pulling down the neighborhood and it almost seemed like his house was ground-zero for a black-hole.

I shrugged. I might not be able to fix the whole neighborhood, but hopefully, I'd be able to remove one bad influence. I jogged across the street and down Jonesy's single-car driveway to his detached garage. There was no fence that blocked off the back yard from the driveway and a bare bulb hung over a dilapidated wooden door to his home. I knocked on the door and turned the knob. It was loose in my hand, but I was able to get the door open. The back entrance was at the corner of the house. Stairs led down to the basement and a half-flight of stairs led up to another door. I could hear the scrape of wooden chair legs across linoleum. Jonesy must have been sitting in the kitchen, because within seconds he swung open the door and peered down at me.

"That you, Army?" Jonesy called.

"It's me. Biggs."

"Good. I was just pouring a snort of whiskey," he said. "Hate to drink alone."

I bounded up the stairs and entered the kitchen. I hadn't been sure what to expect but found Jonesy walking back to a wooden table pushed against the windows that looked out the side of his house. In one hand was a bottle of inexpensive whiskey and in the other, two glasses which he banged onto the table as he sloughed into one of three chairs.

"Ice is in the freezer if you take that," he said. "I don't like to water it down."

I wasn't much of a drinker beyond an occasional beer. I preferred a glass of water, but I wasn't getting out of the whiskey. "How ever you like it," I answered. "Do you mind if I get a glass of water?"

"Help yourself. Glasses are above the sink."

Behind me, I heard the bottle tapping the glasses unevenly as Jonesy's hand shook. The man wasn't in good shape, but he'd served in a tough war and would get nothing but respect from me. I filled my glass with water from the tap and joined him at the table.

"Appreciate your offer," I said.

"Where's that dog of yours?" he asked, grabbing his glass. "She didn't get blown up in your truck, did she?" He looked at me worriedly as he raised his glass. I picked up the whiskey he'd poured for me and took a good drink. The liquid burned my throat and involuntarily I coughed.

"No," I said, my voice hoarse from the harsh treatment. "Diva's okay. How'd you know that was my truck?"

"I saw pictures on the news," he said, downing the rest of his whiskey as if it were water. "After Nam, I was a mechanic. A 1982 truck frame isn't that hard to pick out. And it's just like a grunt to start a new fight while he's in the middle of another one."

"Guilty as charged," I agreed.

"I was serious about the Vic," he said. "Keys are here on the table. Just make sure to change the oil and leave a full tank of gas. Now if you don't mind, I'll be heading off to bed." He grabbed my glass of whiskey and gave me a questioning look. When I nodded, he tossed it back and put the glass back on the table, thumping his chest with the thumb-side of his fist. "Oh. I tossed a pillow and blanket on the couch for ya. I hope that doesn't offend your sensitive backside."

"More than I had an hour ago," I said. "Much appreciated."

"Yup." He walked from the room. I listened to him wheezing all the way down the hall, followed by the sound of an electric motor.

I grabbed my pack, turned off the kitchen light, made my way through the dining room and found what I supposed was the living room. A recliner sat in front of the window overlooking the porch. Beside the recliner was a small table, its top cluttered with books, newspapers, eye glasses and various bits of trash. I sat back on the couch that ran along the far wall, pushing the pillow to one side and stretched out.

It didn't feel like I'd been asleep for more than a moment when I felt a tapping on my forehead. "Hey, Army. Daylight's burning."

Groggily, I sat up and rummaged around in my pack to find my phone. It was seven thirty.

"Were you a drill sergeant?" I asked, noticing a bunch of notifications on the lock screen.

"That damn pack of yours sounds like a Christmas cantata," he said. "Been going off all morning. You want some eggs?"

My stomach growled at the suggestion. "I better get going," I said. "I'm meeting the landlord for the place across the street."

"You looking to rent from Peabody?" he asked. "Hey, it's just as easy to make eggs for two as it is for one."

"His name's Peabody?"

"Ironic, since he reminds me of that old cartoon," he said. "Talk to me while I make breakfast."

I grabbed my bag and followed him back to the kitchen. "What do you know about that place? He's only asking three fifty a month for it."

"Creight ran him out a couple of years back," Jonesy said. "At first, old Peabody tried to fight him. Called the police when Creight would make a ruckus. Well, all that backfired on Peabody because Creight just took it to the next level. Finally forced him to move out. Ever since, Creight hassles anyone who shows interest. Peabody can't sell it, rent it, nothing."

"That's messed up," I said.

"You really thinking about renting?"

"Price is right," I said. "I've had a hard time getting things going after getting out. I've been sponging off my friends and family."

"At least they're not calling you baby killer," he said, cracking eggs into a pan he'd heated up.

"It's my problem," I said.

"Good. Man ought to own his own problems."

Awake enough now, I hit the power button on my phone. I'd missed a number of calls: Snert, Chessen, Pappi and even Nala. "I need to make a call," I said, standing up and walking toward the back door.

"Eggs in five minutes," he said.

I hit the call back for Chessen. Of all the people who'd called, she could cause me the most problems.

She picked up on the first ring. "Where are you, Biggston?"

"Laying low," I said. "Someone tried to take me out at the hospital. You guys collect the shooter?"

"Yeah, we got him," she said. "He's denying everything. Said you had the gun and were shooting at him."

"That's bullshit."

"We're going to need a statement," she said.

"You get what I just said, right? They were trying to take me out."

"The guy's lawyered up," she said. "You're the only witness. If we don't get your statement within forty-eight hours, we're going to have to cut him loose."

"He shot up the hospital," I said. "That's got to be illegal."

"And a security guard said you were acting suspicious," she said.

"Did you talk to the nurse?"

"I did. She agrees with you and for what it's worth, I believe you. Just get down here and make a statement," she said.

"Give me 'til tomorrow," I said.

"Don't do anything stupid," she said and hung up.

By the time I made it back into Jonesy's kitchen, he'd thrown the most pathetic ever looking eggs onto half-burned toast. To make matters worse, he was looking proudly at his creation and holding a fork out expectantly. "Don't let it get cold, now," he said.

It's a funny thing. I hadn't had much solid food in the last few days and as bad as the eggs and toast looked, they tasted delicious. Watching in awe as I devoured the food, Jonesy scraped an egg from his own plate onto mine. "You sure?" I asked.

"I remember when I had an appetite like that," he said. "Now everything tastes like burnt toast."

I suppressed a smile. Maybe his toast tasted burned because it was. Still, it was delicious and I wolfed it down, then picked up our plates, taking them over to the sink.

"Don't worry about that," he said. "What else do I have to do today?"

"Cook shouldn't have to clean," I said and washed off the plates.

"You seem like you're in a hurry," he said. "What would you have done if I hadn't woken you up?"

"Probably missed my meeting with Peabody," I said.

"Not likely," he said, clearing his throat like he was about to start coughing again. "Couch is always open, Army." He held the keys up and jangled them at me. "Whatever you're into, I can take care of myself. Oh, and you'll need to put these registration stickers on the license plate." He pushed away from the table and plucked an envelope from a stack.

"Can't tell you how much I appreciate your help, Jonesy," I said.

"Not the first time the Marines had to bail out the Army," he called after me as I jogged down the back stairs. "Won't be the last."

JONESY'S GARAGE was small and made of the same dark brown brick as his house. I entered from the open side door and found the well-worn, classic, late 1970s vintage Crown Victoria covered by a thick sheet of dust. It wouldn't be a small matter to get it started. Instead of trying to fire her right up, I opened the hood, sneezing at the dust I stirred up. I was surprised to see a newer battery, probably not older than four years. Considering the amount of dust on the car, there wasn't any possibility the battery had held its charge. Scanning the shelves, I happily discovered a battery charger. Plugging it in, I set it on the car's oversized fender and checked the cells for water level. Not unexpectedly, I was also going to need water.

My phone told me I was pushing eight o'clock. Hurriedly, I searched for and found a dusty old cup on one of the shelves. I hustled over to a silcock on the back of the house, first cleaning the cup and then returning to the garage with fresh water to top off the battery cells. Jonesy had been a mechanic, so I wasn't surprised when I discovered the battery charger was a good model. Once connected, the dials told me the battery was just as dead as I'd expected.

Leaving the battery to charge, I donned my pack, exited the garage, and made my way across the street to where a balding man sat inside a parked SUV directly in front of the rental property. He must not have expected me to come from Jonesy's because when I knocked on his window, he jumped and looked like he might flee.

"I'm here to see about a rental?" I called through his closed window.

"Who are you?" He had only rolled the window down a few inches.

"Henry Biggston. We talked on the phone."

The man, whom I assumed was Peabody, got out and stood flat-footed, giving me the once-over. "You're a big one, aren't you?" he said.

"I just want to get this straight," I said. "Three hundred fifty a month?"

"First and last due today. No refunds and the house is in as-is condition. If you stay for six months, we can talk about repairs." He reached into the car and pulled out a clipboard. "Fill this out. I perform a standard background check. If you have a criminal record, I'll give your money back, but I'm afraid I can't rent to you."

"I'm just a few months out of the Army," I said. "Honorable discharge. No criminal record."

Peabody nodded his head in acceptance. "That's good. Now, I'm afraid things are overgrown. I don't get out here very often. It'll be your responsibility to cut the grass and shovel the walks." He pointed to a section of the form he'd asked me to fill out. "Initial there to indicate your agreement. Also, the furnishings in the house belong to me. You have to leave them. That's next line."

"Do you have a lawn mower?" I asked.

He pursed his lips. "I did, but it was stolen. That will be your responsibility." I was okay with that; we had more than one old mower at the farm I could borrow.

"Can we look inside?" I asked.

He raised his eyebrows like he was expecting me to have walked away already. "I have to warn you. It's a mess in there. It'll be up to you to clean it. Vandals got in and broke windows and did unspeakable things to the carpet. I had to have it all pulled up. The wood floors were never refinished, but they look nice."

He fought for a few moments as he tried to unlock the door. Finally, he gave it a push and the door bent, not actually unlocking. "Um, that could use some work, but it's okay for now."

The house was small, with the front door opening directly into the living room. The dining room and kitchen were in the back half of the house, forming a u-shape around stairs to the basement. The place had a bad smell to it that I couldn't quite place and there was trash everywhere as well as a small amount of furniture.

Skipping the basement, Peabody walked me through a tiny passageway that joined the kitchen to a hallway that had three doors. One led to a back bedroom, one to a front bedroom and the middle one to a standard, if grimy, bathroom. The front bedroom was piled with debris and no furniture and while the back bedroom had a bed, it looked like it had been home to poo-throwing monkeys.

Peabody caught my interest in the bed. "If you'd like to discard the bed, I'm fine with that," he said, pursing his lips. His voice was full of despair as he spoke. "Nobody is supposed to have been in here."

We stood in silence for a few seconds. To say it was furnished was laughable as I was pretty sure the only piece of usable furniture was the kitchen table and the two wooden chairs. Everything else was beyond scary.

"I'm in," I said, holding out my hand.

The look on his face was a mixture of disgust and joy. "You'll take it?"

"It's rough, but I'm not exactly in a position to negotiate," I said.

Peabody's jaw clenched. "What are you into, Mr. Biggston? I'm telling you, I'll have you evicted if you are into illicit drugs or their trade." His oddly formal speech reminded me a lot of Snert and I felt a pang of guilt knowing Snert was very likely out of his mind with worry.

"Run the background," I said. "I'm shooting you square. Do we have a deal?"

It took twenty minutes to fill out the paperwork and Peabody took pictures of my driver's license as well as every room in the house. I found it ironic that he thought I could make this house look worse.

"And the money?" he prodded when I handed back the forms.

"Oh, I have a dog," I added, not yet letting go of the papers.

"The lease specifically states you can't have animals," his lip curled in disgust. "I won't have them trashing my home."

I pulled on the papers, noticing that he wasn't letting go. "Look, I've got a lot going on. Three fifty a month and I'll clean this place up and run off the squatters. Diva is house trained, and I can guarantee no uninvited visitors will so much as look twice at your property."

"I don't need people getting hurt," he snipped, but his resolve was waning.

"Peabody, you and I both know you're never going to rent this to anyone nice. What you need is someone with teeth. Take a risk here. I'm a vet who needs a place to live. This works for both of us. Kick me out in six months if you don't like my progress."

"And you'll leave just because I say?" he asked skeptically.

I let go of the papers and placed my hand on his shoulder. He flinched but didn't back away. It took every ounce of courage he possessed to not bolt. "I'm one of the good guys, Peabody. You give me notice and I'll be out at the end of the month."

"End of the next month," he corrected. "You've paid first and last."

I chuckled. "Right. We have a deal?" I extended my hand.

"We do, Mr. Biggston." His arm trembled as he slid his small hand into my own. I gave him my best reassuring smile, which seemed to give him some confidence.

"Call me Biggs. All my friends do," I said. "So, tell me Peabody, what is it you do for a living?"

"I'm an accountant," he said, pulling a key ring from his pocket and handing it to me. He walked to the front door and gave a last, wistful look into the living room. It wasn't lost on me that he had an emotional attachment to the house.

"Money?" I asked, digging into my backpack and pulling out seven one-hundred-dollar bills.

He smiled nervously and accepted the money. "You should always ask for a receipt for cash," he prodded, pulling a piece of paper from the clipboard after writing on it.

"Pretty sure we shook hands, Peabody," I said.

"Keep the receipt, Mr. Biggston," he said, struggling against the broken front door.

"Biggs."

He looked back just as the door shuddered and popped open, giving me a slight smile. "Biggs, then."

I turned back into the house, silently making a list of my top priorities. Given the condition of the main level, I wondered just what hidden horrors the basement might hold, although it would have to wait for another day.

Sutherland wasn't all that different from Afghanistan and discovering that someone was trying to kill me had kicked in old habits. If caught out in the open and behind enemy lines, my first job was to find adequate shelter and blend in. I felt like I'd accomplished that in spades. Rangers were encouraged to think outside the box and act with aggression. We were the guys who took the fight to the enemy and that meant doing so on their home turf. Now that I had a stable base, it was time to get down to business and figure out what was going on.

I shrugged off my pack and set it down on the kitchen table after testing for stability. I pulled out Snert's rugged notebook, fired it up and plugged in DeLovely's USB stick. I couldn't figure how she'd known to send someone to Lambert to take pictures of me working on Lambert Textile's security system. I opened a sheet and added that question, right under how DeLovely had known I was being held by the cops after the warehouse incident. I flipped back to the USB and looked at the root folders.

Aside from the folder with my name on it, there were two more: Richard Manning and Bosian. I assumed Richard was DeLovely's husband but was curious about the Bosian name. Organized crime was active in Sutherland and I was pretty sure I'd heard Pappi mention Franky Bosian as being head of one of the two biggest families.

In the folder were dozens of pictures, all dated over the last few weeks. One by one I ran through the pictures, flipping back and forth to a document where I recorded the information I gathered from each. The pictures had been renamed with what looked like the last names of a few subjects present in each picture.

Someone had added meta data to further identify people or give a description of what was happening. There were a lot of people I didn't recognize, but one caught my attention. Jake Snodgrass, aka Jake the Snake. The notes on the picture called him a high-level enforcer for Franky. Jake was interesting, since he was the man who'd gotten away after shooting at me in Lambert's warehouse. The fact that the notes suggested he was ex-special forces made me question his bad aim that day. I added that to my growing list of questions.

The investigator who'd taken the pictures had done a great job of adding notes. It was a good tradecraft lesson and I'd want to add the same detail to my own. I pushed aside the swirl of speculation forming in my head, trying to stick to the facts. I had one more folder to look through. My target, Richard (Dick) Manning.

The first thing that struck me about Dick was that he looked like a Fortune 500 executive. His perfectly cut hair had a small amount of gray at the temples and framed a well chiseled, deeply-tanned face. In every picture, he wore a suit and tie, each piece probably costing more than my entire net worth. He also didn't drive his own car. That job was reserved for his chauffeur, a man I recognized as Billy Teal-hoff. Billy was the guy I'd taken down in the warehouse and turned over to the cops. I flipped over to add another question to my list. *What was Manning's driver doing in Lambert's warehouse with Franky Bosian's enforcer?* I immediately added the next one. *Was*

Tealhoff working for Manning? ... or Franky? Or, was it one and the same, since Manning worked for Franky?

Something was off. I was missing something fundamental. DeLovely wanted me to follow her husband because she felt he was messing around on her. However, the pictures taken by her investigator showed Manning at Sutherland's exclusive country club, Manning at a number of high-end restaurants, and Manning entering a high-rise office building in Sutherland's busy downtown. There wasn't a single woman in any of the pictures.

The last shots in Manning's file, however, were grainy night pictures. They'd been taken from a long distance and showed the warehouse next to Lambert's. Even though the picture resolution was horrible, I realized I was looking at pictures taken the same night as Lambert's security footage. Hurriedly, I flipped through the three pictures. The last showed a scene that would haunt me for a long time. Amalia Rouca stood at Lambert's front door. What the picture lacked in resolution, it made up for in its wide-angle view. In the foreground was Richard Manning's Mercedes Benz. On the ground in front of the Benz was a crumpled figure.

For several long minutes, I studied the picture, flicking my fingers apart on the screen to zoom in and out. While it would never hold up in court, I felt certain the other girl in the picture was Amalia's sister.

I PULLED out my phone as I crossed back to Jonesy's house. I didn't want to jam Nala up by leaving a record of my call on her phone so I blocked my outgoing number.

"Officer Swede," she answered professionally.

"Can you talk?" I asked.

"Are you crazy?" she answered, her voice changing to a harsh whisper. "Half the force is out looking for you."

"Chessen said she believed me."

"Yeah, well, she hasn't cleared you yet," Nala answered. "That man you left handcuffed at the hospital was Gordie Blondo. He's an epically bad guy and works for Franky Bosian."

I'd seen only one picture of Blondo in the P.I.'s file, but you don't forget the face of someone who tries to kill you. "You don't have to tell me," I said. "He tried to kill me last night."

"You need to know something. He's already out."

"He escaped?"

"No. He was let go," she said.

"They can't do that! He tried to kill me. There's a gun and witnesses. What else do you need!?"

"You're the only witness and you disappeared. They didn't find a gun," she said.

"Bullets in the wall?" I asked.

"No slugs were recovered."

"How is that possible?" I asked. "The cops were there in minutes."

"No one is denying something went down at the hospital. Blondo rolled in a high-powered lawyer and without any evidence, we couldn't hold him," she said.

"I feel like I have a target on my chest." I subconsciously rubbed my chest where the three bullets had impacted.

"You do."

"Who is DeLovely Manning?" I asked. We weren't getting anywhere and Nala wasn't going to convince me to come in, especially after hearing her news.

"DeLovely? What about her?"

"Who is she?"

"Not on the phone," Nala said. "Where can we meet?"

"You'll come alone?"

"You and me, we're more than that, Biggs," she said. "I'm not going to rat you out."

"I'm going out to the farm," I said. "Meet me there?"

"Yeah. I can do that," she said. "It'll take me an hour to get free."

"That works. Thank you, Nala," I said and hung up.

I went directly to Jonesy's garage to work on the Crown Vic. Even though it was morning, the garage was already warm and sweat ran down my back as I checked the battery. It didn't have a full charge, but it appeared to be holding one, and should have enough power for a few starts. I checked the radiator and oil. Both were full, but desperately needed to be changed. Worse yet, the tires were low, with one all the way flat.

I plugged in Jonesy's air-compressor and worked my way around the vehicle. It was slow going, each tire not reading even a few PSI, but eventually I got them filled. There were a million potential problems with an old car, especially one that had been left to sit, but I knew my way around older engines. I was up to the task.

Nothing happened on my first attempt to start the Vic. The motor refused to even turn over. I looked at the dash and noticed we weren't getting power. I'd initially ignored the fuse box, so I hopped out, thinking I had a blown fuse. Before I tracked that down, I noticed a bunch of junk on the battery. I laughed at the situation I found myself in. I was likely being hunted by mob assassins and here I was working on a broken-down car.

I cleaned off the battery terminals, shaking my head at my distraction. I'd seen the residue but had forgotten about it while the battery had been charging. The terminals were loose and once I connected them, I heard beeping come from within the vehicle. Power issue solved.

On my next attempt, the car chuffed as the motor turned over. A moment later, a huge black cloud billowed out as I revved the engine. I coughed as I raced around and opened the garage door. The old girl idled roughly, but it was nothing that couldn't be solved with a bit of attention. I ran the seat back and put her in gear, slowly rolling out of the garage. Through the kitchen window, I saw Jonesy looking out at me, nodding his approval. I gave him a quick wave as I ran back to close the garage.

I was unable to see out any of the windows aside from the front windshield, which I'd brushed off with the windshield wipers. Fortunately, the automatic windows worked, and I rolled them down and then back up. The result wasn't much better, leaving large grimy streaks, but at least I could see.

On the way out of town, I stopped at my favorite auto-parts store, grabbing supplies for an oil change, a large box of yard-sized trash bags, and a bottle of general spray cleaner. I had more important things to do, but if the car stopped running on me, I'd be stranded. I had the perfect cover – no one would be looking for me in a dusty old Crown Vic.

When I pulled into the lane going to the farm, I saw Pappi walk out onto the porch holding a long-gun. It was likely his twelve-gauge but from this distance, it could have been one of his rifles. I slowed and drove into the barn, which was about fifty yards from the house.

A moment later I heard the familiar bang of the kitchen screen door and watched as a blurry bullet of fur and fangs sped across the yard. Diva barked in warning as she closed the distance, hackles raised on her back. She was ready to put some hurt on an intruder, which suggested to me that there was high tension on the farm, an idea backed up by Pappi and his gun.

"Hold on, girl," I said, stepping back toward the car. I wasn't a hundred percent certain she was going to stop or that she had recognized me yet. With an angry snarl, she launched herself.

"*Setzen!*" I ordered, placing a hand on the fender of the car, bracing myself. In mid-air her demeanor changed and her senses caught up with reality. Unable to abort, she twisted, attempting to adjust but it was too late. I turned and took the force of her charge in my chest, the two of us careening back into the car and falling to the ground.

To say Diva was beside herself with joy at my return was an understatement. For several minutes, we rolled around as she attempted to wash off whatever damage she'd caused with her long tongue. It was a painful exercise, but at least I discovered I could still take a hit.

"Henry, we've been so worried," Grandma Pearl said, arriving on the scene a moment later. From the corner of my eye, I'd seen her and Pappi approaching, but couldn't quite break free. "Where have you been?"

"Relax girl," I said, pushing Diva off and accepting Pappi's hand so I could stand back up. I'd barely made it to my feet when Pearl pulled me into a bone crushing hug.

"We've been calling, trying to reach you," Pearl asked, still holding on for dear life.

"I had some bad stuff happen at the hospital," I said. "I need to get clothes."

"You're in danger, Henry," Pappi said. "What you need is to be in protective custody."

"I can't, Pappi," I said once Pearl finally released me.

"This isn't a game, son. These are serious men who will not hesitate to finish the job," he said. "You've stumbled into something big and you need to get clear of it."

"There's a young girl in danger," I said. "I'm not letting this go."

"We can talk about it in the house. I'll call a couple of fellas I know who can bring you in. I'd trust 'em with my life," he said.

I nodded but walked to the barn instead, sliding the door open. Pappi and I had a workshop in the barn. I wanted to get the Crown Vic out of sight where I could finish the work I'd started in Jonesy's garage. "I won't be here long. I need clothes and my Walther. I'm sorry I dragged you into this."

Pappi scowled at my answer and Pearl's voice came loudly across the drive. "Lester! You will not let him go out. They're trying to kill him. The police need to do something about this. Make him stop!"

I kept my head down and walked to the open door of the vehicle. Diva jumped onto the seat and scooted over to the passenger side, clearly not intending to be left behind again.

"I have a friend coming out in an hour. She's a cop," I said, attempting to mollify Pearl. "She's going to help me."

"At least you're talking some sense now," Pearl said, nervously brushing at the front of her dress. "You must be starving. Finish up out here and get inside."

"What does it need?" Pappi asked, giving the Vic a once over as he walked up to the driver's side window.

I fired up the engine and a large blue cloud belched from the exhaust. "More than we have time for," I replied, grinning. I knew Pappi well enough to know that he'd already moved on in the conversation. He wouldn't be pushing me to stay – for a while anyway. "It's a friend's car and I'm going to start with oil and transmission fluid. I think a ring-job is probably out of scope for today."

Pappi nodded as I pulled into the garage. Once in, I partially closed the barn door. We could still see out, but someone approaching the house wouldn't have a good look inside.

Pappi pulled out the oil pan and rolled a tool cart over. "I don't want to leave Pearl alone too long," he said. "How long are you staying?"

"Not very," I said. "I don't want draw anyone out here."

"We can take care of ourselves, Henry," Pappi said. "I still think your best option is to get into protective custody."

"And then what?" I asked. "They let the guy who tried to kill me go. Someone on the force is dirty."

"Careful, Henry," Pappi warned. "That kind of talk is dangerous."

I pulled off the oil filter and watched as a stream of sludge poured into the pan. "I know. I'll be careful," I said. "But how do you explain the bad guy's missing gun? Not to mention, no casings or slugs found at the scene? The cops were there within minutes, and the surveillance videos were all erased while in their custody. It doesn't have to be a cop, but it's definitely someone who's close to this."

"Do you have any idea what you're into? You didn't tell me what was on the video. And what about this girl?" he asked.

"There isn't much," I said. "The video was from the Lambert Textile building in the industrial park. It caught men offloading wooden crates in the middle of the night. One broke open and young girls fell out. They were in horrible shape. Thing is, I recognized one of them. It was one of the girls who tried to steal my tires the other day."

"When you were picking up Dowdy?" he asked, confused.

"That's right. Somehow, by that night, they were in a crate being loaded into the warehouse next to Lambert's," I said. "That next morning, the older of the two was found dead. Detective Chessen showed me her picture."

"Sounds like mob activity," he said. "Only real mob around here is run by the Bosian family and Franky Bosian doesn't run underaged girls."

"How do you know that?" I asked, accepting the dusty air-filter from him and liberating the new one from its packaging.

"Ten years back or so, teen girls, mostly immigrants, were disappearing off the streets. Detectives followed all the leads, but they turned out to be dead ends. One day, the cases came to an end when one of Bosian's lieutenants shows up dead right outside the precinct doors. The man had his business cut off and a message carved into his chest."

"What was the message?" I asked, cringing at the possibility of the man being awake while having his manhood removed.

"No kids," Pappi said.

"Sounds like Franky might not have gotten the right guy."

"You don't want anything to do with Bosian," he said. "Franky won't want any loose ends. You need to steer clear of this thing. I'll go talk to him."

"Bullshit," I said, which earned me an instant frown from Pappi.

"Look, I don't like it any better than you do," he said. "Son, they'll kill you. You'll never see it coming and they won't miss again. I need to get in front of this."

"And what about justice for those girls? You want to tell me that getting murdered was the least horrific thing that happened to them?" I asked, hotly.

"You can't take the weight of the world on your shoulders, Henry," Pappi argued. "That's Chessen's job. Let her do it."

I stared back at my grandfather. He was every bit as stubborn as me and wouldn't easily back down. Fortunately, the tension broke when Diva barked, seconds before we heard gravel crunching under tires in the lane. Pappi grabbed his shotgun and walked toward the slightly opened door. I grabbed a tire iron from the workbench and followed him.

"Heel," I ordered. Diva looked over her shoulder at me and whined. She was on high alert and wanted to deal with the intruder in her own way. Fortunately, her training required that she come around and join me on my left.

"You know anyone who drives an old Civic?" Pappi asked as a weathered red vehicle passed the garage slowly on the way to the house. He slid through the opening and rotated the shotgun so it pointed down as he walked.

The Civic's door opened and one of Nala's heavily-tattooed arms slipped out, followed by the other, showing that she wasn't carrying a weapon. "Mr. Ploughman. I'm on the job and I'm carrying," she called as she slid from her seat and stood, still keeping her hands raised above her shoulders.

Somewhere along the line, Nala had changed clothing and was wearing her leather pants. A revolver was tucked into the waistband, only slightly covered by a leather vest, which appeared to be the only top she was wearing. I'll admit I was distracted by the form-fitting outfit and how it accentuated the tattoos that covered her back and arms.

"Doesn't look like any cop I've ever seen," Pappi mumbled as we approached.

"You can put your hands down, Nala," I called back.

Diva growled but stopped when I clicked my tongue at her. We'd already had an argument about Nala and agreed to disagree on the matter. Diva's instincts about who she liked or didn't were generally based on the perceived threat. Nala smelled like guns, worked out hard, and carried herself with authority. It wasn't hard to recognize why Diva was wary.

"Nala Swede, I'd like to introduce you to my grandfather, Lester Ploughman," I said. "Pappi, Nala works with Sergeant Williams at the Second Precinct."

Pappi shifted the shotgun to his left and extended his hand. "I heard a lot about you, Officer Swede. Grace Caras is your mother, right?"

Nala's lips tightened into a thin line with only the mere hint of a smile. "That's right. George Caras is my uncle."

I wracked my brain to figure out why the conversation was suddenly tense. I knew her family was related to organized crime, but

I couldn't recall any of the other crime-family names. "Seems to me your uncle used to do some work for Franky Bosian."

"You'd have to ask him about that," she answered tightly.

"Pappi, you're being rude," I said.

"No, he's right, Biggs," Nala said. Her tone communicated that she wasn't happy about being called out, though. "You should know who you're hanging out with."

I looked at Pappi. "I already do. Nala told me all about her family connections. She's a cop, Pappi. She's trying to change things."

"You're right," Pappi said. "Just caught me off guard there. Please accept my apologies, Ms. Swede."

"Apology accepted." She smiled, although the smile didn't reach her eyes. "No harm done. I've had to deal with a lot of stereotypes as a female cop, especially one from a notorious family."

"Oh my." I heard Pearl's voice before I saw her. "I didn't realize we were having company. Please, come in out of the sun. I just made lunch."

"Nala and I have some things to talk about," I said. "You mind if we head back to the barn? We'll come back in a few minutes for something to eat."

"I was loading sandwiches onto a plate," she said. "I didn't think you and Lester would be coming in any time soon. I'll just fetch it."

"Please let me help, Mrs. Ploughman," Nala offered, looking at Pappi with a raised eyebrow.

Pappi nodded his head in acceptance and watched as they disappeared into the house.

"Be careful with this one. Her uncle, George Caras, is every bit as dangerous as Franky Bosian," he said, handing me his shotgun. "Grab your Walther when you say good bye to Pearl."

I accepted the gun and thought about what he said as he, too, disappeared into the house. I trusted Nala. She'd been Snert's friend for years and was trying to clean up her life. I wasn't about to hang her for her family.

Nala, followed by Pearl, appeared on the front porch a moment later carrying a plate of multi-grain sandwiches. "Don't forget to bring the plate back," Pearl said, handing me a pitcher of black tea. She didn't immediately let go, instead whispering, "She's beautiful, Henry. Do you like her?"

I chuckled. We had explosions, assassins and missing girls, but Grandma Pearl still had time to wonder about romance.

"I think you taught me that a gentleman keeps that sort of thing to himself." I gave her a hug and then turned to catch up with Nala.

"What was that all about?" Nala asked, suspiciously. She was still burning from Pappi's earlier questioning.

"She wanted to know if we were a thing," I said. "I think she likes you."

Nala's expression transformed in an instant. Her olive-toned skin and jet-black hair offset her bright white teeth as she smiled. This time, her smile lit up her eyes and *wow*, was she gorgeous.

"We might have a better chance if someone wasn't trying to blow you up," Nala said, hooking her free hand under my arm and pulling me closer.

"I don't know. You look pretty hot in your leathers," I said. "I know I haven't thought about hitmen and explosions since you got out of the car."

She released me as I slid through the partially-opened barn door. Before I made it through completely, her hand landed on my butt, surprising me enough that I jumped forward.

"I've always had this fantasy about haylofts," she said, sliding through the door behind me. She put the plate of sandwiches on the workbench. "Does this place have one of those?"

"Seriously?" I asked, setting the shotgun and tea aside. She'd closed the distance between us and was pressing in on me. I allowed my hand to fall onto her exposed waist between her vest and pants. Her skin was hot to the touch. It had been a long time since I'd been with a woman and she had my undivided attention.

Nala bit her lip and looked up into my face. "Biggs, all this time, I thought you were blowing me off. Who knew you saw yourself as a gentleman?"

"We had a date," I said defensively. "We talked for hours."

"And you didn't make a single move," she said. "I showed you my tats and then we were eating donuts."

"You think I can't handle all this?" I ran my hands down from her shoulders, allowing my fingers to trace the definition in her arms. The last time I'd been with a girl had been before entering the service. Her name was Nichole and I'd been with her the summer after high school graduation. The two women could not have been more different. Nichole, while not flabby by any means, probably had never worked out. As if to drive the point home, Nala flexed her bicep and raised a challenging eyebrow.

I reached out and placed my hand behind her neck, guiding her lips to my own. For a moment, the world and its problems disappeared. As we kissed, I allowed my hands to slide down the sleek leather and press her tight bottom, bringing us even closer. I pulled her upward and to me. She responded by bringing both of her hands to the side of my face. She pulled me in, lifting up on her toes and bringing her right leg around to trap mine.

Without breaking for air, we continued to kiss hungrily. I pressed in and slid my hands down her sinewy thighs, lifting her completely off the ground. She responded, wrapping both legs around my waist and frantically devouring my mouth, her tongue darting in and out.

"I don't think we're going to make it into the loft." I breathed heavily, spinning us around and pinning her against the side of the car.

"Take me, Biggs," she groaned, her eyes fluttering.

I set Nala on the hood of the car, pushing her back enough that I could work on the buttons of her leather vest as she worked on my belt. She was faster than I was, tugging my zipper down just as I managed to slide the first smooth metal disc free. I groaned, closing my eyes, as her hand snaked down to aggressively take control of the pace. Getting Nala's vest off now seemed like a lost cause and much more than my brain could handle. I wanted her beyond reason and there were still too many layers of clothing between us. I grabbed her leather waistband, tugging at the buttons that held her pants closed. My hands were shaking like I was sixteen.

"Oh, geez, stop for a second," I huffed. "They're stuck. I can't get the buttons."

Nala released her grip on me, something I wasn't entirely happy about. She straightened and pushed gently on my chest, taking advantage of my conflicting thoughts. With a sexy smile and slow, deliberately-enticing movements, she deftly unbuttoned her vest, proudly exposing small but perfectly formed breasts. Almost hypnotically, my eyes traced the tattoos that swirled across her breasts, disappearing along her ribcage and up over her shoulders. The design surrounded her breasts but stopped at the edge of lighter flesh that she rarely exposed to sunlight. The tan-lines next to the tattoos were almost more than I could take.

She wriggled and hopped until her leather pants slid off onto the ground, pooling on top of her revolver and the shoes she'd already kicked off. In no time at all, she'd gone from fully clothed to wearing only a black, lacy thong.

"Catch me if you can," she said, slipping under my arms. For a moment, all I could do was watch her bound past the car and leap onto a wooden ladder that led up to the storage loft.

"There's no hay up there," I called, buttoning my pants and trailing after her.

"Sorry about the no-hay thing," I said, staring up at the barn's roof. "Wrong side of the barn."

I'd laid out a tarp on the dusty floor and Nala lay nestled in the crook of my arm with her cheek resting against my bare chest.

"It's so peaceful," she said. "I could stay here forever. We could just have sex and do farmer stuff all day. Wouldn't that be amazing?"

Her hand trailed down my stomach and then lower, successfully stirring my interest again. Normally I'd have been quick to respond. However, in the quiet, my subconscious had taken over, allowing me to work through issues I'd been wrestling with. I resisted letting go of the fragile threads, afraid my thoughts, so clear now, would simply disappear.

"Shit," I whispered.

"Shit?" She nuzzled my neck, gently kissing me. "You want me to stop?"

"Oh, no. This I like. Although it makes me wonder how the human species has survived. I think it must be that only a handful of women are allowed to be as ridiculously hot as you are. If all women were like you, we men would never be able to think about anything else."

"Nice save," she said, nibbling on my ear.

I could tell Nala wasn't overly serious about getting hot and heavy again, but if the last hour were any indication, it wouldn't take much to get her thinking in that direction. "I thought Chessen told you to stay clear of me," I said.

"I'm on a temporary leave of absence. Family emergency."

Absently, I traced my hand along the curve of her back, enjoying the feel of her skin as my hand slowly came to rest on the back of her thigh.

"You want me to stop so you can think?" she asked. "Feels like you might be losing your concentration."

"If it were up to me, we'd stay like this forever," I said.

"That's a funny picture," she said.

"How much do you know about what's going on with Chessen's investigation?" I asked.

"Only what you told me after I got you out of the police station," she said.

I still had no memory of that night. "Did I tell you about Amalia Rouca and her sister?"

"The girl who stole your tires?"

"Girls," I corrected.

"Only that you saw one of them in the video that was erased," she said. "I thought that was Amalia."

"It was," I agreed. "So after Chessen kicked you out of the hospital, she showed me a picture of Amalia's sister. Her body had been dumped in an alley."

"What about Amalia? Is she dead too?" Nala asked, pushing off and sitting back on her knees next to me.

"No idea. But I might have a way to find out. Did you know this kind of thing happened ten years ago too?" I asked.

"Street kids getting killed?" Nala asked. "Hate to tell you this, Biggs, but this shit happens all the time."

"Maybe, but someone's trying to clean this up and me with it," I said. "My grandfather said there was a time, ten years ago, when one of Frank Bosian's lieutenants started dealing in underaged girls. It ended poorly for him."

"Yeah, Franky doesn't go for hurting kids. He's a real hero. Once they're eighteen, they're free game," Nala said with more anger than I'd have expected. She stood and stalked over to the ladder.

"Hey, I'm sorry," I called after her, gathering my clothing.

"It's fine," she said. "I just need something to drink."

I hastily buttoned my clothing and by the time I got down the ladder, I found her pulling her shoes on.

"How would you track down this Rouca girl?" she asked, stuffing her holster into her waistband.

I approached and placed a hand on her arm. "Hey, I'm sorry. I didn't mean to touch a nerve back there."

She smiled and some of the strain drained from her face. "Not your fault. We all have shit in our lives to deal with. Tell me about the girl."

I grabbed one of Pearl's sandwiches. The bread was dry, but I was starving and didn't mind.

"I have her phone number," I said. "I'm going to try to call her."

"Chessen could probably run a trace on it."

"Not yet. What can you tell me about DeLovely Manning?" I asked. "Somehow she's mixed up in this."

Nala gave me a furious scowl. "Are you serious? What are you doing with her? Her dad is Franky Bosian. Her husband, Richard Manning, is like number two in the Bosian empire, mostly because of DeLovely. Why are you asking about him?"

"She's got me on a job," I said. "Came through Finkle."

"Wait. A bail bondsman gave you a job from DeLovely Manning? What kind of job?"

"She thinks her husband is cheating on her," I said. "She wants evidence so she can get a divorce."

"Holy shit, Biggs," Nala said. "Do you realize how effed up this whole thing is? Bosians don't do divorces, and everybody knows Richard Manning is a perv and womanizer."

I scratched the back of my head. "I didn't know that."

"Of course not," she said, shaking her head. "You just saw her big boobs, perfectly tucked ass, and blonde hair and decided to spy on the scariest guy in Sutherland. Well, next to Franky, that is."

I gave her half a wry grin. "No fun if they can't bite back."

"Are you serious right now?" she asked. "Richard Manning is a damn great white shark. He'll bite your head off. Shit, Biggs, maybe fight one battle at a time."

"I'll call DeLovely and ask for a little more time," I said. "You know, she was the one who sent that lawyer, Pendleton, to spring me from Chessen's interrogation."

Nala raised her eyebrows at that. Then she changed the subject. "What now?"

"I finish changing the oil in this old Crown Vic and then we're going to see if we can find Amalia Rouca."

"Looks like this old thing has been sitting in the barn too long. We should take my Civic," she said.

"Actually, I drove it here," I dropped to the ground, replaced the oil plug and spun on the filter. "I just came out to the farm so I could get some clothing."

"And do car repairs?" she asked skeptically as I pulled the oil pan out and walked it over to the drum where we kept old oil.

"And that, yup." I tipped a fresh quart of oil into the fill spout.

"You're nuts."

I grabbed my backpack and pulled out DeLovely's burner phone.

BIGGS: *Need to talk. I've been delayed.*

I then pulled out my normal cell and dialed Amalia Rouca's phone. I wasn't overly surprised that she didn't answer. I shrugged and crafted a text message for her.

BIGGS: *This is Biggs. The guy you stole tires from. I think you're in trouble. I want to help.*

I continued working the remaining quarts of oil into the fill pipe. The air and fuel filters weren't in bad shape but I changed them anyway. I was just wrapping up when a chime on my phone caught my attention.

AMALIA: *Fuck off pervert.*

I held the phone so Nala could see the text and she laughed.

"At least you know she's alive," Nala said. "I bet she's terrified."

"That's right."

BIGGS: *I saw what happened to your sister. Give me an address. I'll pick you up. I have food and a place you can stay.*

I stared at the phone, willing Amalia to respond. She was too small and fragile to have survived as long as she had on the streets. The men who'd killed her sister would be looking for her and there were only so many places she could hide.

It took her several minutes to respond and I blew out a hot breath when the message finally appeared.

AMALIA: *Why help me?*

BIGGS: *Give me an hour. Can you get to the bus station?*

I'd picked that location because there was always a lot of foot traffic. The bus schedules were tightly packed, assuring those exiting a bus had to file through the group waiting to get on for the next trip. Amalia would have no trouble blending into the crowd if she was careful.

AMALIA: *Please don't hurt me.*

Ordinarily, I'm not an emotional person. While serving, I saw deplorable things and had to deal with situations I can't easily talk about. For some reason Amalia's simple plea hit me hard and I had to bite my lip. She was in trouble and was willing to place her life in the hands of a complete stranger.

"How'd that go?" Nala asked when I looked up from my phone.

"She'll meet us," I said, burying my feelings.

"Where?" Nala asked.

"Bus station in an hour," I said.

"I can't believe she's made it this far," Nala said. "You should call Chessen and let her deal with it."

"You do understand that every piece of evidence I've given the police has gone missing, right?"

"One flash drive," Nala argued. "And those cards aren't reliable. Maybe you shorted it out in your pocket or something."

"Someone let Blondo go from the hospital. And what about all the bullets he sprayed into my hospital room? Someone had to clean that up."

"I get it. You're blaming cops when it could have been anyone. Blondo probably had someone helping him," she said.

We were interrupted by the burner phone ringing.

"It's Manning," I said, switching phones and flipping it open. "Biggs," I answered.

"Are you out of money yet?" DeLovely asked, her voice silky, like she was trying to seduce me.

"I haven't made much progress," I said. "Other stuff's been getting in the way."

"Not from what I hear. I'd say you're right on schedule," she said.

My tablet pinged from within my backpack.

"Open that up," she continued.

I looked at Nala with some confusion but pulled out Snert's tablet. The email came from an obviously fake address and directed me to a website. Against my better judgment, I tapped the link and a video began playing. Center frame was Nala and me at night, riding on her motorcycle. The camera was moving, like it was being shot from a car following us. I recognized the road, but had no memory of this trip with Nala. It was weird seeing myself on the back of the bike while my head screamed that the images were faked.

Nala sucked in a breath, obviously surprised by the footage. I watched as the bike pulled into the parking lot and I hopped off. After exchanging a few words, Nala drove off, leaving the frame. The Biggs on the screen leaned over. I still had no memory of these events, but it was obvious I was looking for my hide-a-key. Seconds later, I was running from the truck and diving behind the cement base of the closest lamppost just as the truck exploded. It was like I was watching TV. The picture darkened as a fireball rose into the air. When the scene cleared, I saw myself lying on the ground, not moving.

The camera jerked to the side as a dark SUV approached and pulled to a stop, even as truck debris rained onto the parking lot. A blond-haired man jumped out and walked over to me, calm as could be. He leveled a pistol with a silencer at my chest and fired three rounds. The shooter jerked to the side as bullets ricocheted off the pavement behind him. The camera started to move toward where the shots had been fired but remained just long enough for me to see Gordie Blondo running for the SUV. It wasn't lost on me that whoever fired those shots had saved my life. Unfortunately, the video stopped at that instant and I couldn't see who was there.

"You get all that?" Manning asked, then whispered, "delete it." Her voice sounded muted, like she'd covered the phone with her hand.

"Blondo has tried to kill me twice," I said.

"Good, you know his name. You've done your homework," she said.

"What'd you get me into, Manning? What's this got to do with your husband?" I asked.

"Two birds, my dear boy. You were already involved when I hired you. You just didn't know it yet. I took advantage of the situation and hired you to gather evidence on whoever my husband is sleeping with," she said, her voice still sultry. "How are you doing for money?"

"I'm fine," I lied. I was down to twelve hundred dollars and was out a vehicle.

"There'll be a package under the bus bench on the corner of Fourteenth and Apple. I'd like to hire you for another week. Five hundred a day still work for you?"

"When?"

"Any time after five. And I need more frequent updates," she said and hung up.

"Who was that?" Nala asked, still tapping on her phone.

"DeLovely Manning," I said, capturing Nala's attention.

"You need to stop talking to her," she said. "She's put you into the middle of this. Tell her you can't help. Give her money back."

"There's a kid out there who was locked in a box and headed to a life I can't even imagine. Her sister was murdered because they tried to escape," I said. "Which part of this do you think I can drop?"

"The part that gets a mob hitman to take two runs at you," Nala said. "Maybe you don't understand. Gordie Blondo is credited with over a dozen murders. He doesn't miss. We can get word to Franky Bosian that you're leaving whatever this is alone. Maybe he'll call off the hit."

"You think Franky Bosian put the hit on me?" I asked.

"Even if he didn't, he can still stop it," she said.

"Why would he do that? If he's running these girls, he'd rather see me dead. If it's Manning running these girls, he'll want me dead to clean it up," I said. "No part of this ends well if I talk to Franky Bosian. I took Blondo down once. I can do it again."

"Maybe you don't remember the video we just watched. Blondo had you in his sights. You *should* be dead. Whoever is coming after you, they'll just keep sending more men," she said. "That's how this works. This isn't war, Biggs. It's not a fair fight."

"What makes Amalia's life worth less than mine?" I asked. "What about her murdered sister? How does she get justice? I can do something about this. The cost is what it is. And this is exactly like fighting a war. My only question is, are you with me?"

"She's right, Henry," Pappi said from the barn door, catching me off guard. "These men won't stop coming for you."

He was holding a small gym bag in one hand and a shotgun case in the other. His face was ashen as he spoke. I glared at Diva, who'd completely ignored her responsibility to warn me of his approach, and then back to him.

"You think I should let this go?"

"Who's this Amalia?" he asked.

"Guatemalan street kid," Nala answered for me. "He's trying to be noble, but it's going to get him killed."

"It's the girl I was telling you about, Pappi. I don't want you and Pearl involved in this. I shouldn't have come out here, but I needed my Walther."

"Walther's in the bag." He handed me the shotgun and the bag. By its weight, I could tell there were several boxes of ammunition inside. "You know I can't just watch you go, now that I know what's going down, right?"

"Remember our deal," I said. A long time ago when I'd joined the Army and was headed out on my first deployment, he'd offered me a deal. I could tell him anything I wanted to about my experiences and he'd keep them to himself. No matter how ugly things got, he wouldn't share the details with anyone. I'd only taken him up on the deal after shit had gotten really gnarly. Pappi had served and seen combat and knew the damage of not releasing pressure.

He knit his eyebrows in disapproval at my invoking our deal. "That's not fair," he complained.

"Let me do this on my own, Pappi," I said. "This girl needs my help and it's going to get messy. I need you guys to stay clear."

"Then you remember our deal," he said, pushing it back on me. "Don't freeze me out. I'm a cop, Henry. I know the people. I know the streets. You should be talking to me about it."

I nodded, looking down at my watch. It was almost five o'clock and if I took off now, I could pick up the cash from DeLovely's drop before meeting Amalia at the bus station. "Give Pearl a hug for me," I said, stuffing the shotgun into the back seat. I pulled the pistol out of the bag and switched holsters to a back-of-the-pants style.

"Oh no you don't," Pearl called from several yards away. "You're not getting away from me without a hug." She was carrying a second duffle and a grocery bag that I was sure was stuffed with food.

"Grab your car. We can drop it in town," I said to Nala as I turned to my grandmother.

Nala slipped off, allowing me a last moment of privacy. I grabbed

Pearl's parcels, set them inside the Crown Vic and hugged her tightly.

"Be safe, Henry," Pearl said, not wanting to let go. "Lester is worried about you and so am I."

"I have to do this," I said.

She pushed back, still holding my arms, and looked at me. "I know, dear. I was proud when you joined the service. I was proud when you earned your Ranger tab. I'm proud of you now. I just wish it wasn't all so dangerous."

I leaned in, pecked her on the cheek and let her go. "Did you make cookies?" I asked as I rounded the front of the car. Diva beat me to the car door and jumped in when it opened.

"There might be a tin of frozen chocolate chip in there," she answered, smiling.

⸻

We dropped Nala's car off on a residential street near DeLovely's drop. I felt weird about pulling the taped package from beneath the bench, but I was relatively certain I hadn't been seen – at least not by the average passerby who wasn't actively working to conceal themselves.

"How much?" Nala asked as I jumped into the Crown Vic.

"Didn't count it," I said, stuffing the envelope between the wide, faux-leather seats.

"You really need to rethink calling this in," she said, turning in her seat so she faced me. "This girl is a lit stick of dynamite. You pick her up and she's going to explode in your face."

"I've been thinking about what Manning said. She's trying to expose her husband," I said and paused as I pieced things together. "Amalia is the key. If DeLovely can tie her husband to the murder of Amalia's sister, I'm guessing Bosian will take him out. I think that's what DeLovely is trying to accomplish. I'll bet anything it's Richard Manning who's trying to shut me down."

"Shit, Biggs, that's a long shot," Nala said. "How are you tying Dick Manning into this?"

I'm not sure what kept me from telling her about the images I'd seen on the USB of a car just like Manning's, next to Lambert Textile the night Amalia's sister was killed. I suppose I hesitated because it was exactly as Nala was saying, a long shot. My gut, however, told me I was right and that DeLovely Manning's cryptic messages were confirmation.

"Can you come up with a reason why DeLovely Manning wouldn't just tell her father that Richard is running underaged girls?" I asked instead, ignoring her question.

"Because Richard Manning is dangerous. If Franky doesn't buy DeLovely's story, Richard would have her killed – Franky's daughter or not," Nala answered.

"And Franky would put up with that?"

"Doesn't matter if he would or wouldn't," Nala answered. "She'd be just as dead. This way you're taking the risk for her."

I slowed as we approached the bus terminal, doing a quick drive-by. We were twenty minutes later than I'd told Amalia, but it couldn't have been helped.

"I think I see her," Nala said.

I pulled the envelope from between the cushions and stuffed it into my front pants pocket.

"What are you doing with that?" Nala asked.

"Last time I left money in the car it almost got blown up," I said, gliding into a metered parking spot. I lowered the back windows for Diva, left the car running and the A/C on, as we were in a sunny spot.

Nala laughed as she jumped out of the car and surreptitiously transferred the pistol from her waistband to a leather purse she had over one shoulder. Before exiting the car, I chambered a round in the Walther and pushed it into the holster that rested against my back.

"Where'd you see her?" I asked, joining her on the wide sidewalk that led into the brightly lit terminal.

"Over by the buses. I don't see her right now," she said, nodding at a long row of buses where a crowd of people were in different stages of either offloading and collecting bags or waiting in line to board. Amalia was small and would be impossible to see from our position.

We hurried through the crowd and were separated as we worked our way through the chaos. Nala tipped her head meaningfully toward the corner of the terminal where there were open spots for more buses and less activity. As she went in that direction, I caught sight of dark hair and the thin brown arm of a girl about Amalia's size. I quickened my stride, but even before she turned, I realized the girl's clothing was too nice for someone living on the streets.

The crowd thinned as I approached the back of the terminal. The wide loading platform opened to a two-lane, one-way circular drive, beyond which sat a large fenced lot that held buses not in service. The drive was obviously the restricted route when approaching the terminal.

I caught a glimpse of a small figure peeking out from behind a small concrete block building next to the gate that allowed entry to the out-of-service lot. I stepped forward, trying to get a better look.

Nala's hand shot out and pulled me back just as a bus crossed in front of us, turning into the terminal area. "Shit, Biggs, be careful."

"She's over there," I said, nodding at the small building.

"You see her?" Nala asked.

This time I looked down the two-lane road for more buses before I jogged across, slowing as I got closer to the bus lot. "Amalia?" I called, not too loudly. "It's me. Biggs."

I crossed in front of the unoccupied building and almost missed her. She'd sunk to the ground with her arms wrapped around her knees. She looked up at me with dried tear streaks through the dirt on her face. "Are you going to hurt me?" she whispered.

I felt Nala's hand come to rest gently on my back as I slowly lowered to a crouch. I looked across at Amalia and gave her a comforting smile. "No, and I won't let anyone else hurt you, either."

I startled as I felt the Walther slide from my back holster. Pain exploded in the back of my neck. Between being off balance from crouching and the force of the blow, I fell forward, just catching myself. With confusion, I looked back and discovered that Nala had leveled both my Walther and her own revolver directly at me.

"Sorry, Biggs," she said.

"WHAT THE HELL, NALA?" I asked, looking up at the woman I'd trusted in the most intimate way only a few hours ago.

Standing up slowly, I heard Amalia whimpering behind me. I slid my body between her and Nala.

A late-model white Cadillac glided to a stop behind Nala and my heart dropped into my stomach. Behind the wheel was none other than mob hitman, Gordie Blondo. He stepped out of the car, leaving his door open and the engine running.

"I'm doing this for you. It's the only chance you have of getting out of this alive," Nala answered, sliding my Walther into the front of her pants while keeping her revolver on me.

"Only temporary passes today, Luv," Blondo said, not hiding his English accent. "Next I see him, it'll be proper cement shoes for the lad."

She stared at him incredulously. "Manning promised that if I gave up the girl, he'd leave Biggs alone."

Blondo nodded his head. "If he said it, then it's true. Doesn't square me and the Yank, though. He's a bloody black mark on my record. I can't let folks go thinking I'm off my game. We're talking my reputation here."

"I fucking gave you the girl!" Nala argued. "You coming after him wasn't the deal!"

I had started to angle myself closer to Nala during the argument, but Blondo hadn't been fooled. Quick as lightning, he had a .45 caliber semi-auto on me.

"Not so fast there, slick," he said, waving me back while addressing Nala. "Manning agreed to your deal. Not me. After this, Captain America there only has me to worry about."

"That's bullshit," Nala said, swinging her revolver around to aim at Blondo.

Blondo reacted instantly, pulling out a second weapon and leveling it at her. "Think about it, Swede," he said. "What do you think lover boy is going to think when he learns you're our inside girl? Or that you told us when he'd be coming back to pick up his truck at Lambert's? I especially love how you dropped him and scooted out of there quick as a bunny."

The sound of a bus approaching caused the two to shift so their weapons were discreetly hidden. As long as the bus turned into the terminal, we'd remain virtually invisible in the shadow of the small building.

My head spun with this new information from Blondo. All this time I'd thought Nala was on my side. If he was telling the truth, she'd been pinch-hitting for the other team all along and had nearly gotten me blown up.

"You did that?" I asked. "What about the girls? How can you let this happen?"

"Nothing she can do about it, mate," Blondo said. "Because of you, we've decided to do a bit of house cleaning. We'll be fresh out of girls by this time tomorrow."

"You're going to murder all of them?"

Blondo smiled as he read the shock in my face.

"Not if we can help it," he answered. "Lots of market out there for fresh meat."

At least Nala showed regret on her face. I turned and opened my mouth to say something to Blondo when a big white vehicle came flying backward off the circle drive, slamming into Blondo's Cadillac and throwing it forward. The car door missed Blondo by inches as he danced out of the way. I seized the opportunity and lunged for Nala's outstretched hand and her pistol. I must have startled her, because she squeezed off a wild shot, trying to avoid my grasp.

While grappling, I felt the hard-earned strength in her arms as she pulled away. Turns out, I'm more of a brawler than a weightlifter. I pulled back my elbow and slammed it right up into her jaw. I heard a sickly crunch and felt her sag. It was the advantage I needed. In one continuous motion, I finished removing the revolver from her hand and tucked into a roll.

Blondo must have recovered, because he let off a wild shot in my general direction. I was moving at top speed, wanting to put the building between him and me. I turned, lining up a shot while at the same time, assessing the risk to the dozens of innocents in the area. It had been one of the things I hated most about breeching enemy houses in Afghanistan. There were always innocents – usually used as shields – and bullets had no trouble killing them just as easily as the enemy.

A second and third shot pinged off the ground next to me as I surged back toward Blondo.

"You gotta be kidding me, mate," he grunted as I slammed into him, knocking his pistol away.

The man was heavily muscled, much like Nala, but I suspected the assassin hadn't earned all of it in a public gymnasium. I'd had more than one opponent who liked to talk when I fought them. According to my coach, they were trying to psych me out. For the most part, I never heard them.

A slash along my arm got my attention. Blondo had pulled the knife I'd seen on his belt and I partially deflected his strike. We separated and I dropped back into a fighting stance, pulling my t-shirt off and gripping it tightly with both hands. It's a fairly well-known defense against a knife, but Blondo was trying to assess my skills as he circled and set up his next move.

"Aww, now you're just having a go at me," he said. "You brought a t-shirt to a knife fight."

Blondo was fast and didn't telegraph his strike. Instinctively, I knew I needed to do something unpredictable or he'd make real contact and the fight would end just as quickly as it had begun. Instead of wrapping his knife arm in the material, as was the normal move in this situation, I released one end of the shirt. Curling my fingers over and flattening my hand, I threw a right jab into his throat. With my other hand, I accepted the knife into the folds of the cloth and felt the point of his blade slice into the palm of my hand.

The effect was instantaneous. As Blondo choked, I wasted no time and spun into him, grabbing his outstretched arm and pulling against the elbow joint. Together, we fell onto the ground, the impact knocking some of the wind out of me. Then I felt the man regain his wits. Still on my back, I pulled his arm, brought my leg up, and wrapped it behind his neck. He yowled in pain as I pulled his face toward me.

"Do it!" he said angrily. "They'll send ten more in my place."

I finished the move by locking my ankle in place with my other leg and squeezing with all my might. Blondo coughed once and then I heard a crack as I broke the vertebrae in his neck and he slumped against me.

"Crap, Henry, are you okay?" I looked around and found a very worried Snert standing by with a large can of pepper spray in his hands. My eyes flitted from him then up to the damaged back end of the white vehicle. What was he doing here in his over-sized work van? And with a can of pepper spray? There was one thing about Snert, the man was all heart.

Nala groaned and started to sit up.

"How'd you know where I was?" I asked.

"Um, I might have put a GPS on your tablet," he said with an embarrassed shrug. "It's very safe."

I crawled over and retrieved my Walther from Nala. "Damn it, Nala," I said with a sigh. "I thought we had something."

"What?" Snert asked.

"Long story." I opened the revolver and dropped the bullets into my hand, then threw her gun over the fence. I turned to look for Amalia and found her hiding in the corner, trying to make herself as small as possible.

"Crap," I said and tried to be calm as I walked over to her. "Hey, kiddo. Can you come with me?" I asked in as soothing a voice as I could manage.

Amalia responded with a stream of indecipherable Spanish. Her posture and the tone of her voice told me she was terrified and wasn't capable of fighting anymore. She'd given up, but I was pretty sure she'd trust me enough to let me get her out of here. It broke me to see the proud survivor I'd first met reduced to a paralyzed, terrified child.

"Does the Sprinter still run?" I asked, looking back at Snert.

"We can't drive away from an accident," he said.

"And what if more men with guns are coming?"

"I'll check," he said, running over to the van.

I reached down, picked Amalia up, cradling her gently in my arms, and carried her to the back of the van. Amazingly, the reinforced bumper guard had taken most of the damage when Snert rammed Blondo's car, and the rear doors opened easily. Warily, I watched as Nala stood up, not willing to make eye contact with me. "I did this for you," she said. "I'm sorry."

I shook my head and jumped up into Snert's vehicle, pushing aside tech parts that had been thrown to the floor. Amalia was shaking and grabbed at me as I set her down in the aisle and closed the doors behind us.

"No go," she said.

"I won't," I said. "Snert, get out of here and take the next right," I said. "I need to grab Diva and my car."

"No monstruo," Amalia pulled on my arm.

"Diva's not a monster," I said. "Trust me. If I tell her to protect you, no one will dare try to touch you."

"We have to go back for Nala," Snert pushed as he slowed in the bus lane and turned onto the street where Jonesy's car was parked.

"Nala had a gun on me," I said. "She was more than willing to give this girl up to that man I was fighting. Nala's on the wrong side of this."

"That doesn't make sense," he argued.

"Stop here," I said as he pulled ahead of the Crown Vic.

"If I leave the scene, it's a hit-and-run," Snert said. The shock of the encounter was wearing off and he was starting to process the issues.

"Trust me," I said. "No one will report that accident. I'm sorry about your van."

"My van? That guy was going to kill you!" Snert double parked a few cars ahead of Jonesy's car.

"Amalia," I said, kneeling on the floor to make eye contact. "We need to change cars. The bad men are coming and we need to leave."

She looked back at me with wide brown eyes and nodded her head wordlessly. I grabbed her hand, and she gripped it with a strength I wouldn't have attributed to such a small girl.

"Where are we going to meet?" Snert asked.

"Buddy, I'm trying to keep you out of this," I said.

"That's not working, Henry," he called after me as I opened the back door and hopped out onto the pavement. Amalia followed me closely, not letting go of my hand for even a moment.

"You're right," I said. "I'll call you."

"Or I'll track you down again," he said. "Take the shirts. They're right there."

I quickly scanned the bins and cargo netting, locating a box covered in brown postal wrap with a logo in the shape of scope crosshairs. There were no words for what he meant to me. "Thank you, Buddy." I scooped the box up and shut the door.

It took everything in me to not sprint back to the Crown Vic where Diva was going nuts, having seen us exit Snert's truck. I dared a glance back to the terminal building. There was increased activity in the general area where we'd been and I suspected it was only moments before the police would show up. I wondered just how Nala would explain the dead hitman and wrecked car.

"No, no, no," Amalia whined, pulling against me as we approached Diva and the car. For Diva's part, she had given us several happy barks, but I suspected Amalia couldn't interpret happy vs. angry.

"I've got you, kid," I said. "Monstruo es amigo." I was butchering the language, but I also knew she'd understand what I was trying to say.

Climbing into a vehicle with a girl strapped to my side, while carrying a box and trying to keep an exuberant dog off is darn near impossible. Under other circumstances, I might have seen the event as comical. As it was, we were attracting attention and Amalia's complaints were getting louder.

I breathed a premature sigh of relief when I managed to get Diva into the back seat with the package, and slide Amalia and myself into the front seat. Diva, not at all sensitive to Amalia's mood and seeing available space, jumped back into the front passenger seat. She stepped on Amalia as she pushed toward me for our normal greeting, which involved me scratching the sides of her face while avoiding her giant tongue. With a screech, Amalia climbed across me, wedging her back against the window, sitting between me and the steering wheel. Trust me when I say, it was an act of pure contortionist gymnastics.

"*Setzen!*" I ordered.

Diva was taking full advantage of my distractions.

"Back," I pointed to the back seat.

Diva whined, but knew I meant business when I barked out orders. Fortunately, dogs weren't overly literal. Even though I'd told her to both sit and get in the back, she complied, slinking back over the headrest.

I turned to the girl who was responding sluggishly, no doubt shock was setting in. "Hey kiddo, you're going to need to sit on the other side. We need to get out of here before the bad men come."

Amalia looked up at me. I felt like a heel, but helped her move to the center of the bench seat. To say that she had a smell going was an understatement. It was the smell of fear, sweat and a general lack of access to facilities we all take for granted.

I tried to lift my arm to shift, but this apparently was too far. She clung to my arm as if it were her only lifeline. Instead, I reached over with my left arm and pulled the transmission arm into drive and lurched out into the heavy traffic passing in front of the terminal.

I wasn't about to drive back to my rental house, nor was I going to Snert's or the farm. If Blondo had help, it was possible we were being followed. Instead, I simply drove, with no real destination in mind, grateful that I'd filled the gas tank. Thank goodness, Diva had the sense to settle down once we were moving.

"Hungry?" I asked, after a few minutes, remembering the bag Pearl had left for me.

"Si." The problem with that response was that the tiny girl was wrapped around my right arm and made no attempt to release it when I tried to reach into the back seat.

"You'll need to let go for a minute." I gently pulled my arm free and reached into the back seat for the handles of the paper bag. I pulled the bag over and set it on Amalia's lap. While my arm was free, I also grabbed a half-empty water bottle and handed it to her. As expected, she opened the bottle and greedily sucked down the contents.

We pulled up to a stoplight. As far as I could tell we weren't being followed so I opened the bag, popping off the staples Pearl had clipped into the top so Diva wouldn't get overly curious. On top was a tin that I knew held freezer cookies. I moved the sack and set the tin in Amalia's lap. "Que?" she asked.

"Cookies from mi abuela," I answered, proud that I'd formed most of a sentence.

Amalia tore off the top and wordlessly pulled a cookie out, eating it as if it was the last food on Earth.

As the light changed and I started through the intersection, DeLovely's burner phone rang. I considered not answering it, but problems were like dead fish. They didn't smell better with age.

"Biggs," I said, holding the phone to my ear.

"Did you kill Blondo?" DeLovely asked.

"Not really something we can talk about on the phone," I said.

"Don't need to. I know the answer. That was a mistake. This is going to make it up the ladder to Franky, you know," she said. "He's only going to care about one thing - that someone took out one of his enforcers. You should have let Blondo take the girl."

"Man, have you misread me." I rolled my eyes at her callousness. "Do you have a point to this call?"

"Burn the USB. I don't need this coming back on me," she said. "Consider our contract complete, Mr. Biggston."

"Is that all this was for you?" I asked, doing my best to keep the annoyance from giving way to fury. "A way to get Dick out of your life? You don't care about the damage done to these kids? Take a risk for once and do the right thing."

"Don't be naïve," she said. "You're nuclear, Biggston. Don't think that being his daughter will help me escape his wrath."

"Give me twenty-four hours," I said. "I might be able to salvage this yet."

I wasn't sure why I was surprised that DeLovely Manning wasn't willing to stick her neck out. Her attitude pissed me off so much that I struggled not to toss the phone into oncoming traffic.

"I'll deny ever knowing you," she said.

"I think that's the point of a burner phone," I said. "If I can tie this back to Dick, we can both get what we want."

"I'm throwing this phone away in twenty-four hours."

Amalia, initially startled at my anger, relaxed and lay down on the seat cushion. Her eyes fluttered momentarily as she fought sleep, then closed after I rested my arm protectively on her side. I seethed as

I replayed DeLovely's insistence that I should have turned this kid over to a life of unspeakable horrors, one that would likely end within months.

I continued to drive and finally found myself on the outskirts of town, next to a nature preserve popular with runners. It was getting late and only one SUV was left at the end of the parking lot. An empty bicycle rack atop the vehicle told the only story I needed: someone was out for an evening ride. I backed into a spot so I could observe any other vehicles that entered the lot. Finally, after sitting with my motor running for ten minutes, I shut the car off, satisfied that we were alone.

I shuffled out of the car, careful not to wake Amalia and released a very happy Diva from the back. Technically, I was supposed to have her on a leash, but with no one around, I wasn't worried. Diva dashed off and was soon lost in a sea of tall grass that led to a small stream only a few hundred feet away.

I realized I'd never replaced my shirt and that I still had a gash in my hand. Fixing the shirt was easy. I pulled a fresh one from the duffle Pearl had sent along. The gash would be more painful. Most of the blood had dried around the wound but each time I bent my hand, it reopened. Ideally, I should go in for stiches, but I'd have to settle for glue.

I grabbed a sandwich and a cookie from Pearl's treat bag and pulled out my phone. I sighed. Why did all the calls I needed to make remind me of the *dead fish* saying? I was in well over my head and there was no getting around asking for help. But first, I figured I'd review my text messages and put off what would surely be an unpleasant call with Chessen.

SNERT: *Sprinter at mechanic's. I'm back at house.*

BIGGS: *Probably best if you don't open the shop for a couple of days.*

He must have been waiting for my text because he responded immediately.

SNERT: *Okay. Have you heard from police? I can't find any report of the accident.*

BIGGS: *You won't. Mob will cover up.*

SNERT: *What about Nala? I can't believe she's in this.*

BIGGS: *It's complicated. I don't know. I can't trust her, though. You need to be careful.*

SNERT: *Open the box. Put on a t-shirt. I'm wearing one too.*

BIGGS: *Copy that.*

I pulled out the package I'd taken from the van and opened it with my knife. Inside were three white t-shirts padded with thin layers of armor. I was amazed that the lightweight material was supposed to stop any bullet except .357s or .44 mags. I knew for a fact the shirts would stop .22 cal. There was no doubt in my mind that one of these shirts had already saved my life.

SNERT: *What now?*

BIGGS: *Pack a bag. We're going to a safe house.*

SNERT: *You have a safe house?*

BIGGS: *Meet me at pizza place in thirty minutes.*

I smiled as Diva came jumping back out of the grass, her muzzle wet with stream water. For a moment, I wished I was a dog. She enjoyed life minute-by-minute. When I made no move to call her back, she turned and disappeared once again, probably following the scent trail of a ground squirrel or some other animal.

I pulled up my contacts and made the call I was dreading – to Chessen. I would let the chips fall where they may, but first I would ensure Amalia's safety.

"DETECTIVE CHESSEN." She answered her phone on the third ring.

"It's Biggs," I said. "We need to talk."

"That's an understatement," she said. "Come down to the station. Swede's already confessed."

"Confessed to what?"

"We'll talk at the station."

"I'm not coming down there," I said. "There's a contract out on me."

"Look. The D.A. says he'll give you full immunity, protective detail, the works. He wants to get ahead of this thing," she said.

"That's fine, I'll tell you everything, I just need to do it my way," I said. "Seriously, what did Nala confess to?"

"That's not how this works. We hear your story, then we compare them. That way we know if anyone is lying," she said. "If you give us what we need, you get absolution for your sins. You yank us around, you go to the box."

"How bad does the D.A. want this?" I asked.

"He's been looking for something to hang on the Bosian crime family for a long time," she said. "Who knows, maybe our D.A. is looking at a run for mayor."

"They're trafficking illegal immigrants," I said.

"Not on the phone," Chessen warned.

"You know my grandfather?" I asked.

"Of course. Department isn't that big," she said. "He's a good man."

"Think you could get the D.A. out to his farm sometime around dinner tomorrow?" I asked.

"Don't do anything stupid, Biggs," Chessen said.

"Can you get him there?" I asked.

"I'll see what I can do. You know there are a lot of people looking for you right now?"

"Copy that," I said and hung up.

The sun was starting to set as I made my final call for the evening.

"Que? Esto es Melinda."

"I guess that answers my first question," I said, chuckling.

"Who is this?" she asked, her voice friendly but suspicious.

"Biggs," I answered.

"Oh, Biggs. I didn't recognize your phone number. What question did I answer?"

"I wanted to know if you were just a pretty face. I see fluent Spanish is another of your hidden talents."

"I like that you think my face is pretty," she laughed. "It's late. Is everything okay?"

"That's harder to answer than you'd think," I said. "I feel bad for calling, but I don't really know anyone else."

"Are you trying to order Mexican food and need me to translate?" she deadpanned, making me wonder if she was serious.

My stomach growled as I looked over at my forgotten sandwich and waved at the swarm of flies that had made it their home.

"Look. It's a big ask and it might be dangerous, but I need someone who knows more than cusswords and baño," I said.

"What have you gotten into?" she asked, growing more serious. "Tell me you're not mixed up with the Tijuana gang."

"Not sure who that is," I said. "No. There's a girl I need to talk to."

"You're kidding," she said.

I wasn't sure why she suddenly sounded annoyed, so I pushed on. Okay, it should be patently obvious. I'm a dolt, what can I say? "Can you meet Snert and me at Louzari's on Old Cheney in twenty minutes? I know it's a lot to ask, but I really need your help."

"Man, Biggs. You have huevos gigantes."

"Please?" I asked. "You carry, right?"

"This is the weirdest conversation I've ever had."

"Will you come?"

"Forty minutes," she said. "And count on the fact that I'll be packing."

"Oh, one more thing. Could you bring a couple of flashlights?"

━━━

I circled the block. As I came back toward the pizza place, I watched Mel slide out of a new blue F-250 pickup. At no more than five-feet two inches, she was tiny in contrast. I'd already picked up Snert and rearranged things so that he was in the back seat of the Crown Vic with Diva.

"Amalia," I whispered, shaking the still sleeping girl's shoulder. "I need you to wake up."

If I had expected her to be groggy and slow to awaken, I'd have been wrong. Her eyes flew open and her head jerked around as she took in the car's interior. Her eyes quickly came to rest on Snert. Of course Snert, not new to feeling uncomfortable, waved awkwardly, but stayed silent.

I pulled through several open parking spaces and rolled down the window on the passenger side. "Lock your truck and get in," I said, coming alongside and surprising Mel. Not unlike Amalia, Melinda scanned the interior of the car.

"What's going on, Biggs?" she asked, opening the door and getting in next to Amalia. "Who is this?"

"Yeah," Snert said. "I thought we were getting pizza."

Amalia shrank away from Melinda, pulling my right arm up over her head as a shield.

"Guys, this is Amalia," I said. "Amalia, these are my friends, Melinda and Snert."

Even in the midst of all the craziness, Amalia was still able to peek around my arm, crack a small grin, and repeat, "Snert."

I slowly pulled through the parking lot and exited on the opposite side. We wouldn't be getting pizza tonight.

"This is so not what I was thinking it was," Melinda said, shaking her head.

"I'm sorry about the cryptic conversation. I'm afraid my phone might be bugged," I said.

"Give me your phone, Biggs," Snert held his hand out and I tossed it back to him. From the satchel he'd brought along and stashed at his feet, Snert extracted what looked like a grocery bag. Knowing him like I did, I suspected the item was some sort of tech that shielded its contents from radio signals. "Can I have yours too, Melinda?" he asked. "This is a Faraday FOB defender. Of course, we are using the attenuation blocking capability, which is roughly in the sixty to eighty decibels range."

"Okay ... What's going on, Biggs?" Mel asked, handing her phone to Snert.

"Italian mob wants the small person next to me who doesn't speak much English," I said, trying to shield my conversation from Amalia. "I was hoping you could help me talk to her."

"Why do they want her?" she asked.

"Wait," I said, a grin forming on my face. "What did you think this was about?"

"You invited me to a restaurant to eat with you and Snert because you really wanted to talk to some girl," she said. "I wasn't exactly sure what I was getting into."

I laughed and then stopped myself. "You thought I was asking you to double with me and Snert because *my date* couldn't speak English? And you came?"

"Well, you did ask me to bring my carry piece. I figured I could wing you if things went bad," she said. "What's the drill here?"

"First, you need to make a decision. Are you in or are you ..."

She interrupted me mid-sentence. "In."

"Let me finish."

"Suit yourself, but the appendage beneath your arm is all the information I need."

"Seriously," I said. "You can walk right now and nobody will know you're involved. The fact is, we're up against the mob. Earlier today I killed a mob hitman."

"Wow, don't sugarcoat it or anything," she said. "You really killed someone?"

"Gordie Blondo, Bosian family enforcer," I said. "He was trying to get Amalia. I stopped him. In fairness, this was his third run at me."

"You need to call the cops," she said.

"Amalia's sister was murdered by these guys," I said. "There are more girls and I believe they've only got a few hours before they're shipped out of town or killed. If the cops get involved, I ..."

"You're talking crazy," she said. "How do you know they only have a few hours?"

"Blondo let it slip. I think Amalia might be able to help me locate where Manning is holding them."

"I thought you said Bosian," Mel said.

"Potato, po-tah-to," I said. "Richard Manning is a lieutenant of Franky Bosian's, working off-book. Long story: essentially, Bosian would never approve running underaged girls. But killing Blondo might have caused them to circle the wagons. At least that's what the cop I'm working with thinks."

"Then you need to take me back to my truck," she said.

I gave a quick nod of my head and pulled Amalia closer to me. "I respect that, Mel. No hard feelings."

"Are you always this good at reading women?" she asked, giving me an odd look.

We drove in silence for a couple of minutes and I turned into the pizza restaurant's parking lot, pulling to a stop in front of her truck.

"Maybe we can talk after this is over?" I asked. I liked Mel, but I had probably just ruined whatever friendship we'd started.

She jumped out of the car, leaving the car door open "Don't move."

"Do you know what's going on?" I asked, catching Snert's eyes in the rear-view mirror.

"Not for most of my life," he said, shrugging.

When Mel returned, she was carrying a flat bag about four-feet in length in one hand and a plastic ammunition case in the other. Diva popped up, catching a whiff of the weapons. She watched Mel climb back into the car with interest but thumped her tail against the seat.

"I'm not bailing on you, dumbass," she said, closing the door behind her. "It just seems like we might need a little more firepower."

"Are we getting something to eat?" Snert interrupted, a whine starting to creep into his voice. "And where's this safe house? You could have told me to order pizza, you know. My blood sugar's getting low."

"There are sandwiches left in the paper bag back there," I said.

"Hambriento," Amalia whispered, pulling on my arm. I looked down at the small girl. I couldn't imagine how she'd gone from barely existing in my universe to my highest priority. I wasn't sure if I was reacting to the world having royally crapped on her or simply that we'd been through a stressful event together. But at that moment, there wasn't anything I wouldn't do for her.

"She's hungry, Biggs," Mel said and then spoke softly to Amalia in Spanish.

"Bad news on the sandwiches," Snert said, pulling a mostly eaten sandwich away from his mouth. "I got the last one."

"It's almost eleven," Mel said. "We're not far from that all-night burrito truck on Forty-eighth."

I turned on my signal and changed lanes. We were only five minutes away. "Copy that. Did you bring those flashlights?"

"What's your deal with the flashlights?" Mel asked.

"Safe house might not have power," I said. "It's kind of a hole."

"I brought two tactical lights," she said. "There's a grocery store in the same parking lot where the burrito truck is parked. I'll run over while you get food."

We pulled up to a stoplight and I grabbed two hundred-dollar bills from my pocket and handed them to Mel. When she was reluctant to accept, I explained. "I wasn't actually expecting a party tonight. Would you mind grabbing dog food and toilet paper too?"

She snatched the bills out of the air and shook her head ironically. "Not much of a long-term planner, are you?"

"In my defense, this pretty much all broke loose today," I said.

I scanned the parking lot as we pulled in. The Mexican food truck was usually a popular late-night stop for the party crowd, but they were having a slow night. Only a single group of late teens was seated at the picnic tables nearby. I parked, positioning the car between the food truck and the grocery store.

"Back in a flash," Mel said, jumping out of the car.

When I grabbed the door handle to exit so I could order food, Amalia grabbed my arm. "No," she whispered. "No."

"I just need to get some food," I said. "You'll be safe with Diva and Snert."

Snert had been watching the exchange. "I can go," he said, cutting off a renewed complaint from Amalia.

I looked from Snert to Amalia. "Get a lot," I said. "I'm starving and I bet Amalia is too."

Diva whined as Snert got out. She needed a break of her own, but she could hold it long enough for us to get back to my newly rented house.

A few minutes later, Snert returned and the smell of refried beans, roasted peppers and spicy beef quickly filled the car. "No Melinda?" he asked.

I started the car and drove toward the store just in time to catch Mel as she exited, pushing a cart loaded with plastic bags.

"You buy 'em out?" I asked, jumping from the car before Amalia could stop me and circling around to open the trunk.

"You have no food for Diva. You have no cleaning supplies. You have no toilet paper, candles, cups. What about soap and wash cloth? Do you expect me to allow that beautiful child to remain with her face covered in grime?" she asked, her voice not nearly as indicting as her words.

"Right, I think what I should have said was thank you," I said, closing the trunk.

Melinda placed a finger on my chest, smiled and then turned away, her hair brushing against me. "I am pleased to know that you are not completely untrainable."

When I jumped back into the car, I noticed that Amalia had slid over slightly toward the center of the car and Mel. In her right hand was an unwrapped candy bar already half gone. Mel said something to her in Spanish and Amalia responded, her speech rapid but, as far as I could tell, not upset.

On the way to Sycamore Street I kept a lookout for a tail, taking time to circle different blocks and, one time, even parking for a few minutes in a neighborhood. Satisfied that we were alone, I turned toward Jonesy's, finally arriving at the rental.

"Isn't that where Marlin Creight's mom shot you?" Snert asked.

"How'd you know that?" I asked.

"It was on the police report. Before you ask, I found that information without hacking anything," Snert answered.

"I was looking for another run at Creight and saw the rental," I said. "The guy in the brick house across the street owns this Crown Vic. Jonesy's a vet, and we kinda hit it off. Now, before you say anything, the safe house is in pretty rough shape. I'm getting a deal on it because I'm going to help clean it up."

"How rough?" Melinda asked, interrupting the conversation she'd been having with Amalia.

"Third world rough," I said. "Landlord has trouble with squatters."

"Swell," Melinda said. "Wish I'd bought rubber gloves, in that case."

"Amalia, we're going to stay here tonight," I said. "It's safe. I need you to come with me to the house."

"Si," Amalia agreed.

Mel talked with her further. The bits and pieces I could understand let me know Mel was mostly just reassuring her that it would be safe.

"Snert, I need you to bring the food in while Mel and I secure the house," I said.

"You think someone's in there now?" he asked, his voice squeaking.

"No," I said simply. "Mel, you have those tac-lights?"

"Roger," she answered, extracting two thin flashlights from her backpack and handing one to me. She slid forward in her seat, swung the pack onto her back and grabbed the long, flat case she'd brought from her truck. Unzipping it, she pulled out a well-used Sig Sauer M400 AR-15 and attached her own tactical light onto a picatinny rail that ran beneath the barrel. With practiced ease, she slapped a thirty-round magazine into the receiver and cycled the bolt, pulling a round into the chamber.

"Amalia, you stay behind me," I said, making sure I had her attention. "If we see any bad people, you lie down on the ground."

Amalia nodded her head soberly.

I turned the knob on the dome light so it wouldn't turn on when we got out of the car. "Give us a couple of minutes, then come in," I said, handing Jonesy's keys to Snert.

When I opened the car door, Diva whined, her ears standing straight up. No doubt Mel's rifle had put her on alert and she didn't want to be left behind. I helped Amalia out and whistled, giving Diva permission to follow along. A second later, she'd cleared the front seat and was standing next to me.

"Hunt 'em up," I whispered, gesturing away from my body with my left hand.

Silently, Diva leapt ahead, keeping her nose high as she started a sweeping pattern between us and the house. From my back holster, I pulled out my Walther and flicked on the flashlight. I didn't want to draw too much attention but there were no street lights and I was unfamiliar with the terrain.

"How do you want to do this?" Mel asked, coming alongside.

"I'll take point. You're a southpaw?" I asked, noticing she was holding the gun in her left hand. I switched my grip on the Walther to hold it in my left hand. I was only a slightly worse shot with my left hand and we'd be more efficient clearing the house if we were aligned on the same side. The move caused raised eyebrows, but nothing else, so I continued. "Keep Amalia behind me, you can take my left shoulder. We'll move fast, counterclockwise through the house."

"Copy."

Remembering the broken front door, I set my shoulder close to the jamb, turned the door handle and pushed. The cheap door flexed but held. Wood creaking under my increased pressure, it finally gave way, swinging open. Diva burst through the door, rushing ahead through the living room, dining area and kitchen. I waited for her to either signal or return, positioning the rest of our group next to the wall where the central hallway began. Like a machine, as Diva took position in front, we pushed forward, entering the first of two bedrooms. Diva followed my lead and made a quick circuit of the room and closet, holding for a moment as I swept my flashlight across the floor. We continued, checking out the bathroom and finally the master bedroom.

"We're clear," I said, mostly for my own benefit. "Basement."

When a dog catches the scent while hunting game-birds, they're described as getting *birdy*. I'd never hunted birds with Diva, not seeing the point. She'd hunted more dangerous prey and I doubted birds would have been of much interest to her. The term *birdy*, however, very much described her attitude as we descended the shaky wooden stairs into the basement.

"Slow girl," I said, trying to keep her close. In the Army, while on mission, she would only be let off her leash when we were right on top of someone or needed her to run someone down. I couldn't afford to both run her leash and run point, so I had to trust her.

"Where'd she go?" Mel whispered as we reached the bottom of the stairs. There was a door to the left and a wider opening to the right which led into darkness. An excited bark from somewhere ahead in the dark section of the basement drew our attention.

"Clear right," I ordered as we flattened against opposite sides of the opening. Mel scanned right at the same time I illuminated the left, toward Diva's barking. This side of the basement had no windows – or they had been blacked out – so we utilized the cover around the opening until we could see what the room contained. I could feel Amalia's hand on my waist as I swept the room, looking for Diva. There was no end to the clutter and the smell brought me back to Afghanistan. Someone had been cooking meth in this basement.

Diva barked again as I turned a corner and entered a room at the far end of the basement. On the opposite wall was a countertop holding a complete setup for cooking meth, including a large fan that connected to an eight-inch, silver exhaust pipe that ran through a plywood patch over the broken-out window.

"Basement is clear, Biggs," Mel said, her flashlight joining mine to illuminate the scene.

"Looks like my landlord has more than squatters," I said.

"What is it?" Mel asked.

"Drug lab." I flashed my light onto shelves where large, shallow plastic trays were laid out. It looked as if someone had poured Jell-O into them and left them to set up. "That's a lot of meth."

"Are you sure this place is safe?" she asked as we turned to walk back to the stairs. There was no question the basement was a creepy place. The fact that it was an active drug lab had pretty much ruined the *safe* in safe house.

"It does add an interesting wrinkle, doesn't it?"

"Biggs?" Snert's voice called down the stairs. I heard the panic in his voice and, just as importantly, so did Diva. Without a word, she brushed past me at full speed and bolted up the stairs.

If *birdy* was a great way to describe a curious dog with a scent, the word definitely did not fit this situation. All predators have the instinct to fight and protect. The Army takes advantage of these traits and strengthens them with training. Snert was part of our company, or pack, as Diva saw it. When a member of the pack is attacked, the entire pack responds. Without a leash, it's an instinct that's impossible to overcome in dogs – and men alike, as it turns out. Shit was about to break loose.

THE SCREAMING BEGAN as Mel and I raced up the stairs. I turned into the kitchen first, arriving on the scene of a bloody, snarling, furball. The scream I'd heard was from none other than Marlin Creight and he was doing his best to escape from a very pissed off Diva.

"You okay?" I asked Snert, allowing Diva to bring Creight into full submission.

"He grabbed me and had a knife to my throat," Snert said, obviously very upset. "He was going to kill me."

I felt a tap on my shoulder – Mel letting me know she was beside me.

"Okay, buddy. I got this," I said.

I stepped forward and shined my light into Creight's face. "Stop fighting her!"

Creight was on his back, trying to get loose by punching at Diva, who wasn't about to relent. Creight's punches weren't overly effective as Diva was strong and lightning fast. Every time he swung, Diva would shake her head, using powerful neck muscles to tear into his arm. There was no question who had the better of whom.

"It's killing me!" Creight screamed in pure terror.

I understood how he felt. Diva's snarling sounded otherworldly.

"Stop fighting her. Put your hand behind your neck and lie back. She'll stop," I yelled over the chaos.

"Alan, pick up that knife," Mel instructed calmly behind me.

I couldn't focus on him, but my sense was that Snert was frozen and incapable of doing as he'd been told. A moment passed and then a small figure darted across the kitchen floor and scooped up the knife. Amalia, with knife in hand, dashed back to safety near Mel.

I watched Creight relax and follow my instructions. As soon as I gave Diva the release command, Creight grabbed his bloody arm with a whine and rolled into a fetal position.

"Who are you? What do you want? Are you trying to take over this area?" he asked. Diva continued to push at him with her muzzle, dancing around, ready for another fight.

"Diva, heel," I ordered. It was a testament to Angel's training that Diva obeyed.

"Just so you know, my friend there has a 5.56 lined up on you. Play it smart and you'll make it out of this in one piece," I said. "Get stupid and we'll put you down. You copy?"

"I ... I copy," he answered.

Mel pulled a small loop of 550 paracord from her pack and handed it to me. I nodded. I had paracord in my own pack, but that was still in the car. Mentally, I chastised myself. I was being shown up by a weapons tech who had none of my advanced training. When was I going to start acting like I was in the shit?

Unkindly, I rolled Creight over onto his stomach and placed my knee in his back. I was more pissed at myself than him. He was just doing what drug dealers did. Me, on the other hand? I was out of control. Expertly, I yanked his right arm down, tossed a loop around it and then brought his left arm back, securing both with the cord.

"What are you doing here?" I asked, patting down his back, looking for weapons. I found a wallet and his phone, but nothing else. With Mel's lamp still in his eyes, I was pretty sure he hadn't recognized me. I was fine leaving it that way.

"This is my stash house," he said, confused.

"Just not your night," I said, shaking my head. "Guys, head back to the car. We're out."

"You sure?" Mel asked.

"This place is about to get busy," I said, flipping open Creight's phone and dialing Pappi. I could have ordered Diva to guard him, but she was well ahead of me. Every time Creight moved, she flinched and danced, as if she was ready to attack.

Pappi's phone rang ten times before he finally picked up. "Ploughman," he answered, his voice thick with sleep.

"I need your help with a problem," I said.

"Henry?" he asked. "Are you okay? This isn't your phone."

"I'm fine. Remember that Creight guy?" I asked.

"Finkle's bail skip?"

"Right. There are some details you're missing but turns out I'm renting the house next to his. He's been cooking meth in the basement and I've got him secured on the floor," I said. "Thing is, he's got a fresh batch in the basement and I can't get tied up with this right now."

"Batch of crystal meth?" Pappi asked.

"That's right."

"Son, you don't do things in half measures, do you?" he said, chuckling. "You sure you're secure?"

"We're good. Any thoughts? No way am I letting this guy go and I'd hate to see this meth get lost."

"I have a friend," Pappi said. "I can probably buy you a day, but not much more."

"Did I mention I've got Chessen and the D.A. coming out to the farm tomorrow afternoon, around dinner time?" I asked.

He slowly took in a breath. "Not sure I heard that."

"They want to take me into protective custody," I said. Pearl was in the background asking who he was talking to. "Can't say much more over the phone."

"Protective custody? From whom? What happened, Henry?" he asked. "Aw, damnit, never mind. Give me an address."

I recited the address and then hung up the phone, dropping it into the signal-blocking bag Snert held out.

"We need to move," I said, pointing to the knife Amalia held and gesturing for her to hand it to me. She wasn't at all interested in complying and pulled the long knife to her chest. I nodded. If the knife made her feel safe, it was a small concession. "Diva, guard!" I ordered. She whined, looking like she wanted to finish the job she'd started fifteen minutes ago.

"Where now? You have a less desirable place?" Mel asked, irony lacing her words.

"Get in," I said, jumping into the car. I had a limited amount of time I could leave Diva on guard duty without expecting things to degrade. With everyone inside the car, I pulled forward, not bothering with headlights as I turned into Jonesy's driveway.

"You shouldn't do this," Snert said. "This neighborhood. People might not be friendly."

I ignored him and hopped out so I could open the garage door. Back in the car, I pulled forward and then jumped out again to close the garage.

"I didn't want to drag him into this, but ...," I said to the empty garage.

"But since you already had his car, you thought *why not*," I swung around to find Jonesy, standing at the side door to the garage. Having achieved the surprise he was looking for, Jonesy coughed violently for a minute and then spat on the ground. "Look, I told you. Marines have been bailing out Army since before you were born, kid. Why should tonight be any different."

"I was going to ask, first," I said. "Bad people want to hurt this little girl. I'm just looking for a place to lay low for a night."

"What was all that cloak and dagger crap at Peabody's old place? Looks like there was some excitement. Saw a bunch of flashlights," Jonesy said, coughing. "Creight come pay you a visit? I tried to call."

"I've got Creight hog-tied on the floor. Diva's babysitting. I need to get my crew settled and go back. Cops are on their way," I said. "I can't get my friends tied up in this mess."

"Why didn't you say so?" Jonesy asked. "Think I don't got better things than to be standing out here in the middle of the night?"

"I owe you," I said.

"If I see that shit-stain, Creight, roll out in the back of a patrol car, it'll be me that owes you, Army," he said.

"Language," Mel said, stepping out of the car with her Sig Sauer. "There are ladies present."

He blinked and raised his hands, looking at her gun. "Hold on there. Not a shooting offense."

My stomach growled and I realized I was about to miss another meal. "I've got to get back to Diva."

Snert had exited the car with the bag of burritos. I grabbed two and stuffed them into my go-bag. Mel had schooled me once today on being prepared, I wasn't about to make that mistake a second time. My pack wasn't equipped like I wanted, but the auto-parts store had enough to outfit me better than one might expect. I stuffed the burritos into the top and placed a hand on Snert's shoulder. "Keep 'em safe, buddy."

"I will," he answered solemnly.

"When will you be back?" Mel asked.

"My grandfather said he'd tell his buddy not to tie me down. Hopefully just a few minutes," I said. "I need you to talk to Amalia. We only have a few hours before the Bosian family sells the rest of the girls she was with."

"Okay," Mel said. "She's been through a lot. She needs a bath and a good night's sleep."

"Anything you can get," I said.

"Roger that," Mel pulled Amalia close to her. I almost felt jealous at how easily Amalia had transferred her loyalty to Melinda. Their ability to communicate and the fact that Mel was holding an assault rifle might have had something to do with it.

"Thanks." I turned and jogged down Jonesy's driveway. Before entering the street, I checked both directions to make sure we hadn't picked up unexpected visitors. The distant wail of a siren urged me onward, so I sprinted to the dilapidated rental.

A low, throaty growl greeted me as I entered the house. I'd left Creight bound and curled up on the kitchen floor, just out of sight of the entry. I'd also left a flashlight on the floor, pointing directly at his position. I wasn't overly surprised to discover he wasn't where I'd left him. Diva's growl had come from the kitchen, so I hurried around the U-shape, careful to stay hidden in the dark.

"You got guts, Marlin," I said, chuckling, sliding the Walther into my back holster. Creight had rolled onto his stomach and tried to crawl from the kitchen. Diva, not impressed by his attempt, had repositioned, sitting directly in front of him, growling.

"You gotta save me," Creight said. "She bit my ass."

"Diva, heel," I ordered. She whined. It was her way of saying that she didn't agree with my approach but would comply all the same.

I helped Creight into a seated position. "Here's how this is going down tonight," I said, picking up my flashlight.

"Holy shit," he said, interrupting. "You're that bail bondsman my mom shot. Are you fucking kidding me?"

"Cops are on their way," I said. "Narcotics division."

"No proof I'm connected to this," he answered.

"Right. Stick with that," I said. "I'm sure you wore gloves when you were working the meth."

"I'm not even the cook. That's Mom," he said. "I'm just distribution."

"I'm sure they'll like to hear that."

"Fuck off," he said, probably regretting his words. Idiots come in all sizes.

I leaned against the kitchen counter and unslung my go-bag, setting it next to me.

"Think you can behave?" I asked.

"What choice do I have?" he asked, looking sullenly at Diva.

I cut a burrito in two with my tactical knife, dropped half on his lap and fed the other to Diva. I filled an oversized cup from my pack with bottled water and set it on the ground. Diva wasted no time in lapping it up.

"Don't make me regret this." I cut the paracord and lifted Creight's right hand over his head, securing it by tying the rope through the handles of the refrigerator and freezer. It wasn't perfect, but the sirens were nearly on top of us. "You might want to eat. Best food you're likely to get for a while."

Creight telegraphed his move from miles out. His muscles bunched just before he lunged for me, pulling the refrigerator away from the wall.

"I can't go down for this," he roared.

I stepped in and brought my left fist around in what is best described as a haymaker. Cartilage crunched under my fist as I hit the side of his jaw. Upon contact, his body went limp and he splayed onto the floor, pulling the refrigerator down on top of himself.

"Well, shit," I said. I didn't like striking a bound prisoner, but Creight had left me no choice.

A loud rapping at the front door got our attention. Diva barked and rushed out toward the new noise. "Heel," I ordered. With the excitement, my order only succeeded in bringing her to a seated position next to the door. Wisely, whoever was on the other side didn't open the broken door any further.

"Police. Open up," a man ordered.

I pulled the remaining spool of Mel's paracord from my pocket and looped it into Diva's collar. She'd handled a lot of crazy for one night and more angry men with guns wasn't going to make things better.

"I'm opening the door," I said. "I have a leashed dog and a holstered carry weapon."

"Go slow," the voice on the other side of the door said. A bright light shown through the cracks in the door and I braced myself for a potential takedown.

"Easy girl," I soothed, keeping one hand up and slowly opening the door. Diva growled in response to seeing a pair of uniformed officers but stayed seated by my side.

"You Lester Ploughman's boy?" the older of the two officers asked. Both men had hands resting on their service weapons.

"That's me," I said. "I have Marlin Creight in the kitchen. I'm also a bail bondsman. He's my skip."

"You know you can't call to have us pick up your skips, right?" the younger of the two asked.

"I know," I said. I wasn't sure what would happen to Finkle's bond, but it was small potatoes compared to the drugs I'd found in the basement. "Wish I'd had another choice."

"Lester said something about drugs," the older officer said. "This place reeks of it."

"I didn't catch it at first, but you're right. I guess I've been out of it for a while," I said. I don't know if it had just been wishful thinking that I'd convinced myself that the house just smelled of trash.

He tapped the side of his nose. "Been around a lot of it. Let's see this Creight, but first, you mind if I get that carry weapon from you?" I turned and lifted my shirt, exposing the holstered Walther. "Appreciate it." He pushed the pistol into his belt after checking the chamber.

Creight was attempting to push the refrigerator to the side and escape from the kitchen through the back door.

"You tune him up?" the younger officer asked.

"Less than he had coming," I said, earning me an unconcerned shrug.

"I'll need you to walk me through this," the older officer said. "Lester said you needed twenty-four hours. If this adds up, I can make that happen. But first, I need you to secure that dog."

"Sorry, girl," I said, picking up her water cup and adding fresh water. "I'll just put her in this first room." I led her into the first bedroom and closed the door behind me. I was worried she might find something bad amongst the trash, but I was out of options.

"And his drugs?" my grandfather's friend asked.

"We found what looks like a lab in the basement," I said.

"We?"

"Diva and me," I said, quickly covering. "We put a deposit on the house and are renting it."

"This is not a nice place, Ploughman," he said.

"Biggston," I answered, grabbing Mel's tactical flashlight from the counter. "Henry Biggston. Lester is my Mom's foster dad."

"Brooks, take Creight out to the patrol car and read him his rights," the older man said. "Biggston here is the renter. We can book Creight, at a minimum, with breaking and entering. Run his warrants too. If we have a lab, we're going to be here for a while."

"Copy that," the younger officer answered, having already cuffed a compliant Creight and pulled him to his feet.

"His wallet is on the counter, by the sink," I added.

"Thanks," the younger officer said.

"Sergeant Bill Jacobs," the older officer said, holding out his hand after his partner exited the kitchen.

"Glad to know you," I said, shaking. "You're really helping me out tonight: not getting me tied down."

"Why'd you call?" he asked. "You should have taken Creight down to lockup so you could collect your bond."

"I get you guys involved and he goes down for the drugs. I'm only out a few hundred this way," I said, walking over to the basement door.

Jacobs shined a light over my shoulder and got a look down the stairs. The smell coming up was overpowering and he instinctively withdrew his pistol from its holster. "You rented this place?"

I started down the stairs. "Price is right. It just needs a little elbow-grease."

"Good luck with that." Jacobs was a little overweight and he puffed heavily as we descended.

I led him through the darkened room and around to the lab. He whistled appreciatively as his flashlight came to rest on the finished product. "That's fifty ... maybe seventy thousand street value," he said. "You think Creight's the guy?"

"He said he was distribution. His mom's the cook," I said.

"He admitted that?"

"He's not extra smart," I said. "I told him you guys would run prints and wouldn't have trouble tying him to it."

"And he gave up his mom? I'm not even sure she's in the system," he said.

"Pretty sure she is," I said. "She shot me a couple weeks ago. I heard she turned herself in."

He chuckled. "That was you? I heard about that. Didn't you also get blown up over in the industrial park? You've had a busy couple of weeks."

"Are we good?" I asked, noticing that two more patrol cars had arrived. I suspected there would be even more soon.

"Yeah. Beat it," he said. "And thanks for reaching out. A bust like this is going to make me and the kid look pretty good. I can't keep you out of it forever, though. I'll need you to come in tomorrow."

"That's all I need," I said. "I owe you."

"This one's on Lester's account," he said, following me back upstairs. "If I get that promotion. I'll owe *you*."

He handed me my piece, allowed me to retrieve Diva and my pack, and then escorted me to the front door.

"What'd you find?" Officer Brooks asked as we walked out.

"Drug lab in the basement, just like the kid said. You're going to leave him out of your report until tomorrow afternoon, you read me?"

"You're the boss," Brooks answered.

I kept Diva at heel as we walked past the patrol cars, one of them holding a very subdued Creight. I shuffled through the backpack, pulled the last burrito out and bit into it. Together, we crossed the street and walked all the way around the block, behind where Jonesy's house sat. Diva easily cleared the chain-link fence as we snuck across the neighbor's yard. The only light on in Jonesy's house was in the kitchen and I was able to enter without being noticed by anyone across the street.

"Do you ever sleep?" I asked, finding Jonesy seated at his kitchen table.

"Army, when you're my age, sleep is nothing more than a fickle lover," he said.

"Didn't know you were a poet," I said, sitting and accepting a glass of whiskey he'd poured.

"Where'd you find that girl?" he asked. "She's a spitfire."

I wasn't sure which he was referring to, so I played it safe. "Melinda? She's a weapons tech in the guard. We met at the gun range."

"I saw Creight in the squad," he said. "You're a man of your word."

Melinda appeared in the doorframe that was two steps up from the kitchen and led to the second floor. "Pour me one already," she said in a low voice, crossing over to where Jonesy and I sat. I handed her mine and stood, gesturing for her to join us at the table.

"Where are Snert and Amalia?" I asked.

"Snert's asleep in the living room and Amalia fell asleep in the bath," Melinda answered. "Didn't even wake up when I dressed her and put her to bed."

"Where'd you get clothes?" I asked.

"I used one of Jonesy's shirts. I hope you don't mind," she said, looking sheepishly at Jonesy.

"That little black fella on the couch explained what you're up against," he said. "Proud to do my part."

"Did she say anything?" I asked.

"Sorry, Biggs. She fell asleep," Mel answered. "We could try to wake her."

"No," I answered. "I've got one lead I want to run down first."

"What's that?" Mel asked.

"The warehouse next to Lambert Textile," I said, grabbing my go-bag and standing up.

She scowled at me. "Now? It's two in the morning. You haven't had any sleep."

Absently, I pulled out my Walther and checked the magazine and chamber. It was hot-loaded, just as I remembered. "Best time to be looking around," I said, smiling and making eye contact.

"Take my AR," she said. "I've still got my Glock."

"Don't forget my M1 carbine," Jonesy said. "Brought it all the way back from 'Nam."

"What if you need it?" I asked Mel, ignoring Jonesy for the moment.

"Don't be stupid. You're not going to break into a mob warehouse with just your carry weapon," Mel said.

"I have a shotgun in the car."

"Good. I prefer a shotgun for home defense," she said, standing up.

I BACKED SLOWLY down Jonesy's driveway and turned away from the increasingly frenetic activity at Peabody's rental house. I shook my head at the irony. Due to my own actions, I'd likely just forfeited my first-and-last month's rent.

The warehouse next to Lambert's was my only lead, though it was unlikely the girls from the video were still there. I rolled down the passenger window and Diva lazily leaned against the door, resting her head on the frame. She was as tired I was, but if Blondo was to be believed, we were in a race against the clock. I'd struggled with bringing her. I wasn't expert in handling her and if we got into a situation with much gunplay, I wasn't sure I could keep her out of harm's way. On the other hand, searching a warehouse was a daunting task for one person. Add Diva and we'd go more than twice as fast.

About a mile from the industrial park where Lambert's facility was located, my senses lit up. Soldiers often claim to know when they are being watched. Some people dismiss it as nerves. I've experienced both, but no matter what, a smart soldier doesn't dismiss that intuition lightly. They say that just because you're paranoid doesn't mean you're not being followed. It's a true statement.

Search as I might, I couldn't locate the threat. No cars were following us and the main road was all but deserted. If we weren't being watched, it was a no-harm, no-foul situation. The consequences of ignoring the feeling when somebody was out there could be significant.

I pulled up in front of Lambert's building, taking care to park in a marked spot. If anyone happened across the car, I wanted them to believe it had been left behind by an employee. I gathered my go-bag and shuffled the contents, putting Snert's camera on top. If I ran into something interesting, I wanted proof.

If I'd been alone, I would never have gotten the warning. Out of the corner of my eye, I caught Diva's tell - her ear twitched. With a low growl, she took a long look into the sandy field that lay in darkness past the highway. She was looking out to roughly the same vantage point of the mysterious video on DeLovely's USB drive. It took a lot of discipline to act normally and not follow her gaze. If someone was out there, I wasn't about to tip them off that I knew.

"Heel," I ordered. I slid my go-bag onto my back after tightening the AR-15's single-point sling and clipping the rifle into place. The gear wasn't exactly what I'd used in the Rangers, but it would certainly do the job.

Diva slid into her usual spot on my left and I jogged away from the car, careful to stay away from the few remaining lights in Lambert's parking lot. When we finally made it around the corner of Lambert's building, I stopped and ordered Diva to hold the position. She whined, unhappy to be sidelined, but she complied. I dropped my pack and rifle next to her, which seemed to make her a little happier.

If I was being followed, I wanted to know who was doing it. If Diva and I were both imagining things, I'd only lose twenty minutes. I jogged around the back of Lambert's building and followed a fence line to the next building over. It was dark, but there was enough light to navigate. I picked my way carefully, moving between the shadows, all the time scanning the dark horizon for any sign. The highway would be difficult to cross as the lights were well maintained. There were darkened locations between the street lights, but if someone were paying attention, I'd be easily spotted.

I ran in the dark, twenty feet short of the road, heading away from where Diva had focused. I'd be a lot harder to identify if I put some distance between me and whoever was watching. It was almost by accident that I ran into a narrow culvert that went under the highway. Actually, the smell of fetid water caught my attention long before my search revealed the swale where a muddy trickle still remained.

Surprise is often gained by being willing to do things that others aren't. The drainage culvert wasn't the worst thing I'd ever crawled through. This solution put me that much closer to my objective – mainly staying alive – so I was all in. Crawling on my elbows with my pistol in one hand, I focused on everything except the smell of animal waste and decay. When I exited on the opposite side of the road, I was rewarded with the flash of a cell phone screen about two hundred yards from my position. The interior of a car was illuminated for just a moment, but it was enough time for me to learn a lot – primarily, the car's location and orientation. Staying low, I worked through the sandy field, using thick tufts of grass as cover.

As I got closer, I slowed and allowed my lungs to catch up with my body's exertion. The windows of the vehicle were open and whoever was inside exercised considerable discipline. His only tell so far had been that phone call. On my stomach, I slowly crawled around so I came up next to the rear quarter panel of the vehicle. I heard the steady breathing of a patient man and the smell of his aftershave. I recognized the scent.

With heart hammering in my chest, I readied for action. I was tired from my long sneak, but adrenaline quickly pushed that away. I waited for a moment, looking for an opportunity that would up my chances. Movement from within the car gave me my lucky break. I watched as a long telephoto lens poked out past the frame of the car's window. I lunged forward, pulling violently on the lens. I was ready to reach into the car for another strike just in case, but it wasn't necessary. As I'd hoped, the camera strap had been placed securely around the occupant's neck. The guy's head bounced against the window frame.

Having recognized his aftershave, I wasn't at all surprised to find DeLovely Manning's butler flailing in the car. He was pulling hard on the camera's strap, so I released my hold, sending it flying back into his face. I wasn't about to give him any chance to attack me, so I followed the camera in with a hard, balled fist. The butler slumped over in the seat, not unconscious, merely stunned by the violent turn his day had taken. I seized the opportunity and yanked the car door open.

"Stop," he pled, bringing his arms up defensively. I ignored him. I wasn't messing around any longer and I wouldn't be done until I got answers. I dragged him out onto the ground.

"How are you following me?" I whispered roughly.

"Phone," he said. "The phone has tracking."

Mentally, I winced. I'd been so concerned about the cops tracking my normal phone, I hadn't even considered someone might track the burner phone.

I ran my hands over his tight clothing and found a 9mm pistol in an ankle holster. "This registered to you?" I asked, holding the gun in front of his face.

"No serial," he grunted, mostly due to my knee pressing into his back.

"Why is DeLovely following me?" I dropped the gun's magazine and removed the slide, throwing both off into the dark.

"I don't know," he said.

I continued frisking and found another telescoping baton. "What? Was the mob surplus store having a sale on these?" No answer. He got credit for that. The car's interior lights hadn't come on when the door opened. I stepped off him and sat in his seat. "Don't move. We're done with the rough stuff unless you get creative. Got it?"

"I'm no threat," he answered.

The sound of panting caught my attention as Diva showed up. She must have heard the ruckus and decided she needed to check it out more than she needed to sit where I'd told her. Turning back to the interior, I caught the light green glow of a night-vision monocle. I brought it to my eye and scanned the area.

"How'd you miss me?" I asked after giving the car a final search. I'd taken a long circuitous route, but the monocle was high quality and could easily have picked up my approach. He recognized the rhetorical question for what it was and lay still.

"Tell DeLovely I said hey." After I ejected the memory card and battery from his camera, I poked a knife into the sidewall of the rear tire. I considered hitting two, but really, I was just trying to slow him down.

"That's it?" he asked.

"Probably best if you leave me alone for a few days," I replied and broke into a jog back toward Lambert's, glad to find that my pack and rifle hadn't been messed with. I'd left the items in deep shadow and it didn't appear that anyone else was here but leaving them had been a risk. I pulled on the pack and clipped the AR-15 back in place.

I crossed the short distance to the loading dock of the warehouse where I'd seen Amalia and her sister fall from the back of the truck, checking carefully for cameras or other security sensors along the way. Apparently, the person who used the building wasn't interested in any video evidence, at least not on this side of the warehouse. No one had even bothered to remove pieces of wood from the broken crate that were still lying on the ground. I jumped up onto the narrow ledge of the loading dock, placing my ear against the tall metal garage-style door. I didn't expect to hear anything and, of course, I didn't.

I jumped down and worked my way over to a half flight of stairs that led up to a locked door. Diva followed and we both paused to listen, hoping to hear if there was anyone inside. I gave a half-hearted try at opening the thick, steel security door. It was locked and not something I could easily break down – that is, unless I'd brought along a crowbar, say from Jonesy's garage. Luckily, whoever locked the door had failed to secure the deadbolt, which could have been my downfall, at least on this entry. With some effort, I managed to pop the door free.

The cool air that wafted out of the warehouse smelled slightly of diesel, but nothing else. I gripped the rifle and pushed the door open with my hip, flowing into the large room and visually sweeping it while looking through the scope. It was dark and I could see nothing. I closed the door behind me after sweeping the room once again with the night-vision monocle I'd taken from DeLovely's butler.

Two thirds of the large space was empty, but twenty feet back from the loading dock were rows of shelves. They were only half filled with what appeared to be regular shipping boxes, all different sizes and shapes. I didn't see any crates anywhere near the size of the one the girls had been stashed in. I half crouched, half ran through the aisles, inspecting the shelves as quickly as I could. Diva followed right behind me, inspecting with her long snout. When we reached the end, we'd both come up empty on anything interesting. As far as I could tell, it was just a large, open warehouse with possibly a few offices at the front. Furthermore, there appeared to be no one home.

I wasn't ready to abandon my search, so I continued through a door that led toward the front and quickly searched each office. Nothing looked unusual or out of place. Diva and I returned to the main warehouse. There wasn't much left to do except walk the perimeter.

I might have missed the door if Diva hadn't lain down in front of it, refusing to move. The thick metal door looked like every other panel on the wall. I felt around the edges until I found the spring-loaded lock that freed the door to swing toward me. I gripped Mel's AR, signaled Diva and gently tugged on the metal edge. While Diva checked the room, I scanned with the monocle. The room had no windows and was bare except for a grouping of large crates stacked near the center. Diva had circled the room quickly and was now alerting on the stack of crates. My heart thudded in my chest. I couldn't hear any movement, but who knew what shape the girls might be in if they were still in one of those boxes.

I pulled out Jonesy's crowbar and attacked the first crate. The noise of squealing nails filled the space as I peeled off the side of the first box. My heart sank when a huge duffel bag slid off several others, sagged forward and rolled onto the floor. The bag was wrapped in clear plastic and taped at the ends. I pulled the knife from my belt and slashed into the layers, prepared to find the worst. I wasn't sure what I felt when I discovered ziplocks stuffed with pills. The bottom was lined with all sizes of cardboard sleeves and baggies for repackaging. Diva barked excitedly. One of her missions had been to locate drugs and she'd done exactly that.

"Good girl," I praised and rubbed her head, pulling out a toy from my go bag. Just to be certain the girls weren't there, I methodically opened every crate and every bag only to find more drugs.

<hr/>

In the end, Diva had found quite a stash. I crudely estimated the street value to be somewhere north of a million dollars. When I got back to the car, I dialed the police, using DeLovely's burner phone.

"Sutherland police," a surly man answered on the third ring.

"I was driving through the industrial park. It looks like someone broke into the warehouse on the north side of Lambert Textile Research building. I saw someone go in there. He was hauling stuff out to a truck," I said.

"How do you know it was a break-in?" the man asked.

"Truck looked pretty sketchy," I said. "Maybe I'm wrong. Just thought I should call it in."

"What's your name?" he asked, sounding bored.

I hung up.

I'd blown two and a half hours in my search and had nothing to show for it. Dejected, I drove away, knowing I was out of leads. I pulled my personal cell phone out of Snert's Faraday bag and dropped the burner phone into it.

"Any luck?" Mel asked after answering on the third ring.

"Not a bit," I answered. "I don't suppose you'd wake Amalia up?"

"She's awake," Mel answered. "We're just lying here on the bed, talking."

"Could you ask if she has *anything* that could help me?" I asked.

"I did. She said they were at a different place for a few hours," Mel said. "Some of the other girls told Amalia they'd been to that location a few times before. Apparently, it's where someone puts dresses on them and very bad things happen. She wouldn't go into details."

"Yeah, that sucks," I said, swallowing bile. "Any clues on location?"

"Amalia never saw daylight. It's where she and her sister met up with the other girls," Mel said.

Amalia spoke rapidly in Spanish but I didn't understand much of what was being said.

"What was that about?" I asked.

"She said it smelled like animals and she heard machinery, maybe tractors – that sort of thing," Mel said. "I know it's not a lot to go on."

"What kind of animals? Pigs? Horses?" I asked. I suspected Amalia was from the country and if that was the case, she'd know the difference.

"No, pigs," Amalia answered, immediately. "Yes, horses."

"Does that help, Biggs" Mel asked. I could imagine the two, lying on the bed with the phone cradled between them.

"I'm not sure," I answered. "It just might though."

A patrol car with lights flashing rushed past my position going the other way. My guess was that someone at the police station had recognized the address of the warehouse and were suddenly inter-ested – I hoped for the right reasons.

"It might be better to turn this over to the police," Mel said. "It sounds like things are getting serious."

"I need to see this through," I said. "If there's a chance to recover those girls, I don't want to miss it."

"I know," she responded. "Be safe."

I hung up and switched phones again, pulling out DeLovely's burner and shooting her a text.

BIGGS: *We need to talk. Does Dick have a farm?*

I pulled into the parking lot of a motel. I had no idea where I was going, so it no longer made sense to keep driving. I poured out some water for Diva, who'd fallen asleep on the seat next to me. A moment later the phone buzzed.

"One four two one Fairchild Lane," DeLovely said, without any greeting. "You didn't need to rough up my man. We're on the same side here."

"It could have gone a lot worse," I said. "He get home okay?"

"I think the only thing you critically injured was his pride," DeLovely admitted. "You think Dick has girls out at his farm?"

"It's the only lead I have."

"What are you going to do?"

"I'm going to finish this," I said.

"I'm throwing this phone away. I'd suggest you do the same," she said. "Our deal is still good. You get pictures of Dick and those girls, you'll be paid handsomely."

I hung up the phone, took out its battery and broke the phone in half. I jumped out of the car and walked the broken phone over to an overfilled trash can.

On Snert's tablet, I found 1421 Fairchild Lane to be on the opposite side of town from Pappi's farm. I was somewhat familiar with the area, having delivered hay to many of Dick Manning's wealthy neighbors when on summer break in high school.

Traffic was starting to build for the morning rush, but not enough to slow my progress. The address of Dick's farm was twenty minutes out of town, but still on a well-kept, paved road. From my perspective, you weren't on a farm if you had pavement to your front door. That said, I had a difficult time not admiring the miles of beautiful white-painted horse fences and rolling green pastures. I found the correct address and while I couldn't see Manning's barns or home from the road, I had no doubt they were incredible, given the large stone columns that stood sentry on either side of the wide drive.

I was tired enough that the idea of just driving down the lane and knocking on the door was appealing. I dismissed the idea and continued past, looking for the next road that appeared on Snert's tablet. I passed a few more homes and half a mile later, found a gravel road that ran parallel to Manning's property. I turned left and half a block up, eased Jonesy's car onto a turnout that led into a field.

"Let's go, girl," I urged Diva, waking her up. She jumped gingerly from the car and stretched her legs, pushing blood back into them. I poured water into my cup and held it for her. Greedily she emptied it and I gave her a second round. About halfway through she looked up and jogged down into the ditch to take care of business.

I looked at her impatiently. "Are you ready, now?" I asked.

She barked once and wagged her tail.

I'd chosen my parking spot because it was sheltered behind the house and barns closest to the gravel road. In the country, noise travels and it's not difficult to hear things like car doors closing. I wanted a stealthier approach, although this morning, I suspected people in this zip code might have their windows shut and the air conditioning on.

Diva and I ran across into the opposite ditch and I slowed while looking for telltales of the barbed-wire fence in the early morning gloom. It was one thing to have fancy, white wooden fences facing the road, it was another thing entirely to surround your property with them. I stepped on the bottom of the three strands and pulled up on the second, whistling Diva through.

I kept low as we jogged through the field. I was in line-of-sight from the nearest house and wasn't interested in being observed by an early-rising farmer or their live-in hands. I'd counted a total of three properties separating Manning's from the gravel road and watched for the different buildings as we crossed fence after fence.

A mercury-vapor light illuminated the front of a massive barn and a large paved drive in front of it. A second light cast a glow on the side of an equally massive home. Abutting the barn were a number of horse runs adjoining an outdoor arena. I was more concerned with the four black SUVs and the long Mercedes sedan parked along the driveway. The vehicles could hold a max of sixteen, although more likely a dozen comfortably.

Moving closer to Manning's ranch, I snuck around so we came up behind the barn on the opposite side. I had a good view of most of the property, so I motioned for Diva to lie down next to me. She settled in while I scouted around with the night vision monocle.

A man holding an assault rifle sat on a stool back in shadow. He looked to be dozing lightly. I found two more standing on the porch, talking. They were far enough away that I could just make out murmurs of conversation. Where there were three, I suspected there would be more, so I settled in. They didn't look to have night-vision equipment, so for at least the next hour, my position would be solid.

As I observed the area, I became more aware of the noises around me. I could hear the man moving on the stool and occasionally the sound of muted laughter as the men on the porch continued to talk. After half an hour, I'd discovered no further sentries, but thought I could hear a rhythmic tapping from within the barn. The sound was almost imperceptible, but it was definitely repetitive and slightly spasmodic. Apparently, the sentry sitting in the shadows next to the barn also heard it. He banged on the side of the barn, having startled from his light sleep.

"Quiet in there," he growled, but didn't bother to get up. My blood pressure spiked. I wanted more than anything to get into that barn, but if he could hear that tapping, he would certainly hear me opening a door or window. So, I waited, soon getting my reward as the man nodded off again.

"Stay," I ordered, gesturing to Diva. She whined and I froze, expecting the noise to wake the man. He was only twenty yards from our position, but he didn't move.

I slunk across the yard to his position. The man's body odor was clearly from a protein rich diet. I should probably have been concerned about how much muscle this guy had, but didn't have the luxury of more observation. Ignorance is bliss, said no Ranger ever. Instead, I'd just have to up the shock and awe. I wrapped my right arm around his neck and clamped it down with my left, cutting off his air supply. He tried to resist, but I'd pulled him deeper into more shadow, to keep him from gaining his feet or making noise. I held my breath, waiting to see if we'd alerted his friends on the porch. When the guy finally went limp, the two at the house were still laughing together. One down.

The sky was just starting to lighten, so I dragged the man through a side door into the barn. I ejected the cartridge from his weapon and pulled the magazine, dumping the receiver into a pile of loose hay in a nearby stall. With a low whistle, I called Diva into the barn and closed the door behind her, throwing the bolt home. The man would be down for a good ten minutes, if not longer.

"Is someone there?" another man's voice called out quietly. His voice was muffled, like it was behind some sort of structure. He must have heard my whistle or possibly my disarming of the weapon. I gripped my gun and moved toward the sound, trying not to give away my position.

The whimpering of a child came clearly from the opposite row of stalls, away from where the man had spoken. I stopped, carefully swinging my gaze toward the sound. The horse stalls had doors that were about five-foot-tall with steel bars on top. They would serve nicely as cells, especially if someone was tied up.

"I'm Richard Manning," the man continued. "I'm being held against my will. If you free me, I'll pay you fifty thousand dollars."

I'd made it to the stall where he was being held and crouched down. "Where are the girls, Dick?" I asked.

"Fuck the girls," he said. "I can get more, but not if I'm locked up. One hundred thousand. Cash."

I crossed the aisle to where I thought I'd heard a child whimper. I stood so I could look over the stall door. Lying in the hay were four bodies. Through the monocle, the children's eyes looked green and alien as they peered back at me from the floor of the stall. The looks in their faces were devoid of emotion. I'd seen that before when all hope was gone and the spirit had been crushed.

"Shh," I whispered, holding a finger to my mouth.

"Damn it!" Manning whispered hoarsely. "Leave the product alone. They're as good as dead already. Just like you'll be if you don't get me out of here. Fine. One hundred fifty thousand. Now, be a man and get me out."

"You're a sick fuck, Manning." I returning to the door of his stall. "I'd gut you right now if I didn't think I'd wake everyone up."

A rifle shot cracked through the barn. Diva yelped in pain, her legs buckling as she was thrown back into the aisle. She lay still as dim overhead mercury-vapor lights clicked and started to flash dim, strobing light. A smear of blood on the clean cement floor showed the force of the bullet that had knocked her down.

Instinctively, I returned fire, squeezing off a short burst toward the gap in the front sliding barn doors. I went low, diving over to Diva, grabbing her collar, and pulling her to the side, out of the direct line of fire. Two more shots chipped at the ground near me, but I was unharmed.

"Mr. Biggston. You need to put your weapon down," a man called. "We've no quarrel with you."

"You just shot my dog," I said, pulling my backpack off and rummaging for something to stop the blood that poured from Diva's back.

"Henry, you can't win. Franky has twenty men." The voice belonged to none other than DeLovely Manning. "I can get you out of here alive, if you'll just come work for me."

My HANDS SHOOK as adrenaline coursed through my body. I pushed back the anger that threatened to overwhelm as I looked down at Diva, dying on the floor in front of me. What I needed was time. I positioned myself next to a rolling saddle rack with my back to the stall and pushed a thick bandage onto Diva's wound. A shadow darted across the aisle at the front of the barn using the stacked feed and hay bales for cover. I was basically in the open and someone was trying to gain position on me. With my left hand keeping pressure on the bandage, I pulled my Walther and tossed a couple of slugs in their direction.

"Stay back," I said. "I don't care what you do with Manning. Let me and the girls go and we'll call it even."

"That can't happen, Biggs," DeLovely called back. "There's only room for you. You need to kill Dick and give Franky the girls. It's a win for everyone. Dick stops dealing in underaged girls and I get you, a real warrior, to keep me safe. I can make life very nice for you." Her voice was sultry in its attempt to seduce me. I suspected she'd done the same to many men before me.

I pulled the wrap around Diva's torso and cinched it down. "I counted three men on the night shift," I said. "You come at me, there's going to be a body count. Nobody wins."

DeLovely's voice was coming from outside the barn. As far as I could tell, only one man had come inside for a better angle on me. I grabbed my Walther again. It wouldn't take long for him to figure out I was stalling to work on Diva. Sure enough, the guy ducked into view and unloaded a fusillade of rounds down the aisle. I caught a glimpse of movement just before he popped out of hiding, and I dove across the aisle, rolling on my shoulder and popping up onto a knee in one single, fluid motion. The shooter tracked my movement with automatic fire and bullets hit the saddle and then thumped against the stalls going back toward the end of the barn.

The problem with automatics is that they're difficult to control and the guy was firing high. I squeezed the trigger and put two rounds center mass, throwing him back. The 9mm doesn't have a giant punch, but it was enough to send his remaining fire wild and into the roof. I followed the first two shots with two more, hitting him in the lower abdomen before he could make it to the floor. I loved my Walther, but the short barrel, which made it fantastic for concealed carry, is hell on accuracy.

"Stop shooting, Biggs," DeLovely said. "You're pushing Franky into a corner. He won't be able to call his guys off."

"You're dead, kid. She's lying," Manning said from within the stall I was leaning against. "Give me a gun. Two fighting is better than one."

Shadowy figures moved at the end of the barn. I was too open. I grabbed the stall-door handle and yanked it back. More gun fire erupted as I dove into the stall beneath a shower of wooden splinters. I rolled over and looked up into Richard Manning's battered face. He'd been beaten sufficiently that one eye was forced closed and his lip was torn open. From the crustiness of the blood, I estimated he'd been beaten the night before and left in the stall overnight.

"Don't make me regret this," I said and cut his hands free. I had no doubt he'd turn on me if we ever made it out of this barn, but for the moment, our fates were tied together. I handed him my Walther and the remaining two magazines.

"Smartest move you've made tonight," he said, grinning like a shark. I pushed away the anger that urged me to permanently remove that smile from his face.

"How many are there?" I asked. Considering the cars outside and only three on night watch, I guessed their numbers were likely closer to ten than the twenty DeLovely boasted.

"Counting Franky, a dozen tops," he answered, ejecting the magazine and checking his ammo.

"Give me some cover fire," I said.

"Where you goin'?" Richard asked, his perfect English slipping and exposing what sounded more like a New Jersey thug.

"On three, fire at the front of the barn," I said. "Then follow. I'll cover you."

"Your funeral," he said with a shrug.

I kicked at the stall door, sending it flying open. I popped out and fired three quick 5.56 rounds. Without looking, I dove back into the center of the barn and rolled to my feet, sprinting for the end of the stalls where the barn joined with an interior arena. The sound of my Walther popping alerted me that Manning was making his move. I spun down to my knee and lined up. Two men were advancing, one of whom had been grazed by Manning's shot. I fired two rounds into the chest of the first guy and swung back to the injured one. He fired at Manning but missed. I squeezed off a quick triple shot – and I did not miss.

Manning ran past me into the arena and looked around frantically. A new shooter opened up from the far end and bullets whizzed over my head, also missing Manning. To his credit, the guy quickly ducked back out of my line of sight.

"Climb!" I ordered. I didn't want to say it aloud, but Manning was having difficulty identifying the most strategic move at this point: up into the loft overhead. He turned and sprinted to the simple wooden ladder angling down from a hole in the floor above and started climbing. I had no shot on any of DeLovely's men, so I sent a volley in each direction to keep them occupied.

I turned and ran back to where Manning was struggling on the ladder. Apparently, his leg was injured and he was having difficulty ascending. I jumped for the ladder, springing off a lower tread and launching up to the rough-hewn braces that supported the frame of the opening, allowing Mel's AR to swing freely against my back. Hand over hand, I sprung from one piece of wood to the next until I'd bypassed Manning and could poke my head up into the loft.

I shrugged the AR back over my shoulder as more gunfire erupted below and I had little choice but to pull myself all the way through. I kept moving forward in the dim light, scanning the area quickly. A tuft of hay exploded a few feet from my head. We weren't alone in the loft. I barely had time to register the shots before instinctively charging forward and bowling into the stack of hay where the shooter lay hidden, tumbling bales over on top of him. Wildly, he struggled to free himself, but I was quicker. I lashed out with a brutal punch into his cheek, catching the side of his nose. I was about to follow with a second, when I noticed I'd knocked him out with the first hit.

"What's he doing up here?" Manning asked, huffing as he caught up to me.

"Shh," I answered, picking the man's pistol up from the ground and handing it to Manning. He attempted to take it from me, but I nodded to my Walther. I wasn't about to have Richard Manning running around with a gun registered to me if I could avoid it.

Manning was a practical man and traded guns, then turned around to search the thug for additional ammo. I winced as Manning found a knife, viciously driving the man's own blade into his throat. I didn't need to be reminded that he was an animal, but if I had, that did it.

"What now?" he whispered, a manic grin on his face.

Before I could answer, we were interrupted by new gunfire tearing into the floor of the loft. They were shooting randomly and concentrating fire at the back of the loft where we'd come up the ladder. If they got lucky, we'd be in trouble. We had another significant advantage, however. While they were shooting blindly up, I was able to see through cracks in the floorboards. I picked up a bale of hay and tossed it across the space, near the ladder opening. As soon as it thudded on the floor, there were concentrated shots to that position. More importantly, one of the men backed out to get a better angle and crossed into my line of fire. I squeezed off a dozen rounds through the plywood floor until my magazine was empty. I heard the agonized screams of at least two who were wounded.

Racing back to one of the thick posts that supported the roof, I swung my body onto its backside and waited out the return fire. At twenty inches across, their bullets wouldn't penetrate. Of course, if someone had been standing in the arena, I'd be an easy shot. Fortunately, the mobsters hadn't yet entered that side of the barn, having no more desire to stand in the open than I did.

I looked around for Manning and found that he'd scrabbled up onto a stack of the hay bales. I decided not to tell him those bales would provide little block from the bullets.

Return fire came, but it was short-lived. Our attackers were either unable to fire or were retreating. Not one to leave well-enough alone, I quietly scrabbled to the ladder and carefully leaned down into the opening. It was a horrible firing position, but I needed to see what they were doing.

"What do you see?" Manning asked in a low voice.

"They're retreating," I said.

"Where's your car?" he demanded, catching up with me. "We won't have much time before reinforcements arrive."

"Gravel road south of here," I said.

"Give me the keys," he said. "I'm good for the money."

"You know how to drive a tractor?" I asked.

"It's my farm," he said, affronted, following my eyes to a small ford that had a sand rake connected behind it.

I pulled out Jonesy's keys and handed them to Dick. "Crown Vic, straight over on the fence line. We make a break for that tractor. You'll have to drive. Give me a second to pull the rake off, then I'll do my best to keep any shooters off us."

Manning grinned maniacally. I was sure he was planning my demise in that moment, but then I wasn't being entirely honest with him either.

"There's a small path on the other side of this wall," he said, pointing at the east wall of the indoor arena.

The keys were in the tractor and I helped Manning into the seat. He'd be in trouble unless he kept low and went fast. Little tractors, however, could move quickly over rough terrain if a person knew what they were doing. Of course, if people were shooting at you, even a novice could get good in a hurry.

I pulled at the pin which connected the rake to its three-point hitch. The first came out easily, but then Manning jerked the tractor forward, trying to start it without pushing in the clutch. Fortunately, I didn't have to explain the issue to him. I pulled the remaining two pins as he started it up and lifted the small bucket off the ground.

"You'll have to catch up," Manning shouted as the machine lurched forward and crashed through the side of the arena, splintering the two-by material that held thin sheets of steel siding. He had no intention of slowing for me and while there was some chance I could catch him, it wasn't in my plans.

"Asshole!" I yelled after him and sprinted back into the barn towards Diva and, more importantly, my pack. I'd burned through two magazines of ammo and was out. I slid to a stop next to Diva and frantically grabbed for a fresh magazine.

Soft crying from the other side of the stall door caught my attention. I pulled the latch back and swung the door open.

"Estás herido?" I asked, querying if any were hurt.

The look of terror in four pairs of eyes answered the question. Maybe, but they wouldn't be talking to a crazy man holding a gun.

Shouts outside the barn told me the shooters who were still up had discovered Manning's escape attempt. I only had moments to act.

I cut into the bindings on the first girl's hands and continued down the line.

"Shh," I said.

The girls were becoming agitated, crying and pushing away from me. The fact was, I didn't have time to deal with their fear.

I turned back toward the stall door, shouldered my pack and scooped, Diva into my arms. From earlier observations, I knew the stalls on this side of the barn weren't connected to runouts. I unlatched the door to the outside and gently pushed it open. I didn't turn, but heard feet scuffling quietly behind me. I exited the barn just in time to see two of the black SUVs tearing down the drive in pursuit of Manning. The pursuit wasn't going to be a sure thing. A tractor could cross terrain that an SUV would struggle with, although it would give up considerable speed. In reality, I could not have cared less.

"Rapido!" I urged, looking back to the girls. "Please," I begged.

I don't know if they trusted me because I was holding Diva or if I was just the only new face they'd seen in a while, but the girl in the lead nodded, spoke to the others, and got them moving.

We'd made it about halfway between the barn and the driveway when DeLovely Manning's voice startled me from the direction of the house. "Where are you going, Mr. Biggston?" she called. "There's no place you can hide from Franky."

I continued toward the one remaining sedan in the driveway.

"Franky doesn't need to have any part of this," I called back. "My only beef is with Dick. These girls are too traumatized to say anything different."

"Not my decision, Biggs," she answered, shrugging her shoulders. "Franky does what he wants."

I placed Diva gently onto the front seat and gestured for the girls to climb into the back. DeLovely had a pistol in her hand and while she wasn't pointing it at me, I could tell she was trying to make a decision. I pulled at the visor and searched the center console. No keys.

I climbed out of the car and jogged over to the woman. Somehow she didn't look out of place standing on the porch of the country house at six in the morning, wearing a silky evening gown.

"Damnit, DeLovely," I said. "Let me get these girls out of here. You have my word I won't bring you or Franky into it."

She started to raise her pistol and I stepped forward and grabbed the top of it. I was flabbergasted when she pulled back on the gun, using the momentum to lean into me. Instead of struggling for control of the gun, she placed her left hand behind my neck and kissed me roughly.

She tasted of cinnamon and in that moment, I wanted to reciprocate.

"You owe me, Biggs. And I intend to collect," she said breathily, releasing me. The smile on her face told me she knew, at some level, I'd enjoyed the moment as well.

"I need the keys," I said.

She reached between her breasts and extracted a single key on a ring.

I looked from the key to her chest and then into her face. "You're fucking nuts." I grabbed the key and bolted back to the car.

"Don't forget it," she called after me. "I'll work things out with Franky."

I was almost surprised when the car started. After driving Jonesy's piece of crap, I was amazed at how quiet the vehicle was and how much power it exerted when I mashed the accelerator. As I sped down the lane, I rummaged through my go-bag, finally finding my phone. I dialed as I turned onto the highway, only narrowly avoiding an oncoming car.

"Henry, where are you?" Snert answered.

"I need you to get Amalia out to Pappi's farm," I said. "Can you do that?"

"I'm headed back to Jonesy's right now," he answered.

"Back? Where were you?"

"I took a car service over to Lazario's and grabbed Melinda's truck," he said. "You left us without transportation. Mel says that's dangerous."

"Shit. Right," I said. "You guys need to get out there. You copy?"

"Are you okay?" he asked.

"No time to talk." I hung up and dialed Pappi.

"Henry?" He answered immediately.

"I'm on the north side of town. I have four girls in bad shape. Diva's hurt," I said. "I stepped in a wasp's nest. Any thoughts on my next move? I told Alan and Melinda to come out to the farm. You okay with that?"

"You're early, but keep coming," he said. "I'll make some calls. How bad is Diva?"

"Bad. She might be dead," I said, a single tear escaping and rolling down my cheek.

"I'll call Doc Mosley," he said. "Just get here safely."

I hung up and set the phone down. It rang again and I picked it up, assuming it was probably Pappi.

"You forget something?" I asked.

"Have you lost your mind?"

I paused. What? Who? It took a moment for my mind to negotiate through the mess of the morning. Why was my uncle calling me? "Finkle?"

"You called the cops to pick up Creight? Do you know the shit that causes?" he screamed into the phone. "Now I'm going to need to beg some judge to let me keep the bond."

"Hey, look, I'm in the middle of something," I said. "He was in the act of committing a crime, so I had to call the cops."

"Oh?" Finkle asked. "A big crime?"

"Couple of felonies, as far as I can tell," I answered.

You could hear the sound of the cash register dinging in his mind. "Well. Maybe this thing isn't entirely a disaster."

"You get that bond, I want my cut," I said.

"When hell freezes over," he said.

I hung the phone up. I'd deal with Finkle later.

The beltway around the city was out of my way, but I'd be able to keep moving at speed and wouldn't have to deal with the morning traffic.

"Shit!" Without warning, the car's speakers started blaring. I could only guess I was hearing a ringtone. It was the theme to the old detective show, *Dragnet*. I shook my head at the perversity of a mobster using that particular ringtone. It took me a moment to find the steering wheel button to answer.

"Biggston," I said, dreading the conversation I was sure was coming.

"You got a lot of balls, kid."

"So I do, Franky," I answered.

"That's Mr. Bosian to you."

"No need for you to be involved in this, Franky. Give me your word that you'll leave me alone and I'll keep you out of it," I said.

"What's a jerkoff like you know about a man's word?" he asked.

"My grandfather taught me that a man's word is his bond," I replied. "Look, I'm going to meet with the D.A. in a couple of hours. Probably best if we work this out."

"Manning's dead," he said. "Who's this Gabriel Jones fella?"

"Just a guy I boosted a car from," I said.

"You're not a very good liar, Mr. Biggston," Franky said. "Tell you what. You keep my name out of things and I'll leave Manning's body somewhere the D.A. can find it. You cross me and I'll kill your Grandma Pearl, Granddaddy Lester and your little friend Snerdly. You read me, soldier? Oh, I'll take out this Gabriel Jones guy too. We have a deal?"

"We do, Franky," I said.

"I told you to call me Mr. Bosian."

"Let me make things clear with you, *Franky*," I said. "I'd suggest you come at me first, because if anything happens to my family, I'll make you my sole mission."

"You fucking punk," he growled. "You can't talk ..."

I hung up the phone. It wasn't smart to rile a man as powerful as Franky Bosian, but I knew that if he sensed weakness, he'd own me.

———

When I turned off the pavement onto the gravel road leading to Pappi and Pearl's farm, I noticed several clouds of dust ahead of me. I worried the cars ahead of me would slow me down, but I was surprised to find them moving just as fast as I was. Even more surprising was that all three vehicles turned down the lane that led to the property.

I turned in, but before I reached the end of the lane, I discovered two trucks sitting sideways, flanking the road. One of them looked suspiciously like Melinda's; the other one was Pappi's. The vehicles ahead of me were allowed to enter, but when I approached, I found Pappi standing in the center of the road. Then I realized he was holding his double-barreled shot gun and pointing it directly at me.

I slammed on the brakes and skidded on the gravel, turning sideways in the road. This expensive sedan with black-tinted windows probably deserved that reception. I rolled down the window so he could see me.

"Damn, son," he said. "I about shot you in that rig."

"Glad you didn't," I said.

"Vet's in the house. George's girl, Melinda, is in with Pearl. You have anything to do with her being here?" he asked.

"Long story." I backed up, straightened the car on the road, and headed to the house. Two older men, whose faces I recognized but names I couldn't recall, moved the pickups out of the way.

"Close it up," Pappi ordered circling his arm in the air. "Everyone's here but the D.A."

"I APOLOGIZE FOR BEING LATE. It appears you've been a busy man, Mr. Biggston." Derek Turner, Sutherland's district attorney, sat across from me at Grandma Pearl's kitchen table. It was seven o'clock that evening and most of the day had been devoted to helping the girls I'd rescued. The vet, Doctor Mosley, had taken Diva with her. The bullet had passed right through her back and there was internal bleeding. It was too early to tell if Diva would survive. If she did, she might not walk again.

Long before D.A. Turner had shown up with Detective Chessen, a whole host of squad cars and Health and Human Services personnel had come and gone. Pearl had flown into action, going into the deep freeze to heat up her emergency stew and chili reserves. Every time she had to send one of the officers down to the locked room in the basement for supplies like water bottles, rice, emergency blankets and toilet paper from her Zombie Apocalypse stash, she smiled and thumped Pappi on the chest.

With interpreters, the girls had been evaluated by medical personnel, given food and water based on their condition and finally escorted to different locations. Activity had finally slowed and those of us who were left found a quiet spot to talk. *Almost* everyone had gone, I guess. Through the closed kitchen door, I heard Pearl arguing with someone, although she wasn't overly fired up.

Next to Turner, Detective Chessen sat on the edge of her seat, her back straight and an unpleasant look on her face. I wasn't sure what her issue was, but I suspected the D.A. could make her life miserable – if he hadn't already.

Next to me sat Jason Halter, a criminal defense lawyer Pappi trusted. He was a middle-aged man in a rumpled suit with wavy gray hair that looked like it was hard to manage. He'd shown up only minutes before the D.A., and his advice had been simple: keep my mouth shut. Halter's tired frumpy look was in stark contrast to the D.A. whose suit was perfectly pressed. Turner looked like he'd just showered and dressed, and his white shirt stood out in stark contrast to his deeply tanned, unwrinkled face.

"Given your grandfather's position on the force, I don't feel I should have to tell you that there's no place for vigilantism in Sutherland."

I returned his gaze but didn't respond. I'd been dressed down by harder men than him. Plus, I was smart enough to know that no question had been asked.

"Richard Manning was found dead at his farm early this afternoon." He paused for dramatic effect and then hit the punch line. "He was mutilated – his genitals removed."

Again, he stared at me, trying to read my face. He was weighing something in his mind, trying to pull information from me as he might a witness in court. I found it curious that he'd started only with statements and no questions.

I could wait.

After nearly a minute, he broke the silence and continued. "There's evidence of a significant fight in the barn. Neighbors reported hearing gunfire."

We locked eyes again. I could feel his struggle. He was trying to figure out my part in everything that had happened.

"Detective Chessen, what's your read on this? Is Henry Biggston an out-of-control vigilante?" he asked.

"We don't know the extent of Mr. Biggston's involvement in what happened at Richard Manning's farm this morning," she said.

"That wasn't my question," he shot back.

Chessen looked at me and then back to Turner. "There is no question that Henry Biggston is involved in this whole affair. In my professional opinion, I think he accidentally precipitated the events when he stepped on a big mob turd. No one was ever supposed to see the video he found. His mistake was not coming to my department at that moment."

"So not a vigilante?"

"There's an aspect of that in his actions," she answered.

"If I released him into your custody, what would you do?"

"He's wanted for questioning in several outstanding cases," she said.

"Is he good for any of them?"

"Not right now," Chessen answered. "We're still processing Manning's farm. We might find something there. Gordie Blondo's death is a judgment call. I'd defer to your department on whether to pursue charges."

"Can you wait outside, please?" Turner asked.

Chessen pursed her lips and stood. She clearly didn't appreciate being dismissed.

"I have a problem," Turner said, once Chessen exited the room. "I'm out on a limb here. I've been after Manning for years. He's done unspeakable things, but never anything we could pin on him. I don't believe any death for that man would have been too horrible. The problem is, someone went outside of the justice system and people don't feel safe when that happens. People want to feel safe, Mr. Biggston."

We stared at each other for almost a minute until he finally shook his head, frustrated. "Damn it, Biggston! Do you ever talk?"

"Yes, sir," I answered. "My training has removed all desire to answer rhetorical questions. You're a powerful man and I'm certain you haven't come out here to just share facts with me."

"Do you believe every person has at least one super power, Mr. Biggston?"

"I'm not sure I follow."

"Like me, for example. My super power is reading people." he said. "The problem is, I can't read you. I honestly have no idea if you're a psychopath, a vigilante, or just a war-hero who stood up to the most powerful criminal organization in Sutherland. I'm going to ask you one time and I need an honest answer. Did you kill Gordie Blondo and Richard Manning?"

Halter stepped in before I could speak, placing a hand on my forearm. "Careful, Henry. The D.A.'s testimony on anything you might say would be very compelling to a jury. Admission of guilt here would be admissible in court."

Turner rolled his eyes.

"I caused no harm to Richard Manning," I said. "I had hoped to bring him here to meet you this afternoon once I found the location of the girls he was abusing. I'll be honest, though. Some laws were no doubt bent in the process."

"Murder?" he asked.

"Don't answer that." Halter stepped in. "Derek, Henry Biggston is an honorably discharged, highly decorated Army Ranger. You've already offered immunity. Where's the agreement? Mr. Biggston isn't talking without an immunity agreement."

"I don't like how that plays in the press," Turner said. "The good citizens of Sutherland tend to think giving immunity is going soft on crime – which I certainly am not."

"Henry, don't say another word," Halter said, starting to stand. "Mr. Turner, this conversation is done."

"I have something better," Turner said. "But I want something first."

"You must think I'm stupid," Halter answered.

Turner ignored Halter and turned to me. "Who killed Gordie Blondo?"

"Don't answer that," Halter said, attempting to get between us, but the table was too wide.

"I did," I said, holding eye contact with Turner.

Turner smiled. It wasn't a friendly smile as much as it was the smile a shark might make after a good meal. He pulled a sheet of paper from his briefcase and slid it across the table to Halter.

My lawyer reviewed the paper and slid it to me, asking Turner, "Are you serious?"

I had to read it through a couple of times. The best I could tell, it was an employment contract for the District Attorney's office. I was to be a special investigator. The most confusing part however was that it was dated three weeks ago and had already been signed by Turner himself.

"You want me to work for you?" I asked.

"As far as I'm concerned, you already do," he said.

"I don't want a boss," I said.

"You'll have your independence," he said.

"Why?" I asked.

"The headline writes itself." Turner gestured air quotes, "Highly decorated soldier and undercover investigator, on orders from the D.A. himself, infiltrates and exposes organized crime boss Richard Manning's involvement in a child-sex ring."

"Pretty wordy for a headline," Halter said, peevishly.

"There's no salary on this employment offer," I said, pushing it back.

He pulled a thin leather wallet from his pocket, dropped it on the paper and slid them both across the table. "Investigators get sixty bucks an hour. Submit an invoice along with your report."

"I want you to go easy on Nala Swede," I said, opening the wallet. Inside was a gold badge. "She was trying to keep me from getting murdered by the mob."

"Too late, she pled out earlier this morning," Manning answered.

"Twelve months for tampering with evidence in a criminal investigation. She'll be out in six."

"She's going to jail?" I asked.

"I'm surprised to see you sticking up for her," Turner said. "I saw the video where she held you at gunpoint. She admitted her part in delivering you to slaughter when your truck was blown up."

His question about killing Blondo had been a test. He'd already seen the video and knew I'd killed the assassin.

"Nala didn't know my truck was rigged," I said.

"That just makes her stupid," he said. "Although she was the one who called it in. She also admitted to going back to the scene and running your assassin off. She says it was Blondo. Is that how you remember it?"

"I still don't have any memory of that night. If it helps, Blondo admitted as much at the bus station," I answered and turned to Halter. "Am I okay to sign this?"

Halter gave an uncomfortable shrug. "It's not as good as an immunity deal. If someone in the D.A.'s office decides you acted illegally, you could still be prosecuted."

"And you would, no doubt, point out that I offered a back-dated contract," Turner said.

"How does this work? I report next Monday for work?" I asked, accepting the pen from Turner. My lawyer was uncomfortable, but this was the only deal Turner was offering.

"Oh, hell no!" Turner answered. "The only reason we're having this conversation is because you managed something the entire Sutherland P.D. has been incapable of: tagging Richard Manning with something not even his lawyers can crawl out from under. You're a loose cannon, Biggston. No, your employment is on more of an *as-needed* basis. I wouldn't be counting on a regular check."

"I got help from a couple of friends. I might have borrowed a gun from one of them." I signed the contract and slid it back to Turner.

"Put it in your report," Turner whisked the papers into his briefcase and extended his hand. "Good to have you on the team, Sergeant Biggston."

⊏ ⊐

I'm not sure why I found it perverse that the visiting room at county jail resembled a high school cafeteria. I almost missed Nala, who was already seated at a table. As a cop or in street clothing, she had seemed bigger than life. At the table, wearing the bright-orange over-sized jumpsuit, she was tiny.

As I approached, she refused to lift her eyes to meet mine.

"I can't believe you came," she said, pushing a piece of dust across the table with her finger.

I sat at the table and placed my hand on top of hers.

"You were meant to die in that explosion."

I couldn't see her face behind the curtain of her hair, but a fat tear splashed onto the table. Her next words were ragged as she struggled to talk. "I had no idea I was bringing you to a hit."

"You came back and stopped Blondo from finishing the job," I said. "You put yourself on the line for me."

"I didn't know what to do," she said, her breathing still ragged.

"Why did you destroy that memory card?" I asked.

"They said they'd kill you if I didn't."

"Manning or Bosian?" I asked.

"I don't know," she answered. "Word came through my uncle. I thought you would drop the whole thing. I'm so sorry." As she spoke, she tipped her head back and made eye contact. She wanted to gauge my response.

"The only place where we're not square is when you held a gun on me and told me to turn Amalia over to Blondo," I said.

Fresh tears of shame ran down her face. "Franky had a hit out on you. I was told they'd cancel it if I got that girl back. I know it was wrong. I'd have killed Blondo myself if it would have stopped the hit. I was so scared, I didn't know what to do."

"I joined the Army because I believe in freedom for everyone. There are a lot of bad people out there. We're the good guys. We protect the innocent. If you want to be one of my friends, you're going to have to get on board with that."

She wiped at the tears on her cheek. "I hate it when I cry," she said, laughing nervously. "All I can say is I'll try."

"That's all any of us can do," I said, smiling.

I was surprised when only a few minutes later a chime sounded.

"I gotta go," Nala said, standing up straight. She pulled her hair from her face and captured it with a band that had been around here wrist. "I'm glad you came, Biggs. Really glad."

I stepped in and gave her a hug. She wrapped her arms around me and for a moment, I remembered the two of us, lying in Pappi's barn together. I think both of us knew there was no way back to that moment. I held on to her anyway until I felt a tap on the shoulder and a prison guard broke us up.

A beep from Mel's blue, jacked-up pickup caught my attention as its engine fired. I waved, acknowledging that I'd seen her and jogged over. I smiled as I approached and noticed that Snert had changed position, taking the front seat. I knew he'd developed a crush on Melinda and felt a certain amusement at his maneuver. He'd never expressed much of an interest in women, but something about Mel was pulling him out of his shell.

I opened the back door and slid in behind Mel. "Thanks for waiting, guys." I looked over at Diva, who lay on the bed we'd made behind Snert's seat. She was heavily medicated but managed a few slow thumps of her tail when she became aware of my presence.

"How was Nala?" Snert asked. "I heard they're hard on ex-police in jail."

"They're treating her okay," I said. "I don't think anyone would make a move on her, not with her family connections."

"You did the right thing going to visit her, Biggs," Mel said, catching my eyes in the rear-view mirror. Something about her expression suggested she wasn't as enthused as she suggested. "I know you were tight. You think you can get past all that?"

"Hard to say," I said. I wasn't overly comfortable discussing my love life with another woman, especially someone as interesting as Mel.

"I can't believe she held a gun on you," Snert added. "You think you know someone ..."

"She made a tough call," I said. "Wasn't the call I'd have made. Can't even say I completely understand it."

"Of course," Mel said. A ghost of a smile crossed her face and vanished just as quickly as it had appeared. "That's too bad," she quickly added, "but I understand."

"Thanks for bringing me out here," I said. "I really needed to see her. It's just you think you know someone."

"Like you said, Biggs. She made a tough call," Mel said.

I sat back and allowed my eyes to close as my head came to rest on the door frame. I didn't think I'd fallen asleep, but the next thing I knew, I heard dinging and a whine from the still unmoving Diva.

"Rise and shine, cupcake," Mel said, opening the truck door. The sound of Mexican ranchera music drew my attention as it wafted over the recently cut hay-field-turned-parking lot.

"That's a lot of people," I said, climbing out.

"You haven't said anything about my dress," Mel prompted. She slowly spun in front of me, the hem of her brightly-colored summer dress flaring out. She wasn't a tall woman and was no one's definition of model thin, but that was just fine by me. She'd turned into a loyal friend and was beautiful in what my friends called a *country way*. Any man who wasn't captured by her smile had to be half-dead.

"I think you're amazing looking," Snert cut in while I was still admiring her.

Mel gave me a mischievous look and grabbed Snert's arm so he could escort her. "Why, thank you, Alan"

I chuckled at her good-natured flirting. It felt good to laugh.

"A little help with the wagon?" I asked as the two of them walked away from the truck.

"Oh, right," Alan said, turning around.

The three of us settled Diva into the child's wagon Mel lent me. Diva thumped her tail and attempted to stand up. I knelt and stroked her muzzle, speaking to her in a reassuring voice, "I got you, girl."

"Look out!" Mel said, giggling as we approached the gathering. A group of girls ran past us, all wearing simple pastel dresses with ribbons in their hair.

I suffered a moment of complete shock when one of the girls peeled off and ran to me. It was Amalia, only she hardly looked anything like what I remembered.

"Biggs!" she cried, wrapping her arms around me.

"What? How?" I asked, hugging her back.

"Didn't I tell you?" Mel asked. "Health and Human Services can't find records for any of the girls. We have a lot of friends who are registered foster families for at-risk teens. Amalia is living with my cousin, Camila, until her family is found."

Amalia bent down and kissed Diva on the nose only to be joined by two more girls that I barely recognized.

"I will take care – Diva," Amalia said, her English still broken but improving.

"She needs to be in the shade, where it's quiet," I said. "And she needs water."

Amalia smiled as she nodded and ripped off a string of Spanish I couldn't possibly follow. The two girls who'd joined her giggled as she picked up the wagon's handle and slowly pulled Diva toward one of the tents.

"That was nice of you," Mel said. "Even though they are laughing, they are still hurting. Diva is good for them."

"Was it all a lie?" my uncle, Chester Finkle, asked as he approached.

"Alan and I will grab drinks and be back," Mel said, recognizing that she didn't want to get mixed up in that conversation. "Do you want anything?"

"Water would be fine," I said.

"Light beer it is," she said, tugging on Snert's arm to drag him away.

"Good to see you, Chester," I said, holding out my hand in greeting. "Was what all a lie?"

"Aw, give the man a minute to breathe, Chester," Pappi said, joining us. "He just got here."

"I just want to know if you all were using me, so Biggs here could establish his undercover identity?"

"Nope," I said. "Still need the job. And next time, how about no hookups with the mob boss's daughter."

Pappi turned his shoulders toward Finkle and tipped his head forward with a disapproving look. It would have been more effective if he'd had his glasses on, but Pappi hadn't lost his ability to give the cop stink-eye. It was very satisfying to see Finkle squirm.

"Not in the habit of saying no to DeLovely Manning," he said. "Not what you would call a good career move."

"Whatever happened with Creight?" I asked. "Did you get your bond back?"

"Most of it," he said, extracting an envelope from his pocket and handing it to me. "Seven fifty. I only got seventy-five percent, so that's what you get."

Pappi shook his head disapprovingly. I gave him a shrug before accepting the money. Detective Chessen caught my attention, so I smiled, tapping the envelope on Finkle's chest. "I'll stop by next week and see what you have going on. Now, if you'll excuse me, I have someone I need to talk to."

Chessen tipped her head back in acknowledgement as I approached. "Mr. Biggston," she said, sizing me up. Her response was neither friendly nor unfriendly.

"We good?" I asked.

"Until we're not," she shrugged, taking a drink from a plastic cup filled with red punch of some sort. "I hear you've been undercover for the D.A.'s office. Thing is, you don't smell like a cop."

I nodded in acknowledgment. I wasn't about to play coy with her. "It's a recent thing," I said.

Her face warmed slightly and she chuckled. I suspected she wasn't used to honesty in her day-to-day conversations. "Good piece of work bringing Manning down. Pisses me off that D.A. Turner took all the credit. Shit, he didn't even mention your name. Said he needed to keep your identity a secret. Fucking grab for headlines was all it was."

"You know better than that. I know you've seen those girls running around," I said.

She nodded. "Nobody said it can't be both. Fact is, happy endings are one in a thousand," she said. "By the time I get involved, it's always a dead body. That's why nobody over at the Second Precinct is going to give this another look. Bad guy mobster got what's coming to him. Between you and me, we found a lot of blood out at that farm and no bodies, but they have a way of turning up at the wrong time. You need to know who your friends are. You read me?"

"Loud and clear, Lieutenant," I said. "Next time you're in the loop or I'll find my ass hanging in the wind."

I must have caught her off guard, as she choked on her drink and coughed. "Well shit, Biggs. You're not one for subtlety, are you?"

"I prefer we're all working from the same play book," I said.

"You know, I wasn't going to say anything, but I've got this other case ..."

But of course, that's another story entirely.

ABOUT THE AUTHOR

Jamie McFarlane is happily married, the father of three and lives in Lincoln, Nebraska. He spends his days engaged in a hi-tech career and his nights and weekends writing works of fiction.

Word-of-mouth is crucial for any author to succeed. If you enjoyed this book, please consider leaving a review, even if it's only a line or two; it would make all the difference and would be very much appreciated.

FREE DOWNLOAD

If you'd like to receive automatic email when Jamie's next book is available, please visit http://fickledragon.com. Your email address will never be shared and you can unsubscribe at any time.

For more information
www.fickledragon.com
jamie@fickledragon.com

ACKNOWLEDGMENTS

To Diane Greenwood Muir for excellence in editing and fine word-smithery. My wife, Janet, for carefully and kindly pointing out my poor grammatical habits. I cannot imagine working through these projects without you both.

To my beta readers: Carol Greenwood, Barbara Simmons, Linda Baker, Matt Strbjak and Nancy Higgins Quist for wonderful and thoughtful suggestions. It is a joy to work with this intelligent and considerate group of people. Also, to my advanced reading team, you're a zany, fun group of people who I look forward to bouncing ideas off.

Finally, to Elsa Mathern, cover artist extraordinaire.

ALSO BY JAMIE MCFARLANE

Privateer Tales Series

Privateer Tales Universe

Witchy World

51382624R00150

Made in the USA
Columbia, SC
18 February 2019